BOBBY CINEMA'S SECOND LIBRARIAN DETECTIVE SERIES

ENGLISH

BOBBY CINEMA

authorHOUSE®

AuthorHouse™
1663 Liberty Drive
Bloomington, IN 47403
www.authorhouse.com
Phone: 1 (800) 839-8640

Published by AuthorHouse   07/16/2015

ISBN: 978-1-5049-2337-8 (sc)
ISBN: 978-1-5049-2338-5 (e)

Library of Congress Control Number: 2015911375

Print information available on the last page.

*Any people depicted in stock imagery provided by Thinkstock are models,
and such images are being used for illustrative purposes only.
Certain stock imagery © Thinkstock.*

This book is printed on acid-free paper.

WAHLBERG P.I.

By: Bobby Cinema

Synopsis

Robert Mark Wahlberg is a box office champ in the movies. He was a star in the *Nitro* movie series, where he played a treasure hunter discovering treasure in exotic places in the 1960s. He made six movies that star him as Dr. Nitro Bones and are set in the Vietnam War era, where he has to race for treasure against mobsters and the Russian KGB who want it. Mark became a movie star after he and his brother started a singing group with their best friend Logan, called M-D-L. Mark wanted to join the LAPD after doing a cop movie called *LA Beat* that was a box office flop. Donnie Ronald Wahlberg, his brother, was the screenwriter for the original *LA Beat* and he has the green light to do a reboot and to make the movie better. But Mark never actually prepared for the movie and he needs to do so to make this reboot better. Mark wants to join LAPD reserve unit, but he can't because of his record, he assaulted a man once when he was sixteen years old. He went to Juvie and was released after one year. He wanted to join the reserve unit to get into his character, but he can't. Donnie found a way to help him get into his character. When Mark asked him how, Donnie told him he can work with the police as a private investigator. All he had to do was apply for a P.I. license and start advertising with the LAPD, the DA, or the FBI. Mark is skeptical at first, but he will do it. Donnie and Mark's friend Logan is an LAPD consultant with the studio, and he will do the advertisement with the LAPD to see if they want to hire Mark. Mark applied for the P.I. license and after two weeks he got his P.I. badge and ID. Donnie got him an office at the L.A. Public Library. Mark is feeling comfortable in his office at the Public Library, but the LAPD, FBI and DA turned him down for a consultant job. Until one person responded. His name was Captain Jake Johnson. He is from the LAPD's internal affairs, and he hired him as a consultant on a case. He suspects that one of the cops from Narcotics and Counterfeiting is taking bribes. This detective may be working for somebody, and Johnson asks Mark if he wants to take the case. He needs somebody outside the department to find out who is on the take. One of the detectives might be working for a top drug lord. Mark will consider it, but with a couple of conditions: he needs an LAPD detective badge, a gun, and the authorization to get into places that he usually can't to take the case. Johnson is reluctant at first, and doesn't know if he can trust Mark, but he has nothing on the detectives who are on the mysterious drug lord's payroll. He will accept. Mark gets the LAPD badge, gun, and authorization to start the case. He also signs a waiver that LAPD won't be responsible for any damages if he gets killed or shot. His brother Donnie, his friend Logan Myers, and Detective Sergeant Linda Myers who works with internal affairs, and was placed on the case by Johnson, make up his team.

A limousine enters the LA Harbor at night and it stops. The limo driver exits the limousine, and moves to open the back door. Mark Wahlberg steps out of the back of the limo wearing an Armani suit, Ray-Ban sunglasses, and carrying a briefcase.

The limo driver closes the door behind him, and tells Mark, "Sir, they are waiting for you."

Mark tells the limo driver, "Thank you Bertie." Mark sees the warehouse and goes inside to make the deal of the century. As Mark enters the warehouse, he sees five gentleman waiting for him. Two of the gentlemen go over to see Mark.

Gentleman 1 tells the others, "Search him."

Two of the gentleman search Mark and tell their boss, Gentleman 1, "He's clean."

Gentleman 1 tells Mark, "No gun? I'm impressed."

Mark, speaking with a British accent, tells Gentleman 1, "Like I said, I usually hate guns. Let's get to business, gentlemen."

Gentleman 1 asks Mark "Mr. Ross, how much are willing to pay for this baby? For your baby?"

Mark says, "I am willing to pay five big ones. If it is the best. My clients only want the best they have for their parties."

Gentleman 1 sees the briefcase on the table and opens it. He shows the briefcase to Mark. Mark sees five hundred pounds of Ketamine.

Mark tells Gentleman 1, "Five hundred pounds of K? Excellent."

Gentleman 1 asks Mark, "So Mr. Ross will you take the offer?"

Mark tells Gentleman 1, "I'll take it. It's a done deal."

Gentleman 1 tells Mark, "I appreciate that offer. Now the money, and the K is all yours."

Mark puts his briefcase on the table, and tells Gentleman 1, "Here it is Mr. Roveman."

Roveman opens the briefcase and sees a few hundred dollars strapped around rolls of paper, and Roveman knows that the money is fake. Roveman is upset and tells Mark, "What is going on? I've been had. This money is fake."

Mark speaks with an American accent, and tells Roveman, "The money is fake and this is a con." Mark takes out his LAPD badge and shows it to Roveman, telling him, "Roveman, did I forget to tell you? I'm LAPD, and it's true I don't have a gun. Because you searched in the wrong place." Mark pulls up his long sleeve shirt, revealing his Glock 19 taped on his chest. He takes his gun and aims it on Roveman and his crew. Mark tells Roveman, "You're under arrest. Hands up."

Roveman's men get their hands up, but Roveman doesn't and he tells Mark, "Before I get my hands up, I need to take something out first."

Mark tells Roveman, "Take it out slowly and so I can see it."

Roveman takes his gun out of his holster and tells Mark, "Maybe I will take it out faster since you forgot to tell us drop our guns."

Mark says, "What the…?"

Roveman takes out his gun and so do his four gentleman. Roveman aims his gun at Mark. Roveman fires his gun and three bullets hit the table near Mark, but miss him. Mark dives down on the floor and rolls to a nearby barrel where three more bullets come from Roveman, and he fires his gun at Roveman. One bullet hits Roveman in the shoulder and he falls down on the floor. Roveman is aching and a SWAT team enters the warehouse, just in time. Mark gets up from the floor and tells them, "Hands up now."

A voice comes out of nowhere, "Cut!" The director and the rest of the crew enters the warehouse since they were in the movie studio.

Mark tells the director, "Donnie, I almost had it down this time."

Donnie tells Mark, "That is what you said on the fifth take Mark. Come one, we have to get the scene right before we get to the next part."

Mark tells Donnie, "I can't believe we're doing *LA Beat* again."

Donnie tells Mark, "Were doing a reboot. Last time we did *LA Beat*, three years ago, the movie failed in the premiere and everyone almost lynched us. It was never out in theaters after that. But the studio is giving me a second chance to make a reboot, and to make it better."

Mark tells Donnie, "Donnie this is the same scene we're doing, and all the others that were in the same movie that failed in the box office in the first place. We've got to do something different in this movie."

Donnie asks Mark, "Like what? It's not like I know anything about the LAPD anyway."

Mark tells Donnie, "Donnie, we were a great successful singing group, M-D-L. We recorded nine albums that each went triple platinum, and we were nominated for a Grammy 12 times. We grossed 100 or 200 million dollars and sold-out concerts back then."

Donnie tells Mark, "We had a record deal in 1990 and broke up in 2000. We wanted to go our separate ways."

Mark talks to Donnie and tells him, "Logan and I wanted to join the police force. Actually I wanted to. But I kind of dragged Logan into it. Because we wanted to make a difference, and make people see us as more than a singing group. Logan got into the academy, because he has a clean record, but they saw my record and I was disqualified from joining."

Donnie tells Mark, "Mark we grew up in south Boston. Dad died when I was 18 and you were 17. Mom had a drinking problem. She was never the same after Dad died."

Mark tells Donnie, "Dad was with the Boston P.D. He was buried in his work."

Mark tells Donnie, "Before he died, when I was 17, I went to juvie for vandalism after I joined the Red Dragons, so I wouldn't get beat up every day by them. But we got in trouble, and Dad warned me about them. But the leader of the Red Dragons set me up, and told me that if I wanted to join their club, all I had to do was vandalize this shop, and I did. They set me up and left, and I got arrested."

Donnie tells Mark, "I thought Dad would use his power to get the charges dropped."

Mark tells Donnie, "No, he used his powers to get me arrested and he was disappointed with my rap sheet. I can't be a cop. I ended up in juvie and I was let out when I was eighteen. I wasn't there when he died, because I was in juvie. I drove him six feet under after that day. After I got out, I went to live with you and we found out we had a great singing talent. We recorded and performed together with Logan, our best friend, that we've known since we were nine, and who warned us about the Red Dragons. I didn't listen, and I should have. But, we forgave each other and formed our own singing group with the songs I wrote in juvie, and that got us a record deal and the rest is history."

Donnie tells Mark, "But this movie is a disaster, we barely learned anything about doing a cop movie, even though Dad was a cop his whole life, we didn't pay attention."

Mark tells Donnie, "It's too bad we don't have a police consultant to help us on this movie."

Donnie asks Mark, "Who do we know that can help us out on the film? If this movie fails in the box office, I could lose my contract with the studio. No one in the industry will hire me if this movie fails."

Mark tells Donnie, "Donnie, you forgot about Logan! He made detective two years ago. I'm the one who encouraged him to join the force. I helped him get through to the academy and pass his detective exam. He's owes me."

Donnie asks Mark, "Mark, how come Logan didn't help us last time?"

Mark tells Donnie, "He was really busy, and plus we never asked him. I think I will ask him now."

Donnie asks Mark, "You think he will be too busy to talk to us?"

Mark tells Donnie, "He is always busy with police work. He even bragged once that he aced the last test that scored him top of his class in the academy. Man, he loved to rub my face in that one. But I will give it a shot."

Donnie tells Mark, "Okay, good luck. Our fate in this movie is in your hands. I really want this movie to be a box office gold."

Mark tells Donnie, "Don't worry big bro, our father may be disappointed in our career changes. But he wouldn't be disappointed in this movie."

Detective Logan Myers is a detective in the LAPD, and is at the headquarters of the 8th precinct, in the Narcotics and counterfeiting department. He is typing in his report on his drug bust at his desk. Logan is thinking about what to type in, but can't think of anything right now. Logan finishes his report with how he shot the suspect in the leg and arrested him. Logan tells himself, "That's it. I think once the captain sees my report, and once my suspect tells me who his supplier is, I will have to find his operation and shut it down. Put him and his posse behind bars. The captain and I will get a lot of recognition for what we did. Now all I have to do is print and take my report to the boss, and it will be smooth sailing." Logan presses the print button and grabs his report from his desk and takes it to his boss, Captain Matthew Smithson.

Captain Smithson is working at his desk inside his office. He hears a knock at the door and tells the person who is outside his office, "Come in."

The door opens and it's Logan. Logan tells Smithson, "Hello Captain Smithson!"

Captain Smithson greets Logan and tells him, "Hi Myers!"

Logan tells Smithson, "My report is done sir. You want me to leave it in my desk?"

Captain Smithson tells Logan, "No, let me take a look at it for a minute."

Logan tells Captain Smithson, "Okay sir."

Logan goes over to Captain Smithson's desk. Logan hands in the report to Captain Smithson and Smithson grabs the report and reads over it for a minute. Smithson tells Logan, "Myers I need you to sit down for a minute, there is something I want to talk to you about."

Logan tells Smithson, "What is it Captain?"

Smithson tells Logan, "Sit down and I will tell you. It is really important that you hear this."

Logan tells Smithson, "Yes sir!' Logan sits down in his chair and asks Captain Smithson, "Captain, what do you want to talk to me about?"

Smithson tells Logan, "I heard you arrested your suspect, Marvin Keltner, the one who was selling heroin."

Logan tells Smithson, "Yes sir. I got a warrant to search his place from Assistant D.A. Eugene Medford sir."

Smithson tells Logan, "Myers, in your report, you shot him in the leg because he was resisting arrest."

Logan tells Smithson, "Yes sir, he was resisting arrest. I found bags of heroin in his place, and once I've interrogated him about who his supplier is, I will have my chance to find this mysterious kingpin, and put him away and shut down his operation once and for all."

Smithson tells Logan, "That sounds great Myers, but we got one problem."

Logan tells Smithson, "What's that, sir?"

Smithson tells Logan, "I got a call from Keltner's lawyer. The warrant that Medford signed on was fake. He never signed a warrant."

Logan tells Smithson, "What do you mean? He signed on the warrant. I have his signature and he gave me full authorization to search Keltner's place and arrest him."

Smithson tells Logan, "I don't know whose signature you have, but it is not Medford's. It was probably a gag from a court clerk who was playing you. Even though forging a signature is illegal. But I'm sure Medford will overlook it, since he was part of the gag."

Logan tells Smithson, "What does this mean?"

Smithson tells Logan, "It means, Keltner's lawyer is considering pressing charges for illegally searching his place for heroin and shooting him in the leg. Keltner is considering suing this department for harassment. So, in other words, all the charges against him are dropped."

Logan tells Smithson, "He walks. I can't believe it."

Smithson tells Logan, "That's right. Myers, I know you are upset about this whole situation."

Logan tells Smithson, "Why would I be upset. Since I arrested Keltner, who was going to lead me to his boss, who is a mysterious drug lord that I been after for a year and since no one can find. How could I be upset? But hey, I can find another lead to find this guy."

Smithson tells Logan, "That's the other problem we have to talk about."

Logan tells Smithson, "What is it, Captain?"

Smithson tells Logan, "You know Keltner's Lawyer was going to sue this department for the harassment of his client that you brought up on charges. So, I had no choice."

Logan tells Smithson, "What choice is that?"

Smithson tells Logan, "I had no choice but to suspend you for one week with no pay."

Logan can't believe he is hearing this, and tells Smithson, "What! I can't believe it. What about finding this mysterious drug lord who is supplying heroin in L.A. I've been after this guy for a year, none of us could ever find him. So, who is going to handle the mysterious drug lord case?"

Smithson tells Logan, "I am tossing out this case. Since we have no leads, I have no choice but to toss it out. Until then, you are suspended from this case."

Logan is really upset about this, and tells himself, "Oh man."

Smithson tells Logan, "I need your piece and shield on my desk."

Logan gets up from his chair, takes out his LAPD detective badge from his left pants pocket and his Beretta 92F from the back of his pants and places them on Smithson's desk.

Smithson tells Logan, "I am sorry about this Myers. I did what I could with the Chief to keep you on the force, but he didn't give me a choice."

Logan tells Smithson, "What choice is that Captain?"

Smithson tells Logan, "I have to either fire you or suspend you. Or he will fire both of us."

Logan tells Smithson, "I guess it wasn't my job, it was yours. I'm sorry you had go through that, sir."

Smithson tells Logan, "Don't be. I'll do what I can with the Chief of Police to lift your suspension. Until then, you can finish out the day. But please stay out of trouble and stay off this case. Or next time you will be off the force permanently."

Logan tells Smithson, "Yes sir."

Smithson tells Logan, "Good luck, kid."

Logan tells Smithson, "You too, sir."

Logan shakes Smithson's hand and exits the office.

Donnie is working in his office in his production company, M.D.L. Productions. Donnie hears a knock at the door, and tells the person outside his office, "Come in."

The door opens and Mark enters Donnie's office and closes the door behind him. Mark is carrying a small package in his left hand and tells his brother, "Hey big bro, our worries are over."

Donnie asks Mark, "You get a hold of Logan?"

Mark tells Logan, "Not yet, but I have something better."

Donnie asks Mark, "What is it Mark?"

Mark tells Donnie, "I took a P.I. exam last night. Take a look at this." Mark opens the package and takes out two P.I. badges and two Beretta 92F guns and places them on Donnie's desk. Mark tells Donnie, "Here it is our very own P.I. badges. I took the test yesterday and both of us are now licensed Private Investigators. Now we can work with the LAPD as consultants or other clients who needs us."

Donnie asks Mark, "Mark are you telling me we are officially Private Investigators?"

Mark tells Donnie, "Yeah."

Donnie looks upset for a minute.

Mark tells Donnie, "I know that look, it's the I did something stupid look and you are going to kill me right now."

Donnie tells Mark, "I can't believe it Mark. I got one thing say to you." Mark looks frightened and Donnie tells Mark, "That is awesome! Thanks man. Now we are officially P.I.s, now we get to do things that we can't do in the movies."

Mark is excited about this too. Mark tells Donnie, "I know it's amazing."

Donnie tells Mark, with a concerned look, "You are not playing me are you, these P.I. badges, they're not props that you got from the studio are they?"

Mark tells Donnie, "No, they are real."

Donnie tells Mark, "These guns are props right? They do look real."

Mark tells Donnie, "No, they are real."

Donnie is upset and tells Mark, "What do you mean they are real? Mark, I told you I hate guns."

Mark tells Donnie, "So do I, but we need it for protection. For life and death situations."

Donnie tells Mark, "Please tell me they are not loaded."

Mark tells Donnie, "Of course not."

Donnie tells Mark, "Thank goodness."

Mark tells Donnie, "I have the bullets in my office. So we don't have to worry about that."

Donnie tells Mark, "That makes me feel a lot better."

Mark tells Donnie, "Relax Donnie, I locked the shell casings in my desk. So no one can open it."

Donnie tells Mark, "Where did you get these guns anyway?"

Mark tells Donnie, "Logan registered us for guns when he made detective two years ago for our protection, and if I ever want to become a P.I. and work with him someday. So I placed an order for our guns and took out the casings and put them in my desk with a lock and key to use it sometimes. Since I passed my P.I. exam and they sent me the package of my P.I. badges. I put the unloaded guns in the package to surprise you. Tell me, Donnie, you are surprised right?"

Donnie tells Mark, "Yeah, I'm surprised and speechless Mark."

Mark tells Donnie, "I knew you would be thrilled when I got this license."

Donnie tells Mark, "Mark, how is being a P.I. is going to help us with *L.A. Beat*?"

Mark tells Donnie, "We have never experienced what it is like to be detectives. We have never eaten, breathed or felt like cops. We need to get into character, and see what it is like to be a detective, and how they work and how live with the tough choices they have."

Donnie tells Mark, "Yeah well Dad lived it. He even ate, breathed and knew what it was like to be a cop."

Mark tells Donnie, "I never did. I wanted to be like him. I wanted to change the world like he did. Look what it got me back then."

Donnie tells Mark, "What did it get you?"

Mark tells Donnie, "I got in trouble with the law, and I was in juvenile hall. I was 17, and I was in there for one year, until I turned 18 and got released. Dad didn't even fight for me, he just let me rot there for one year."

Donnie tells Mark, "All because you were a disappointment to him. When you fell in that wrong crowd."

Mark tells Donnie, "Hey, I was young and stupid, and besides you know we were bullied in high school. C'mon you know I joined the Red Dragons so I wouldn't get beat up every day. Besides, these are the guys who made our lives hell."

Donnie tells Mark, "And that's why you joined those guys? So they wouldn't beat you up?"

Mark tells Donnie, "Exactly, man Dad was really disappointed in me when I joined that crowd. But he disappointed me a lot more when he ignored me my whole life. You know, I wanted to join the force to be like him, but he told me it was a waste of time, because nobody could do what he did. Even after I got in trouble for vandalism, he was the arresting officer, and he wanted to teach me a lesson. With a record, I wasn't able to join the force."

Donnie tells Mark, "You know, that explains why you didn't forgive him before he died."

Mark tells Donnie, "Yeah, well he died after I was sent in. I always felt like I was responsible for his heart attack."

Donnie tells Mark, "I don't think it was your fault. Besides, he didn't want us to join the force."

Mark tells Donnie, "Because he told you that you didn't have the chops."

Donnie tells Mark, "You know, we both told him off when he died. Those were the last words we said to him before he died. We never actually had any closure, or actually talked to the guy."

Donnie tells Mark, "The only reason is because the guy was unreasonable. Besides he wouldn't ever listen to me, and I was afraid we were going to turn into him."

Mark tells Donnie, "Huh, we have nothing to worry about. I don't think either of us are anything like him. I mean Ben is more like Dad, but we're nothing like him."

Donnie tells Mark, "Yeah, I guess you're right. Besides, Ben is the oldest. And he did follow in his footsteps."

Mark tells Donnie, "Did you get a hold of him? We all lost touch when our singing career took off right after I got out of juvie."

Donnie tells Mark, "Well, I got ahold of Mom. I heard he got transferred to the LAPD. Now he's actually working narcotics."

Mark tells Donnie, "I bet he won't talk to us because he was jealous of us because we made it big and he didn't."

Donnie tells Mark, "Man that's not true. Besides, Ben was Dad's favorite. He was grooming him to be his replacement."

Mark tells Donnie, "Well, trust me, this P.I. job will help us get me into character for *LA Beat*. And trust me, we need to learn everything about police work if we want this movie to succeed."

Donnie tells Mark, "It's going to take more than working that police work to get you into character. Like you said, we need to eat, breathe, and think like cops."

Mark tells Donnie, "That's why we have these P.I. jobs. So, we can be police consultants for the LAPD. Luckily, Logan, who's in the LAPD can get us in."

Donnie tells Mark, "What makes you think he's going to put in a good word for us?"

Mark tells Donnie, "Well, we have to try, and besides he does owe us. I'm the one who helped him get into the academy. I tutored him from the entrance exams. I even helped him pass the detective exam too. So, he kind of owes me."

Donnie tells Mark, "Only because joining the LAPD was kind of your idea. It was too late for you, but Logan could still get us in, since he was a member of our singing group M-D-L."

Mark tells Donnie, "Well, you know we broke up after a few years. You wanted to get into the movies, and me and Logan wanted to join the police force. I couldn't, because I was ineligible, but Logan wasn't. So, he does owe us."

Donnie tells Mark, "You still have his number?"

Mark tells Donnie, "Yeah. I have his number. I think I'm gonna give him a call. Donnie, I need to ask you, we need to find a base of operations to work from."

Donnie tells Mark, "What do you mean a base of operations to work from?"

Mark tells Donnie, "I mean an office to work out of. Just find us a building or an office space somewhere so that we can work. Besides, I don't think anyone is going to work with us out of a car or someplace."

Donnie tells Mark, "Hey, what about a library?"

Mark tells Donnie, "What about it?"

Donnie tells Mark, "They have an office space in the library we can use."

Mark tells Donnie, "Library? Like the L.A. Public Library?"

Donnie tells Mark, "Yes. The head librarian is a fan of ours, I hang out there all the time. I could talk to the head librarian, he owes me a couple favors, and I think he can let us use the office space there."

Mark tells Donnie, "What kind of favors?"

Donnie tells Mark, "We made some public appearances that helped the library out a lot. Plus we spoke on that campaign remember?"

Mark tells Donnie, "Oh yeah, I forgot about that. Go talk to the head librarian, and get us an office space, and I'll call Logan and see if he can get us a job."

Back in the LAPD, Logan is looking over some of the files from the case that he was suspended for, and he tells himself, "Man, something's not right here. I remember Medford signed a warrant, but this is a forged signature? He never signed it? I guess Keltner walks. Man, I was this close to finding his supplier. Too bad I'm a by-the-book cop, 'cause if I wasn't I could find out who Keltner was working for. He must have an inside guy or something, which I really doubt. Too bad I'm not in IA, 'cause even I couldn't figure it out."

An LAPD detective enters, and goes over to Logan's desk to talk to him. The detective tells Logan, "Hey Logan!"

18

Logan tells the detective, "Hey Ben! How's the new job?"

Ben tells Logan, "Hey, you know it's really kind of cool. Besides I'm usually a beat cop, but I finally passed the detective exam, so I moved to L.A. so I could take on real criminals."

Logan tells Ben, "That's why all of us became detectives, because this is the real action."

Ben tells Logan, "Hey, you know it's been a long time since I've seen you guys in the neighborhood."

Logan tells Ben, "Yeah, well while me, Donnie, and Mark's singing careers took off, you stayed to become a cop."

Ben tells Logan, "You know, I was jealous of you guys, becoming rich and successful, and travelling around the world. But, I'm kind of glad I became a cop, because I was my father's favorite, and I wanted to join the force and be like him. You know Mark wanted to be like him too, but deep down Dad didn't see any potential in him. He always told him he was a disappointment, and didn't have what it took to make it in the force."

Logan tells Ben, "And how come your dad, or you, never got him out of that gang. He only joined the Red Dragons so he wouldn't get beat up all the time. They had been bullying us our whole lives in school."

Ben tells Logan, "Hey, I wanted to get him out of there. There was nothing to be done. Besides Mark was too interested in fitting in somewhere. When he got in trouble with vandalism, I always knew what it would get him."

Logan tells Ben, "I'll tell you what it got him, a one year stint in juvenile hall. Besides, your father was the arresting officer, and he wanted to teach him a lesson to stay away from gangs. Besides, he didn't want him to join the force, so I bet this little lesson helped him out."

Ben tells Logan, "Well, even with that heart attack that he had, what really killed him was when Mark went behind bars. But, I really got to hand it to you. You following our father's footsteps. Besides, I knew you'd come to your senses, that singing group was a waste of time."

Logan tells Ben, "Heh, a minute ago you were jealous of us, and now the singing group was a waste of time?"

Ben tells Logan, "Of course it was a waste of time, besides I was only playing you. You think I wanted to share some sympathy with Donnie or Mark? Let's face it, those guys were a huge disappointment to Dad and me."

Logan tells Ben, "Yeah, except our singing group was successful. We even recorded a few songs with Mark when he was in. We put some recording equipment in juvenile hall to record a few songs and sent them to a record company. And we were signed, and got a few platinum records. Good think the warden was a music fan, or we would have had to wait a year for him to get out."

Ben tells Logan, sarcastically, "Oh silly me, and I thought I was showing a little sympathy here, yeah right. Like I said, Logan, I'm kind of glad Smithson fired you. Since you're off the case, I'm back on it. Once it's over, I'll probably get a promotion and a medal for finding this mysterious drug lord."

Logan tells Ben, "I wasn't fired, I was suspended. Besides it's only one week, I bet I can look over this case file for a week and see what went wrong, and once I find out what went wrong, I will find this drug kingpin and arrest him, and they'll have no choice but to lift my suspension."

Ben tells Logan, "Just like my brothers, they think they were wasting time playing cop, no you're wasting time playing cop. If you weren't weak, you could bust him. I'm a by-the-book cop too, but I eat, breathe, and live cop. You're just some washed up singer trying to play the part."

Logan tells Ben "We'll see Ben once I wrap up this case."

Ben tells Logan, "Hey don't you remember that Smithson assigned me to this case. That means I'm in charge of this case, and so all files and documents will go to me, so either way you will have no authorization to work on this case. Why don't you hit the road, and I'll take over."

Logan stands up and tells Ben, loudly, "Why don't *you* hit the road, and get out."

Ben starts laughing, and tells Logan, "Heh, excellent comeback, no wonder you're never good at making comebacks. But, hey, I'll leave you alone for a couple minutes to sulk before you have to leave, and I take over. Oh, by the way, your case file belongs to me so, bye-bye." Ben leaves, and takes the case file with him.

Logan is still upset, and tells himself, "Man, I wonder if it's too late to plant heroin on him, and put it in his desk. Nah, he'd probably get away with it. I can't even shoot the guy, there's too many witnesses around." Logan sits back down in his chair, and sulks for a minute. The phone rings, and Logan picks up the phone and talks to the guy on the other line, "Hello?"

Mark's voice tells Logan, "Hey Logan, it's Mark. Listen, I need a favor."

Logan tells Mark, "Look, Mark, whatever it is, now's not a good time."

Mark tells Logan, "Look there's something I need to tell you. It's really important."

Logan tells Mark, "Well, since I have all the time in the world, what is it?"

Mark tells Logan, "Here's the favor: Me and Donnie are working on this remake of *LA Beat*."

Logan tells Mark, "*LA Beat*? Didn't you make that movie a few years ago? It was really terrible."

Mark tells Logan, "The studio is giving us another chance. We're redoing the movie."

Logan tells Mark, "Well that sounds good, but when you loaned me that script. That movie was still terrible."

Mark tells Logan, "Yeah, I know that. But, Donnie did rewrite the movie, so it's better. The only problem is I don't know anything about being a cop."

Logan laughs for a minute, and tells Mark, "You do realize that your father was a cop? And your older brother Ben, who I ran into a couple minutes ago, already rubbed it in my face that he is a better cop than me?"

Mark tells Logan, "Well, Ben was Dad's favorite. Me and Donnie were called the disappointments. Or the sons he wished he never had."

Logan tells Mark, "You got that right. Anyways, what about *LA Beat*?"

Mark tells Logan, "The only problem is, I don't know what it's like to be a cop. I don't know how to live, eat, and breathe being a cop. I always wanted to join the force, but my dad always told me I wouldn't make it. That I didn't have what it takes to get in."

Logan tells Mark, "Well, you were a geeky, wimpy kid back then."

Mark was shocked and tells Logan, "Hey!"

Logan starts laughing, "I'm only kidding, man."

Mark tells Logan, "Hey, a few weeks in the academy would have pumped me up. Or I would've ended up working desk duty, but thanks to my stupid choice in joining the Red Dragons, the wrong crowd, that got me barred from joining the police force. I couldn't even join the L.A. reserves because of my record."

Logan tells Mark, "Hey, I'm really sorry about the man. You know, I did try to pull some strings in the academy back then, after I graduated. But rules are rules."

Mark tells Logan, "The leader of the academy actually said that?"

Logan tells Mark, "Actually, the academy leader was never a fan of yours. I think that's one reason they never let you in. And the deputy mayor really hated your movies back then, that's why he black-balled you from being a cop."

Mark tells Logan, "I always thought the mayor had the authorization, not the deputy mayor, to black-ball me."

Logan tells Mark, "The leader of the academy owed the deputy mayor a favor, so that was that. But anyway, Mark, if there was any way I could get you in, I would."

Mark tells Logan, "I think there is a way. Me and Donnie just applied for P.I. licenses, and we're gonna start our own detective agency."

Logan is shocked for a minute, and tells Mark, "A P.I. agency?"

Mark tells Logan, "Yeah a P.I. agency. We're going to work with the police and help them work on cases."

Logan tells Mark, "Wow, just like Sherlock Holmes. Since you guys are P.I.s, what's the favor?"

Mark tells Logan, "I wonder if you could put in a good word for us, see if anybody from the department wants to hire us on any cases that you guys can't solve yourselves."

Logan tells Mark, "Well, there was a case I was supposed to be working on, but I got suspended because I messed up."

Mark tells Logan, "What was the case?"

Logan tells Mark, "We arrested some guy who was dealing drugs, he was going to lead us to his supplier. His name was Luke Keltner. He was selling heroin outside of an industrial plant. He was going to give us information about who this mysterious drug lord was, but since the district attorney's search warrant was forged by the court house clerk or somebody, he walks. So, we're back at square one."

Mark tells Logan, "Hey, maybe I could help you find this guy!"

Logan tells Mark, "Look, Mark, I'd love to help you out, but I'm suspended since I messed up on this case. I've been after this mysterious drug lord for two years, and we still haven't found him."

Mark tells Logan, "Look, Logan, you can trust me. We can do this job."

Logan tells Mark, "Look, right now the department is not going to ask for outside help to bag this mysterious drug lord. Besides these guys are very strict about asking private investigators to help with our investigations."

Mark tells Logan, "You know, Logan, you do owe me. I'm the one who tutored you for the entrance exam and the detective exam. You owe me. I just thought you could put a good word in for me with somebody."

Logan tells Mark, "Look right now, I'm not exactly the department's favorite. I've been messing up a lot of cases. If I wasn't by-the-book, I could probably solve a lot more cases. Just once, I wish I wasn't a screw-up."

Mark tells Logan, "Yeah well, Logan, one thing I've always learned? People who screw often do a better job than people who think they're perfect or flawless."

Logan tells Mark, "Well, if there weren't any screw-ups out there, I'd make these guys look like wimps."

Mark tells Logan, "So there's nothing you can do?"

Logan tells Mark, "Sorry man."

Mark tells Logan, "Well, I understand. Thanks anyway. Maybe I'll just have to talk to Donnie and scrap the project anyway. I know the studio's probably gonna fire Donnie and me for this. Once they find out that we can't make this movie a blockbuster they're gonna terminate our contracts. But hey, it's our problem, not yours. Alright, see ya Logan."

Logan tells Mark, "I'm sorry man. I wish there was something I could do." Logan hangs up the phone.

Back in the production office, Donnie is in his office, and sees Mark hanging up. Mark tells himself, "Man, I wish there was something you could do. I hate to break it Donnie once we lose our jobs for this. I wonder if I can get a cardboard box out of the studio to live in, since me and Donnie are gonna be on the street. And I bet Ben will be loving this too."

Mark reenters Donnie's office and Donnie tells Mark, "Hey, did Logan help us out? Did he find any cops that can ask us for some help?"

Mark tells Donnie, "Listen Donnie, there's something I need to talk to you about. I don't think you're gonna like this."

Donnie is totally shocked and he's not really happy about what Mark's going to say.

Mark tells Donnie, "I think you may want to sit down for this."

Donnie sits down on his chair, and covers his eyes for a minute because he's angry that he may not like the news.

Back in the police department, Logan is still looking at a copy of case file before he has to leave the department. Until a police captain enters and walks to his desk and talks to Logan. The police captain tells Logan, "Excuse me are you Detective Logan Myers?"

"Yes sir, who are you?" said Logan.

The police captain takes out his LAPD badge, and shows it to Logan and tells him, "I'm Captain Jake Johnson. I'm running Internal Affairs for this department."

Logan is shocked for a minute, and tells Captain Johnson, "Your IA?"

Captain Johnson tells Logan, "That's right, I'm IA."

Logan is scared for a minute, and is freaking out a little bit and tells Captain Johnson, "I swear I didn't take any bribes. I never did anything illegal."

Captain Johnson stops Logan's rambling, and tells him, "Take it easy Myers, I'm not here to bust you for anything. Besides I heard you got suspended on a lousy drug bust."

Logan tells Captain Johnson, "How do you know that?"

Captain Johnson tells Logan, "Hey, we're IA. We hear everything. And, one of the officers from here told one of our IA guys about what was going on. I thought maybe I could use your help on something."

Logan tells Captain Johnson, "You do realize you're Internal Affairs? You're not exactly liked in this department. Half these guys want to lynch you when you stick your heads into our cases, or try to hammer us for taking bribes or doing anything illegal."

"Well, I'm practically new here," says Captain Johnson.

Logan tells Captain Johnson, "So when did you start?"

"I just started today, and I looked at the case file on this drug bust you had against Keltner. The search warrant was signed by the DA, and it wasn't forged. It was misplaced. I think this might be an inside job."

Logan tells Captain Johnson, "What makes you think it's an inside job?"

Captain Johnson tells Logan, "Because this mysterious drug lord has somebody in the department on his payroll."

Logan tells Captain Johnson, "Any idea who it is?"

"We don't know, it could be anybody in the department. Every time we try to find this guy, he slips away. And mostly, when it reaches operations, half the stuff is already gone, like he'd moved the operation elsewhere. Like somebody must have tipped him off."

Logan tells Captain Johnson, "So he must have an inside guy, since Keltner walked, we still want to know who he is. You know, if I wasn't suspended on this case I would try to find out who he is. But, like you said, there's a leak in the department, and I can't find out who it is."

Captain Johnson tells Logan, "That's where you come in. Since you were working on this case, I thought you could help me out here."

Logan tells Captain Johnson, "Sir, you do realize I'm suspended? Plus, I'm off this case."

Captain Johnson tells Logan, "By Captain Smithson, not by me. You'll be working for us on this case. Plus, I think you need to work outside the area, since this mysterious drug kingpin has his inside guy watching everyone."

Logan tells Captain Johnson, "Well, if I'm going to be working on this case, I wonder if you can do me a favor."

"Sure anything," said Captain Johnson.

Logan tells Captain Johnson, "I know you need me for this case because you want to find your inside guy, and I'm the only one you can trust. I just gotta ask, how far would you go to find this guy?"

Captain Johnson tells Logan, "Hey, I'll do whatever it takes to find this guy. I want this drug kingpin off the street. You guys have been after him for a couple of years, and I want to shut him down for good."

Logan tells Captain Johnson, "That's where I need the favor."

Captain Johnson tells Logan, "What's the favor?"

Logan smiles at Captain Johnson, and tells him the favor quietly.

Back at the production office, after Mark finishes telling Donnie the news.

Donnie tells Mark, "I guess we're finished. Logan was our only hope to finish this movie, and our butts are riding on getting it done. I really worked hard to get this movie made. Do you know how many favors I had to put in at the studio to get it done?"

Mark tells Donnie, "You know, I get it. We put our savings in to fund this movie, and since there's not going to be a movie, we're going to be on the streets. Because we wanted to do this movie our whole lives, and we had another chance to get this thing right. Man, if there was a sign we could get another chance, I'd be all for it."

Donnie tells Mark, "Well, whatever the sign is, I think it's long gone right now. I guess we'll have to tell everybody that we're going to shut down the office."

Mark tells Donnie, "So who tells our crew that we're shutting down?"

Donnie tells Mark, "You know, I'm the oldest, and I am in charge of M.D.L. Productions, so I think I should tell them."

Mark tells Donnie, "We are gonna put a hundred people out of work, once we tell them the production company will be out of business."

Donnie tells Mark, "You know, Mark, you said something about a sign, let's wait to see if it comes. If it doesn't, I'll go out and tell everybody we're done."

Mark tells Donnie, "How about five seconds?"

Donnie tells Mark, "Alright, time me."

Mark winds his watch for five seconds, and waits.

The watch's alarm goes off, and the five seconds are up, and Donnie tells Mark, "I guess time's up, I have to go tell them."

Mark tells Donnie, "I'm sorry, big bro."

Donnie tells Mark, "Yeah, me too."

Donnie was about to get up from his chair, until he hears the phone ring.

Mark answers the phone, and tells the caller, "Hello M.D.L. Production, er, I mean ex-M.D.L. Productions, whatever it is, I think you should talk to the studio head, because we're out of business."

Logan's voiceover tells Mark, "Hey, uh, Mark, it's me Logan. Good news."

Mark sarcastically tells Logan, "Hey, Kate Upton finally return your phone calls?"

Logan laughs for a minute, and tells Mark, "I think I found you a case I'm working on. I need your help."

Mark was a little bit excited, and shocked, and tells Logan, "The Keltner case? I thought you were suspended on it?"

Logan tells Mark, "I was suspended on the case, but the new guy, Captain Jake Johnson, he's from IA, he's assigned me to the case because he thinks there's somebody in my department working for this mysterious drug kingpin. This might be an inside job, and I need your help to find our leak, and figure out who this mysterious drug kingpin is."

Mark tells Logan, "Okay, if I'm going to work on this case there will be a couple conditions you need to work out with your captain."

Logan tells Mark, "Sure, what is it?"

Mark tells Logan on the phone, "We need 2 LAPD detective badges, so we can get inside places, and interview any suspects, or make any arrests if we're gonna find this guy. In other words, I need full authorizations to work on this case. You know, handcuffs, guns, all of it, everything."

Logan tells Mark, on the phone, "Done. I'll call Captain Johnson and tell him the arrangements. Where do you want to meet?"

Mark tells Logan on the phone, "I know a place, Donnie's already got it set up, we'll meet there."

Logan tells Mark, "So, where is this place?"

"Alright I'll tell you where it is, but no questions asked."

Logan tells Mark, "Okay."

Mark tells Logan, "Okay, just meet me at the LA Public Library. Come over at 10. I'll meet you at the front door."

Logan tells Mark, "Alright, Mark, I'm going to say this. Why the library?"

Mark tells Logan, "I'll explain later. But, like I said, no questions asked. I'll see you tomorrow at 10 AM. See ya Logan."

Logan tells Mark, "Alright man."

Mark hangs up the phone, and Donnie asks Mark, "Who was it?"

Mark tells Donnie, "It was Logan. Good news! We're back in."

Donnie tells Mark, "You mean, we're in. We've got ourselves a case?"

Mark tells Donnie, "Yup, we're in. I guess we can save our movie after all."

Donnie and Mark celebrate for a minute, high-fiving each other. Donnie tells Mark, "Look, Mark, before we start. Do we know anything about detective work? What do we know about investigating a crime?"

Mark tells Donnie, "Hey, you forget, Logan taught us everything about detective work. And we've watched a lot of movies. We even wrote a movie! We know a lot about detective work, it's just that we've never gotten into character on it before."

Donnie tells Mark, "You know that's true. I guess we did learn something. I just hope we can still learn our detective skills that Logan taught us."

Mark tells Donnie, "I hope so too. Man, Logan really was a lousy cop, no offense."

Donnie tells Mark, "None taken. Just hope we know what we're doing."

Mark tells Donnie, "Yeah, me too. Besides, we're a little bit rusty, but I think we'll be fine."

Donnie tells Mark, "I hope so too."

At 10 AM, inside the Los Angeles Public Library, Logan enters the first floor with the case file that he was working on, and he is carrying all the equipment that Mark asked for in three shopping bags. Logan sees Mark, and goes over to talk to him, "Hey, you're way early Mark."

Mark tells Logan, "Hey, I had to make a good impression. And besides, one thing you've always known about me, I'm always on time."

Logan tells Mark, "Yeah, except you've been late to five recording sessions, and a few of our concerts when we were on tour."

Mark tells Logan, "Hey, those arenas are so big, it's hard to find anything. It's like you need a map to figure out where you are. Especially in recording studios."

Logan tells Mark, "Yeah, that's true. Besides, I was late with you too. Okay, I got the equipment. So tell us, where's this secret place we have to meet?"

Mark tells Logan, "I'll show you. And you wanted to ask why we're meeting in this library?"

Logan tells Mark, "Uh, yeah."

Mark tells Logan, "Because this is the last place on Earth that anyone is going to look for us, or do any detective work. Besides, you said there's a leak in the department, right? This is the only place they can't figure out what we're up to."

Logan tells Mark, "Good thinking. So, where is this place anyway?"

Mark tells Logan, "Follow me."

Mark shows Logan where they're going to work. They see the elevator and Mark presses elevator button, and the door opens, and they go inside the elevator. Mark shows Logan their secret location. The elevator door closes when they get to the secret location. Inside the computer room, the door opens, and Mark and Logan enter the computer room. Donnie is there on one of the computers waiting for them, sitting in his chair. Donnie sees Logan, and they haven't spoken for about five years, since Logan joined the force. Donnie goes over to greet him, and hugs him, saying, "Man Logan, it's been a long time since we've seen each other. I really missed you."

Logan tells Donnie, "Yeah, I know, it's been a long time Donnie. I've really missed you too."

Donnie lets go of Logan, and tells him, "Man, how's the police business?"

Logan tells Donnie, "Donnie, you do realize that Mark told you I got suspended from a case, and he told you that I've been a lousy detective for the last three years, since I made detective."

Donnie tells Logan, "Yeah, I know, I was just testing you. I wanted to keep you on your toes."

Logan starts laughing, and tells Donnie, "Funny, Donnie. Cute, but funny."

Mark tells Logan, "So, do you have the case files to work on?"

Logan tells Mark, "Yeah, I have them right here."

Donnie tells them, "Alright, let's see what you've got on this mysterious drug lord case that you're working on."

They all three sit down, and Logan hands the files over to Mark and Donnie, and they both look them over.

Donnie tells Logan, "Logan, the guy you arrested, Marvin Keltner, right? He was going to lead you to this mysterious drug lord."

Logan tells Donnie, "Yeah, of course. Since the search warrant was never signed by the assistant DA he walked, so we're back at square one."

Mark looks at the file for a minute, and sees Keltner's picture, and he tells Logan, "I don't think Keltner's your guy. I don't think he's going to lead you anywhere."

Logan tells Mark, "What do you mean he wasn't going to lead me anywhere?"

Mark tells Logan, "Because the heroin inside his apartment? I think that stuff was planted there. Besides, it looks like someone needed a scapegoat. Sure, he may work for this kingpin, but I don't think he knew what he was running drugs. I think he was set up as fall guy."

Logan is a little bit upset, and tells Mark, "What do you mean he was a fall guy?"

Donnie tells Logan, "Simple. Logan, what is the one thing you always have to know about bad guys?"

Logan tells Donnie, "What's that?"

Donnie tells Logan, "Every bad guy is always two steps ahead of you. They'd know you'd be tracking them down, so the only way to get away is to plant the evidence on someone else. Like Keltner. Even though he had a rap sheet with drugs, he wanted out. His PO was the one who got him a job in his industry because he needed to make ends meet, but he doesn't know who he's working for. Why don't you think he was the perfect scapegoat?"

Logan thinks for a minute, and tells them, "That way they cover their tracks, so that they wouldn't find out who the real kingpin was. I think he works in the same place as Keltner. He wasn't buying drugs from somewhere else, he was buying drugs inside the place he works in."

Mark tells Donnie, "I know the place that he was working at Steel Industries, it's a steel plant about 20 blocks from Culver City owned by John Steel. I think that's where Keltner was working. I think his boss may be the mysterious drug lord."

Logan tells them, "Well I checked John Steel, he's pretty clean. Besides, I doubt there were any drugs inside of his steel plant."

Mark tells Logan, "Maybe not in one of his plants, he must own a warehouse. Plus, he wouldn't just put drugs inside of a box or something. He'd need some place to hide it, like molten steel."

Donnie tells them, "Why liquid steel?"

Logan tells them, "Simple, that way he can get rid of the smell, he could drive the scent off in five seconds. If you hid heroin in liquid steel you would drive the smell off in five seconds, besides no one would expect a bunch of heroin inside liquid steel."

Donnie turns on the computer, and got the password to the FBI and LAPD, and looked up John Steel.

Logan tells Donnie, "Hey Donnie, how'd you get into the computers? I was going to help you with that. How'd you get into the FBI database?"

Donnie tells Logan, "The FBI director is a fan of ours, and besides I gave him an autographed copy of a CD and Mark and I sang a few songs at her daughter's birthday party, so she owes us."

Logan also tells Donnie, "How did we get the computer room all to ourselves anyway?"

Mark tells Logan, "The head librarian is a fan of ours."

Logan tells them, "Man, that explains a lot."

Donnie looks up the files about John Steel, and tells them, "I found out about John Steel. Two years ago, one of his employees was suspected of heroin dealing."

Logan tells Donnie, "You know who it is?"

Donnie tells Logan, "Yeah, his name is Marcus Redneck, he was vice president of Steel Industries. He was suspected of earning some extra cash selling heroin on the side, but the police never had any proof that he was connected to the drug dealing."

Mark tells them, "Unless Redneck was just the middle man, he was just small time. Logan, you said there was a leak in the department?"

Logan tells them, "Yeah there is."

Mark tells them, "That explains how he covered his tracks. Your leak must've tipped him off that the police were gonna raid the warehouse, and him."

Logan tells them, "You think Redneck might be the mastermind? Or he's working for Steel?"

Donnie tells them, "I don't know, but I think both of them might be in on this. But, one thing I do know, there's always competition. That's one thing about every business, there is always a competitor."

Logan tells them, "Somebody wanted to put them out of business, so they do whatever it takes to get them out."

Mark figured out something, "Hey, I think I know why Keltner was being set up. We know he was being set up by his company, but why? Because Keltner is a corporate spy from another company."

Donnie tells Mark, "Like who?"

Mark tells them, "Had to be something they had to fight over a contract for. Must be something really big."

Donnie checks over the computer, and tells them, "I think I figured out what they were competing for. It's for the Navy. The Navy is looking for new steel for their battleships. They're paying one of these companies, like, 500 million dollars for their new naval carriers."

Mark tells Donnie, "What's the name of the company that Steel Industries may be competing against?"

Donnie tells them, "You're not going to believe this, but it's a start-up company. It's Bruce Steel Incorporated. It's another steel company about 20 blocks from here. They're both competing for the Navy contract."

Logan tells them, "Bruce Steel? I think I remember that guy. That's John's brother. John Steel Sr. was the founder of Steel Industries, when he died he must have left the company and all of its assets to John Jr. Man, Bruce was always competing against him, trying to earn his father's trust, but he was always never good enough, a disappointment. But he was left a little bit of industry money."

Mark tells them, "That explains a lot about Keltner. His PO must have sent him to that industry. Keltner was trying to make some extra money, so Bruce must have hired him to figure out what John was up to. Keltner looked at more than just John's plans on the Navy contract, he also found out that he was running a heroin business on the side."

Logan tells them, "You know there was an anonymous tip about Keltner buying and selling drugs in the factory. It explains a lot about why we raided the place and arrested him. We interrogated him and tried to figure out who he was working for. His boss was right in front of us the whole time. I didn't know the company he was working for was running a drug business on the side."

Mark tells them, "We've got to get a hold of Bruce Steel. I think he might be able to tell us about his brother's side-business. Or if he found out that he was running a drug business. Or if he was about to tell the police about what his brother was doing."

Donnie looks at his computer, and tells them, "Well, I don't think we're going to be able to talk to him anytime soon. He's on a business trip in DC. He's talking to one of the navy admirals about the navy contract. I think he might be close to closing the deal."

Logan tells them, "How close?"

"I think on Friday. They just need Bruce's signature and he's gonna get 500 million dollars to use the steel to build the navy carriers."

Logan tells them, "I know John wants that navy contract, and it looks like he's gonna be fighting for it. Besides, if he wanted to put his brother out of business, why didn't he plant the drugs on him, why just put it on Keltner?"

Mark tells them, "I think there might be a bigger play here. I think he wants Bruce to get that contract signed. I think he's planning on bigger drugs in his warehouse pretty soon. I think they're going to attempt to plant drugs in Bruce's warehouse. If they find drugs with Bruce's steel, they'll have no choice but to tear up the contract and sign with John."

Donnie tells them, "Even if they get Bruce's signature, it's signed and sealed. They don't have to tear up the contract even if they find drugs. They can still use Bruce's steel, since it's signed and sealed."

Mark tells them, "There's always a loophole in the contract. And to tell you the truth, only the Navy Admiral can tear it up or dismiss the deal, if their client is involved in any wrongdoing. Either way John still might get the contract. Lucky for me, I could took a couple business classes at USC before Donnie and I started the production company."

Logan tells them, "Let me guess, the dean of admissions is a fan of ours too?"

Mark and Donnie say, "Yup, you bet'cha."

Logan tells them, "Sometimes, it's good to be a celebrity."

Mark tells them, "I think the only person we should talk to is John Steel himself. I think we should pay him a visit and see what he's up to."

Donnie tells them, "Are you guys just going to arrest him and try to interrogate him, like they do in the movies or those procedural police shows?"

Logan tells them, "Hey, even I don't do any of that stuff. Besides I don't even play good cop/bad cop, because deep down I know I'm no good at either. And they never let me into the interrogation box. Not even my ex-partner would let me in. And besides, I know the business. We interrogate them, they won't tell us a thing, and even if they did they would tell us less, and then they'd get their high priced attorney to let them out, and we're back at square one."

Mark tells them, "Well, we're not going to do that. Because we're going to go in disguise."

Logan tells them, "If we're going as Masters of Disguise, what are we going as?"

Mark tells Logan, "I'll explain later what we're going as. But right now, we need to change. Lucky the wardrobe department has a closet full of clothes we can use for a disguise."

Logan tells Mark, "What kind of disguise can we use to get in to talk to Steel?"

Mark tells Logan, "I think I know one, and I know exactly how to get in. But, you know, we don't need the wardrobe department, just some new suits."

Donnie tells them, "Yeah, besides, I checked Steel's itinerary. He's off for the day. He won't be back in his office until tomorrow morning. If we want to pay him a visit, we'll have to wait until 9 AM tomorrow."

Mark tells them, "If we want to pay a visit to Steel, we're going to have to go as like investors or a charity organization to get him to talk to us."

Logan tells them, "That sounds like a great idea, but there's just one problem. Mark's too recognizable. Unless he hasn't seen any of the six *Nitro* movies, he'll be able to spot him right away."

Mark tells them, "I don't think we'll have to worry about that. Lucky for me, there is a wig that I can use to disguise myself, or I could just use a better look."

Logan tells Mark, "What better look is that? Because either way you're still recognizable. He'll still be able to spot you."

Mark tells Logan, "I don't think we're going to have to worry about it. I may be recognizable, but I won't be me. Besides, there's a million doppelgangers that look like me, so I don't think we'll have to worry about that. All we have to do is put on a couple suits, gel our hair, and wear some Ray-Ban sunglasses, and he won't be able to recognize us."

Donnie tells them, "Okay, now since we've got that covered, who's going to go and pay him a visit?"

Mark tells Donnie, "Simple, Donnie, me and Logan will go. I need you to run the computer, and do some research for us."

Donnie tells Mark, "Okay, but there's something else I should tell you guys."

Mark tells Donnie, "What is it?"

Donnie tells Mark, "Even if you guys go as business men. You need somebody to spot you, someone to introduce you."

Mark tells Donnie, "You've got a point, Donnie. We need like a personal assistant who can help us. Who we can we get?"

Logan thinks for a moment, and he tells them, "Hey, I think I know somebody that can help. Plus, she is a dire M-D-L fan, and she loved the six *Nitro* movies. I think she can help us."

Donnie tells Logan, "Who is it?"

Mark tells Logan, "You think she can help us?"

Logan tells them, "Of course, she's a huge fan. She would do anything for us."

Donnie tells them, "Can you get her to meet us in the computer room at around 8 o'clock so we can get her started?"

Logan tells Donnie, "Sure thing. I have to get back to the department, and meet up with Captain Johnson. I'm going to tell him that we may have found our drug kingpin, but we still haven't found our leak yet."

Donnie tells Logan, "Sure thing. No problemo. Just make sure to get her here to the library. I'll get her an outfit too, to help us out."

Logan tells Donnie, "Okay. Donnie, there's one thing I wanted to ask you before I go."

Donnie tells Logan, "Sure what is it Logan?"

Logan tells Donnie, "What about your movie *LA Beat*? I thought you guys were filming?"

Donnie tells Logan, "We're going to put in a two-week delay, and stop productions for two weeks, so that we have plenty of time to solve

39

this case. Plus, we need to get into character for the movie. Besides, I think I'll have a rewrite to do soon."

Logan tells Donnie, "Alright, I was just checking. I'll see you guys tomorrow at 8 AM. Bye guys."

Donnie and Mark tell Logan, "See ya, man."

Logan gets up from his chair and exits the computer room.

At 9 PM, outside Club Car, Marcus Redneck and Marvin Keltner are about to enter the club. Keltner tells Redneck, "Are you sure the boss wants to meet me in this club?"

Redneck tells Keltner, "Yeah, of course. He needs to have a word with you."

Keltner tells Redneck, "Do you know what it's about?"

Redneck tells Keltner, "Well, I have no idea, but I think it has something to with your job. Since Mr. Steel told me you're doing an excellent job with us, he probably wants to offer you a raise or a promotion, and he wants to tell you in his club."

Keltner sounds very excited, and tells Redneck, "Man, I'm really excited. I hope it's a big raise, because I worked really hard for the guy. I'm sure he'd be really surprised when I tell him the news."

Redneck tells Keltner, "Don't worry he'll be surprised. He'll be definitely surprised."

Keltner and Redneck are about to head inside the club, until a masked figure grabs both of their shirts and brings them back into the alley. The masked figure, in a hood and sunglasses, his voice dubbed, tells Keltner and Redneck, "Hands up! I want your wallets. Now!"

Keltner and Redneck give him their wallets, and Keltner is very scared. Keltner tells the mugger, "Look, here's the wallet, just take it and go alright? Just don't hurt us."

The mugger tells them, "I want more than your wallet, pretty boy. I heard somebody is spying on Mr. Steel, and he doesn't like it. He doesn't like when somebody takes something that's his."

Keltner is a little frightened, and he tells the mugger, "Wait a minute, you work for Mr. Steel? Who are you?"

The mugger tells Keltner, "A man whose about to take your life. Like this." The mugger kicks Keltner in the groin and two bullets fire from his gun into Keltner's head. Keltner falls to the floor, dead.

Redneck puts his hands down, and tells the mugger, "We got him. At least Steel's brother won't be spying on us anymore."

The mugger tells Redneck, "Yeah, of course he won't be spying on us anymore. Because you won't be spying on Mr. Steel anymore. Because I know you were trying to steal his business."

Now Redneck is a little bit frightened, and the mugger aims his gun at Redneck. Redneck tells the mugger, "I swear I'm not stealing business from Mr. Steel I swear."

The mugger tells Redneck, "Oh really, huh? Because Mr. Steel asked me to take a look into your place, and I saw drawers of heroin, and money on your shelf. He doesn't like anybody stealing his business."

Redneck tells the mugger, "Please, I'll give the money back, and the drugs. I didn't mean to run a side business on him. I'll give it all back."

The mugger tells Redneck, "Of course you'll give it back, with interest." The mugger punches Redneck in the stomach, and roundhouse kicks him in the face, and Redneck falls to the floor. The mugger kicks him in the stomach three times, and tells Redneck, "That's just so you don't forget, and you are going to pay with interest, starting now."

Redneck is begging for his life to the mugger, and he tells him, "Please, please, please, I'll give it back I swear."

The mugger fires his gun. Four bullets hit Redneck in the chest, and he dies, and the mugger takes off the hood, his face still hidden in the dark. The mugger tells himself, "Like Mr. Steel said. Nobody steals from family, nobody. Not even me. This was personal." He looks at Keltner's body, and says, "And you were that close to spilling the beans to my boss, and me, but like I said, Keltner, nobody stops Steel, nobody, not even me."

At 8 AM, outside the computer room at the L.A. Public Library, Logan shows his ex-partner, who transferred from IA, Detective Sergeant Linda Myers, into the room. Logan tells Linda, "Hey sis, thanks for helping me out, I really owe ya."

Linda tells Logan, "Hey, I would do anything to see Mark. You know, I've had a crush on him since I was 12."

Logan tells Linda, "Yeah, I know. Since me and Donnie and Mark started our singing group, you'd always drool over him, every time we played a concert, or when I brought him to dinner with Mom and Dad at home."

Linda tells Logan, "You know, I know I never said anything, but I was young and stupid back then. Besides, I was 12 and you guys were 18, Dad would have killed him if I he had asked me out."

Logan tells Linda, "Well, I know Dad loved Mark and Donnie, but he's really protective about who you date."

Linda tells Logan, "Hey, I understand. That's the reason I never wanted to get on Dad's bad side. But, since I'm grown up now, I think he's decided to back off a little. I think he's a lot more worried about my work since we joined the police force."

Logan tells Linda, "Well Dad worked in the glass factory for thirty years, he wanted us to get a safe job, but we wanted something better from our lives. You and I both wanted to join the police force but he was scared that he would lose us. But, I think he is okay with it."

Linda tells Logan, "Yeah, I just transferred from Boston PD about a week ago, after I made detective. Besides I kind of owe you for getting me into IA."

Logan tells Linda, "You do realize that IA is the most hated department ever? Not a lot of cops like internal affairs."

Linda tells Logan, "Hey, I know that. Besides, I wanted to work on Narcotics. But then you got suspended before my transfer, and you talked to Captain Johnson, and he wanted us to work together, so that was that."

Logan opens the door to the computer room and enters. Logan and Linda see Donnie waiting for them.

Donnie recognizes Linda, and says, "Linda? Is that really you?"

Linda tells Donnie, "Hey Donnie! Man, it's been a long time."

Donnie tells Linda, "Man, a very long time."

Donnie hugs Linda for a minute, and he has a little bit of a crush on her, but he doesn't say anything, and Logan tells Donnie, "Yo, 007, you can let go of her now. She has to breathe."

Donnie lets go of Linda, and tells Logan, "Sorry, man. It's been a while since we've seen your sister. Man, she's really grown up." Donnie sees Linda, and sees how attractive and beautiful she is. Donnie tells Logan, "Man, I can't believe that's Linda. Your sister is really hot."

Logan is a little bit upset, and tells Donnie, "Hey hey hey, that's my sister! If you ever say anything like again Donnie, I'll kick your ass in five seconds."

Donnie tells Logan, "Sorry man, but she is hot."

Logan tells Donnie, "Hey don't make me punch you."

Donnie tells Logan, "Yet again, still sorry. Anyway, Mark will be out in a minute."

Logan tells Donnie, "Does he have our suits ready for us?"

Donnie tells Logan, "Yeah, he should be out of the closet in a minute to get you in your suits."

The closet door opens, and Mark steps out, carrying three dress suits on hangers, but he's only wearing his boxer shorts, not having changed yet. Linda is a little bit shocked, and Logan tells Mark, "Dude, put a shirt on! And some pants! I don't like looking at your body. I don't even like looking at my body."

Mark tells Logan, "Sorry man. Hey, I didn't know you were bringing…?" Mark sees Linda, and he is shocked. Mark tells Linda and Logan, "Linda? Is that you? Wow, you've really grown…?"

Logan tells Mark, "Mark don't even think about it."

Mark tells Logan, "Sorry man. Besides, I didn't expect you to come way early. And I didn't know you were bringing Linda. Wasn't she your ex-partner?"

Logan tells Mark, "Just for a couple of days, I had to work on this narcotics case alone. So we decided to separate a little, and she had to do her own thing."

Donnie tells Logan, "What was her own thing?"

Logan tells Donnie, "She got shot in the leg at a drug bust, and she was out of action for a couple days. But she's fine, the doctor cleared her for duty."

Mark tells them, "Well, I'm glad she's doing okay. We need all the help we can get. And Linda, I was going to ask…?"

Logan sees Linda is a little bit gun shy when she sees Mark. Logan tells Mark, "Dude, what did I tell ya? Don't even think about it."

Mark tells Logan, "Sorry man. I better go back in the closet and change. By the way I got your suits for you. There's a study room there that you can use."

Linda tells Mark, "Yeah, thanks Mark. I really appreciate that. You know, you are, uh, really hot."

Mark tells Linda, "Thanks, I appreciate that. Besides I was on the cover of the *World's Most Beautiful People* magazine last year."

Linda tells Mark, "I could tell."

Logan tells them, "Guys, I'm standing right here."

Mark and Linda tell Logan, "Sorry."

Logan tells Linda, "C'mon Linda, let's go change."

Linda tells Logan, "Okay."

Linda and Logan grab their suits from the hangars that Mark had set on the table. Mark went back into the closet to change as well.

Mark parked his BMW 640i Coupe inside the parking lot outside of Steel Industries. Linda exits the BMW, and the front door window is down. Linda is wearing her business suit and Ray-Ban sunglasses.

Mark tells Linda, "Okay, Linda, just go talk to the secretary at the front desk. Introduce us and see if Steel is in."

Linda tells Mark, "Okay."

Linda goes inside Steel Industries, and sees the lady at the front desk. The front desk lady is working, but sees Linda, and tells her, "Hi, can I help you?"

Linda puts her briefcase on the desk, and takes out a business card to show to the lady at the front desk. The front desk lady grabs it and observes it for a minute. Linda tells the lady at the front desk, "Hi, I'm Linda Myers. I represent Patrick Investments. We're here to make an investment. My bosses Robert and Logan Patrick, brothers, want to make an investment in Mr. Steel's company. They're considering investing about 500 million dollars in the company because of the new project that you're working on for the Navy. We want to invest in this company to help him out."

The lady at the front desk asks Linda, "How do you know about the Navy contract?"

Linda tells the lady at the front desk, "We have some friends in high places." The lady at the desk looks at Linda for a minute, and Linda tells her the truth, "They read the Wall Street Journal every day, and that's how they heard about your company and decided they wanted to invest. We're worth millions. I just wanted to see if Mr. Steel was in today, or if we needed to make an appointment. The Patrick brothers are willing to pay top dollar for this company, and it will really help Mr. Steel if they invest in this company. Not only will it make Mr. Steel rich, it will make the Patrick brothers a lot richer."

The lady at the front desk tells Linda, "Well, I'll check to see if Mr. Steel is in. If he is in, I'll tell him the news. When can Mr. Steel meet with the Patrick brothers?"

Linda tells the lady at the front desk, "Oh, they are already here. I just want to talk to Mr. Steel first, to see if he's in and if he would like to make an appointment. They are waiting outside to see if Mr. Steel wants to meet us."

The lady at the front desk tells Linda, "I'll see if Mr. Steel is busy." The lady at the front desk picks up her phone, and calls Mr. Steel's office. She tells the secretary at Mr. Steel's office, "Excuse me Patty, is Mr. Steel in his office today?... He is? Okay thank you. I have a couple investors here that would like to meet with Mr. Steel. They're willing to pay top dollar for this company, and they do not like to be kept waiting. Okay, thank you Patty." The lady at the front desk hangs up the phone, and tells Linda, "Mr. Steel is ready to see them right now."

Linda tells her, "Well, thank you. We really appreciate it."

The lady at the front desk tells Linda, "His office is on the 25th floor. The elevator is to the right over there."

Linda tells the lady at the front desk, "Thank you ma'am."

The lady at the front desk tells Linda, "I'm just here to help."

Linda shakes the lady at the front desk's hand. Linda sees Mark and Logan outside, and gives them the hand signal that they're in.

Mark tells Logan, "We're in, let's go." Mark and Logan enter the lobby, and they go over to talk to Linda. Mark tells Linda, "What floor?"

Linda tells them, "25th."

Mark, Logan, and Linda head to the right to the elevator, and press the button to summon the elevator. The doors open, and they enter the elevator. The doors close and it heads to the 25th floor.

Inside Steel's office, Mr. Steel is working. He hears the phone ring, and he picks up the receiver, "Hello? Hi Patty. Okay bring them in." Steel hangs up the phone and waits for them.

Outside of Steel's office, Patty tells Mark, Linda, and Logan, "Mr. Steel is ready to see you now."

Mark tells Patty, "Thank you, we appreciate that."

Logan tells Linda, "Linda, you stay outside."

Linda tells him, "Sure, no problem, just pray you come out of there alive."

Mark tells Linda, "Don't worry. By the way, if there's any hooting or hollering going on in that office, you better call in the cavalry."

Logan tells Linda, "And the marines too. Because I think we need those guys much more."

Linda tells them, "Just be careful."

Mark and Logan tell Linda, "Yeah, you too."

They were whispering, so that way Patty wouldn't hear anything.

Inside Steel's office, Mr. Steel is waiting for them. The door opens, and Mark and Logan enter. Steel gets up from his chair, and Mark and Logan go over to greet Steel. Steel tells them, "Hello, Mr. Patrick. I'm Mr. Jonathon Steel. I'm CEO and owner of Steel Industries."

Mark tells him, "Well, it's a pleasure to meet you Mr. Steel." Mark shakes his hand and he tells him, "I'm Mr. Robert Patrick, and this my brother and business partner Logan Patrick."

He lets go, and Mr. Steel goes to shake Logan's hand, and Logan tells him, "It's a pleasure to meet you Mr. Steel."

Steel tells Logan, "It's a pleasure to meet you too." Steel lets go of Logan's hand, and tells them, "Can I get you guys some coffee or something?"

Logan tells him, "You know, we could take a couple of coffees."

But Mark stops him and tells Logan, "No, we're good. So, let's get to business Mr. Steel, about why we're here."

Steel tells Mark, "Yeah, of course, let's get down to business. Have a seat gentlemen." Steel, Logan, and Mark sit down in their chairs. Mark and Logan put their briefcases down. Steel tells them, "So, I heard you guys wanted to make an investment due to the Navy contract that I'm getting."

Mark picks up his briefcase, puts it in his lap and opens it. He takes out a financial portfolio, and then closes his briefcase and sets it back on the floor. Mark tells Steel, "Yeah, we're here to make a huge investment in your company. We heard that if you get this navy contract your stock is going to go through the roof."

Logan tells Steel, "It means your fortune is going to triple once you get the contract. And that's why we're here, we want to help invest in your project, because we want to make money too."

Steel tells them, "Well, I haven't gotten the navy contract yet. I'm still in a bidding war against another company, Bruce Steel Incorporated."

Mark tells Steel, "Bruce Steel Incorporated? That's your brother's company right?"

Steel tells them, "Yes. And that wimp thinks he can steal *my* contract. I was always disappointed in him, that he had to leave this company, and use his trust fund to start his own company, all because he didn't like our business practices. I always thought he was kind of weak. But don't worry those navy contracts are going to be mine. Sorry about that. I don't mean to offend you guys, but that guy is just so weak, he doesn't have what it takes to run a business."

Logan tells Steel, "Hey, none taken."

Mark tells Steel, "Mr. Steel, we know what it is like to have a sibling rivalry. We argue all the time, but we always find a compromise, and we end up working well together because of it."

Logan tells Steel, "Plus, we have nothing to argue about right now. We may not agree on everything, but we did both agree on investing in your company. We might have gone to the other Mr. Steel, but like you said, he has no work ethic. We wanted to invest in someone who could really push to get the job done, and stomp on the little guy."

Mark shows Steel his financial portfolio. Steel takes it and observes it for a minute. Mark tells Steel, "This is our financial portfolio. We can make anyone wealthy. Trust me, we've made a few start-up companies into fortune 500s."

Steel tells Mark, "What are the names of the other companies that you've helped?"

Logan tells Steel, "Well we're not here to brag but we can give you two. One of them is called Zalten Incorporated, and then there's the Schwinn Company. We turned those small companies into billion dollar industries."

Steel tells them, "Yeah, I've read about those guys in the Fortune 500. They've made a lot of money."

Mark tells Steel, "Yup, like I said, when we invest, we invest in small too big. And your company may be big, but we invest and it goes from big to gigantic."

Steel tells them, after reading the financial portfolio, "This is a wonderful portfolio, I mean it's really excellent. I'd be happy to have you guys invest in my company."

Mark tells Steel, "We appreciate that, sir. We'll send you a check electronically in a couple of days, after you get started with the Navy project."

Steel tells them, "I appreciate that gentlemen. Once, I get the check, I'll get busy with the project, once I get the contract. The navy won't give my signature in a week. Because I have nothing to worry about, it's in the bag."

Logan tells Steel, "I'm sure it is sir, and trust me you will get your navy contract signed. I bet you wanted to ask us about how much we're willing to invest in your company?"

Steel tells them, "You know, I forgot about that. I was so excited about having some investors that I completely forgot about asking how much you were going to invest. So gentlemen, how much were you thinking to invest?"

Mark tells Steel, "About 500 million dollars, that's how much we're willing to invest in your company on this project."

Steel is excited and tells them, "Wow! 500 million dollars, I appreciate that gentlemen, I really do."

Mark tells Steel, "Hey, no problem. Like I said, we take big risks, and we always come out big, and you are the best risk ever, sir."

Steel tells Mark, "Well thank you Mr. Patrick. Oh, by the way, has anybody ever tell you that you two look like a singing group I used to know?"

Mark and Logan tell Steel, "No, we didn't know that. We have some of those faces."

Steel tells them, "Well, I can't believe how much you like those guys. You could pass as their twins."

Mark and Logan blush a little, and Mark tells him, "Gee, I appreciate that sir. Oh by the way, before we go, there's something we wanted to ask you about."

Steel tells Mark, "Sure, what is it Mr. Patrick?"

Mark tells Steel, "We read about a heroin bust two years ago. There was a mysterious drug kingpin that the LAPD was after, even the FBI couldn't find him. Everybody was after this guy, and I hear he lurked in the shadows."

Logan tells Steel, "Since nobody knew who he is, somebody had to be really smart to cover his tracks. I always thought that this kingpin would have somebody on his payroll. Like a cop or a fed in his back pocket, how else could he cover his tracks that well?"

Steel looks a bit nervous, and a little bit upset.

Mark tells Steel, "You know, I don't think that he has to be a he, he might be a she, but this mysterious drug kingpin is pretty sloppy. I don't think they are actually that good at covering their tracks. There's got to be a top detective out there looking for this guy. They've got to be trying to find him. Maybe by busting one of his dealers."

Logan tells Steel, "What was his name? I think it was Marvin Keltner. I heard they busted this guy, and had him for nearly a week. They had a search warrant and found bags of heroin. He was going to lead the police to his supplier, but the search warrant was faked, and so he walked. But I think he was innocent, because all those drugs were planted. Who would want to frame someone who just got out of jail? And who did he work for?"

Mark tells Steel, "Sorry, this guy wasn't a drug dealer. He probably had to be some corporate spy. You know somebody from a rival company that was trying to figure out what they were up to. Or trying to make sure they don't steal from them. And he was trying to figure out what they were up too."

Logan tells Steel, "You know all this stuff I read in *The Los Angeles Times*, and in the paper today, I read that Marvin Keltner was killed outside of a night club called Club Car last night, but he never went inside, and what would some ex-con like Keltner be worth killing over? He was trying to clean up his act. I know he had to be some kind of corporate spy, and maybe he found out something dangerous, like the rival company was running a big drug scam, and he was close to finding out who the mysterious drug kingpin is. And figuring out that he was hiding drugs inside molten steel, can you believe that?"

Mark tells Steel, "But, I'm sure that is just a rumor. It's not like this rival company has a drug lab somewhere around here where they're making tons of heroin, where they're selling it to Chinese mobs. This big kingpin would want to sell it to a bigger buyer. But it's all just rumor. *The Los Angeles Times* is nothing but rumors."

Steel tells them, laughing, "Yeah, well you can't believe everything you read in the paper. Besides this guy is probably crazy. I hope he gets what's coming to him. As for that rival company, they better keep their nose to themselves, because if they try to spy on their financial documents again, they would probably get killed or reported to the feds, since no company can do that. But, anyways, it's only a rumor. Anyways gentlemen, it's been a pleasure doing business with you."

Mark, Logan, and Steel all stand. Mark shakes Steel's hand and tells him, "Well, it's a pleasure doing business with you sir. And we'll send the check to you in a couple days. Go ahead and start the project. And I hope you get those navy contracts, because I want to make you a fortune, and our company too."

Steel lets go of Mark's hand, and Logan takes Steel's hand, "Yeah, I hope so too. Anyway, I hope this rival company gets what he deserves."

Steel tells Logan, "I'm sure they will, Mr. Patrick."

Logan tells Steel, "We'll see you Mr. Steel."

Logan lets go of Steel's hand, and Logan grinds his teeth, really wanting to punch him out. Mark and Logan exchange goodbyes with Steel. Logan and Mark exit Steel's office, and Steel sits down in his chair for a minute. Steel thinks about Mark and Logan, and sees something familiar about them.

Outside of Steel's office, they see Linda sitting in a chair. Logan tells Linda, "C'mon Linda, the meeting is over. Let's go."

Linda tells Logan, "Sure thing." They exit Mr. Steel's office, and head to the elevator. Linda tells them, "So do you think Steel suspects anything."

Mark and Linda are carrying their briefcases, and Mark tells Linda, "I'm not sure yet, but I think he will. I mean not right now, but soon."

Back in Steel's office, Steel is still thinking about Mark and Logan entering his office, and he picks up the phone and tells the person on the other end, "Macy, transfer me to security. Alright, thanks." Steel waits for a minute and then the phone connects. "Jackson, you have a security camera surveying my office right? You do? Good. Listen, do you have a DVD or a tape of that? Good, I need it right now. There were a couple guys in my office, and I need to see that footage. Okay, send the DVD to my office. Bye." Steel hangs up the phone, and asks himself, "Who are those guys?"

Back outside of Steel Industries, Mark, Logan, and Linda are entering Mark's car. Logan tells them, "Look, if we were going to bust Steel and his drug operation, we need to figure out who he is selling his drugs to. And figure out where his lab is, and where the deal is."

Linda tells them, "It could be anywhere."

Mark tells them, "You guys have some sources, some inside guy who knows where to find it right?"

Logan tells Mark, "Man, my sources are dried up Mark. Besides, even if I had one, I don't know where I'd find it. We've got to find somebody who Steel would never suspect, or even look at."

Mark thinks for a minute, and has an idea. He tells them, "Hey, I know somebody that could help us. I have to make a call, but he's one that could help me out. Hang on for a minute." Mark takes out his cell phone, and puts his briefcase down, and makes a call to his source. Mark calls, and the answer on the other end of the line to, "Hello? Hello Margaret, is he in? Okay, could you tell him I need a favor? Okay, I'll hang on a minute."

Linda looks at Mark for a minute, and Logan tells her, "You really like him, don't you?"

Linda is shocked for a minute, and tells Logan, "No, I don't like him like that. Besides, this guy is an ex-con, and some bad boy type. Besides, I don't date guys like that anyway."

Logan tells Linda, "You had a crush on him for a long time. Even when we had that singing group, M-D-L, you were always drooling over him. Besides he only got in trouble because his Dad called him a disappointment, and he fell in with the wrong crowd. Besides, he only hung out with that gang for a couple of weeks before taking the fall for vandalism."

Linda tells Logan, "Hey, I know that, besides, he doesn't look or act like an ex-con. I just kind of get really nervous looking at him."

Logan tells Linda, "You know, Linda, there is something that I should tell you. I joined that crowd with Mark."

Linda is totally shocked by this. Linda tells Logan, "No way, you? Besides you were...?"

Logan tells Linda, "I'm the one who dragged Mark into the crowd, alright, the Red Dragons. It's true, me and Mark got in trouble with vandalism, but I got out quickly and he covered my tracks. So he took the fall for me and he went to juvenile hall. You know, I thought his dad would help him out, but he didn't. He let him rot out there. And he died of a heart attack after Mark went in. So after he got out, I felt like I owed Mark my life, and we still talked about having a singing group or joining the force. So we did the singing group first, and maybe it was too late for Mark to join the force, but it wasn't too late for me. And Mark did whatever he could to get me into the academy, and also to help me pass the detective exam. One of us had to live out our dream." Logan looks at Mark, and sees him smiling, and Logan tells Linda, "Maybe Mark couldn't join the force like his dad, but I think he has a better job than anyone. To tell you the truth, I think he likes being a P.I. better than he would have liked being a cop."

Linda looks at Mark, "That explains why I like him a lot." Linda smiles at Mark.

Mark finishes his conversation on the phone with his source. Mark tells the source, "Alright, thanks. Alright, I'll meet you there. Bye." Mark hangs up his phone and tells them, "You guys okay? It's like you saw the Loch Ness monster or something."

Logan and Linda both snap out of it, "No, no, no, of course not."

Mark tells them, "Anyway, I got a hold of my source, he says we can meet him right now."

Logan tells Mark, "Who is this guy anyway?"

Mark tells them, "I'll tell you on the way. You know, guys, I think I might have an idea of who might be the leak in the department. It's kind of weird but when I was reading the files a couple of minutes ago, it got me thinking about who might be the leak."

Logan tells Mark, "Like who? Besides, we don't know who it is, it could be anybody."

Mark tells Logan, "Logan, I think it might be my brother, Ben, and also your boss Captain Matthew Smithson."

Logan is a little bit upset and tells Mark, "C'mon it can't be Smithson, or your brother. I know they can both be jerks, but they can't actually work for Steel."

Mark tells Logan, "I don't know, it's just an instinct. Besides, I read the file. I knew Smithson ordered you to Keltner's place and search for drugs, and he gave you a search warrant signed by Medford to give you full authorization to search his place."

Logan tells Mark, "What, are you saying, that Smithson set me up?"

Linda tells Logan, "Well Smithson may need a scapegoat, and I did reading Smithson's files. Mostly rumors that he was taking bribes, but there was no proof to it."

Mark tells Logan, "And guess who initiated the bribe?"

"Our mysterious drug kingpin, John Steel," said Linda.

Logan was thinking too, and tells them, "I think you might be right, guys. As for Ben, I think he might be connected to Steel's drug operation."

Mark tells Logan, "I know Ben was Dad's favorite, and he always had it in for me and Donnie because he was jealous of our success. Besides, I think Dad might have been crooked too. I saw an old man talking to my Dad one time in the house. They were discussing something important, I thought he was a detective or a fed, but I don't think so. This guy had a few more people with him waiting outside the house in suits and sunglasses, and I really doubt they were secret service agents, or FBI."

Logan tells Mark, "You think the old man might actually have been John's father?"

Mark snaps his fingers and tells Logan, "I think so, I forgot Steel Industries was founded in Boston, that they have another location. When John and his brother, Bruce, took over the L.A. Division, they moved the whole company to L.A. after their father died."

Linda tells them, "Is there anything more about John's father?"

Mark tells them, "I'll get ahold of Donnie, and tell him to look up John's father before we go. Logan you drive, I'll make the call to Donnie."

Logan tells Mark, "No problem."

Mark pulls his keys from his right pants pocket, and gives them to Logan so he can drive. Logan unlocks the car, and he and Linda get in the car, while Mark makes a call to Donnie. He tells Donnie, "Listen, Donnie, I need a favor."

Inside Steel's warehouse, a garage door opens, and a limousine enters. The chauffer exits the limo, and opens the back door where Steel exits the limo, carrying a briefcase and wearing Armani sunglasses. Steel sees the manager's office upstairs, and goes to climb the stairs. He nods to the chauffer to close the door. Steel heads to the office upstairs, and sees eight workers working on the drug lab. All the heroin they're making is being hidden inside molten steel inside of a box. Steel goes upstairs to the manager's office.

Inside the manager's office, Ben Wahlberg and Matthew Smithson are sitting down in their chairs and they hear a knock at the door. Smithson is working at the desk, and tells the person outside the door, "Come in!"

The door opens and Steel comes inside the office, and talks to Smithson and Ben, "Smithson, how's everything going with our deal?"

Smithson tells Steel, "Everything is going great Mr. Steel. All the heroin inside the molten steel is gonna eliminate the stench to get through customs."

"Excellent," says Steel.

Ben tells Steel, "Mr. Steel, what brings you here today?"

Steel tells them, "There's something I need you men to look at."

Steel puts his briefcase on the desk, and opens it, and shows them a DVD, "Smithson, I want you to play this DVD, there's something I want to show you."

Smithson tells Steel, "Sure, what is it Mr. Steel?"

Steel tells Smithson, "Play the DVD on the laptop and I'll show you." Steel gives the DVD to Smithson, and he plays the DVD on the laptop. Steel tells Smithson, "Smithson, I wanted to ask, did you tell anybody who you were working for? Or tell anybody about my heroin business? Or my deal with my big clients?"

Smithson is a little bit scared, and tells Steel, "I swear I didn't tell anybody you were the mysterious drug kingpin, or about your big deal. I didn't tell anybody anything. Besides, nobody is going to figure out that you are hiding heroin inside of molten steel, or that you are running the big drug business. Besides, me and Ben are the ones who covered your tracks."

Steel is a bit amused and tells them, "Men, come here for a minute. I want to tell you something in person, something I want to whisper to you."

Ben tells Steel, "Sure, what is it Mr. Steel?"

Steel tells them, "Come right here. There is a little secret I want to whisper to you guys."

Ben and Smithson go over to Steel, and he's about to whisper the secret to them.

Ben tells Steel, "Sir, what it is? What's this secret that you want to talk to us about?"

Steel tells them, "I won't tell you, but I will show you." Steel kicks Ben in the stomach, and gives him a roundhouse kick in the face, and Ben falls down on the floor. Steel grabs Smithson by the ears, and grabs his nose really hard when he lets go of his other ear. Steel tells Smithson, "Smithson, do you know what they serve in ball games?"

Smithson is panicking and hurting, and tells Steel, "No, I don't know, what?"

Steel tells Smithson, "A bag of peanuts!" Steel punches Smithson in the groin, and lets go of his nose. Smithson's groin is hurting, and

Steel punches him in the face, and he falls down on the floor. Steel is upset, and tells them, "I thought you guys cared about me. I thought I took care of you guys. I'm the one who gave you the money, who gave you a great life, and this is how you repay me, two wannabe business guys coming in and asking me questions. I want to show you some security footage." Steel grabs the laptop and turns it around and shows it to them. Smithson looks at the security tape, seeing Mark and Logan talking to Steel in his office. Steel tells them, "You guys were good at covering my tracks from the feds and the LAPD, but I don't think you guys covered them well enough. Because why are these two geeks asking me questions about my heroin deal, and about being a drug kingpin?"

Smithson looks at the monitor, and tells Steel, "It's kind of weird, I almost recognize one of them, but he looks pretty different." Ben looks at the monitor too, but is unaware that it is actually his brother. Smithson doesn't know that it is Logan and Mark either, because they are too unrecognizable. Smithson tells them, "He looks familiar to me too, but I couldn't place them. Who are they, feds? Or IA?"

Steel tells them, "Boy, I have no idea who they are, but they've been asking me questions. I have no idea if they are LAPD, IA, or feds, running around my operation, because you covered my tracks. And if they are cops I bet they're lousy at, because I don't think these losers could actually be cops."

Smithson tells them, "So what do you want us to do sir?"

Steel tells Smithson, "Call one of your friends in the police department, and make an ID on these guys. Figure out who they are."

Smithson tells Steel, "Yes sir."

Smithson and Ben get up from the floor, both still sore, and Steel tells Ben, "You know, Ben, I know you helped me frame Keltner, and took the rap for me, and I want to say thank you for that."

Smithson goes back to his chair and picks up the phone and makes a call to a friend in the LAPD, and tells them, "Roy, listen, I need a favor. I need you to make an ID on a couple of guys, I'll e-mail it to you in a minute. Hang on."

Steel continues talking to Ben, "You know, it was kind of good that he was my scapegoat. But were you actually aware that Keltner was working for my brother, that he thought he could horn in on my business? But he wasn't just horning in, he was trying to find out about me. He was just about to spill the beans to my brother, but I have to thank you for taking care of him before he could spill the beans."

Ben tells Steel, "I appreciate that, sir."

Steel tells Ben, "You know, Smithson's been telling me that you've been skimming out of my drug money. That you've been trying to steal some of my money, and some of my heroin on the side. You can tell me if it's not true, that you weren't trying to steal my drugs and my money, and trying to go into business yourself. Because I don't like it when someone tries to steal from me and go into another business."

Ben is a little bit frightened and tells Steel, "Look I swear, sir. I didn't mean to steal any of the heroin. I thought I could sell a little extra on the side, and make some money, since you don't pay me much. I thought I could run a little on the side, and have a little business."

Steel laughs a little bit, and tells Ben, "You know, your father tried to skim a little from my father. And you know what he did?"

Ben tells Steel, "No, what?"

Steel puts his arm around Ben's neck and Steel takes a Glock 17 out of his pants, and aims the gun on Ben, three bullets come out of his gun, and hit Ben in the chest, and Ben falls down on the floor and dies. Steel looks at Smithson, and tells him, "This is what happens when people try to steal from me, or run their own business behind my back. You don't do that to me, right Smithson?"

Smithson is a little bit frightened, and tells Steel, "No sir. No sir, I would never ever do that to you."

Steel tells Smithson, "How long will it take to ID these guys?"

Smithson tells Steel, "My guy is gonna take nearly half an hour to get it ready."

Steel tells Smithson, "Okay, then we'll wait. Because as for now, if I see these two guys show up at my operation or my deal, I will not only shoot them in the head, I will crush their faces with my boot, and then I will kill you for letting it happen. Is that clear Captain?"

Smithson tells Steel, "Yes, Mr. Steel, and I would never let that happen."

Steel tells Smithson, "Alright, Smithson, call the guys and get this body removed. Have them take it somewhere. Oh, how about the furnace, I'm in the mood for burning something. And I think I'm in the mood for a bit of human flesh to make it warm in here."

Smithson tells Steel, "Yes sir."

Outside of Barney's Bowlarama, Mark's car pulls into the parking lot, and parks. Mark, Linda, and Logan exit the car and enter the bowling alley. Linda tells Mark, "So, Mark, who is this guy anyway?"

Mark tells Linda, "Just an old friend. If anyone can help us, it'll be my guy." Mark, Linda, and Logan enter the bowling alley, and head to the concession stand.

Logan tells Mark, "Are you sure this guy can help us out?"

Mark tells Logan, "Of course he can help us. Besides, he owes me a couple of favors. Trust me, he has political connections everywhere. If you want to find somebody, or know somebody, or find something stolen, he's your guy."

Linda tells Mark, "So, how do you know this guy?"

Mark tells Linda, "I'll explain later." Mark sees the attractive girl at the concession stand and goes over and talks to her. Mark tells the girl at the concession stand, "Hey Bonnie."

Bonnie tells Mark, "Hey Mark. Hey, it's really great to see you. You here to bowl a couple games?"

Mark tells Bonnie, "Uh, actually maybe later. Anyway, hey is Ralph here? I need to see him."

Bonnie tells Mark, "Yeah, sure he's in his office."

Mark tells Bonnie, "Can you get him? We need to see him."

Bonnie tells Mark, "Sure. Hey, could you introduce me to your hot friend there?" Bonnie was looking at Logan, and he blushes.

Mark introduces him to Bonnie, "Bonnie this is Detective Sergeant Logan Myers, and his sister Linda."

Bonnie tells Mark, "Thank god."

Logan shakes Bonnie's hand, and she's a little bit shy, but he starts to flirt with her, "Hey, it's a pleasure to meet you Bonnie."

Bonnie tells Logan, "It's a pleasure to meet you too. I hope you stick around and bowl with us."

Logan tells Bonnie, "Well, later, but we need to see your boss for a minute."

Bonnie tells Logan, "I'll be right back. But, I was gonna ask, are you doing to anything today? I get off at 4 PM, I wonder if you and I could...?"

Linda slaps Logan on the right arm, and tells Logan, "Logan, while we're young."

Logan tells Bonnie, "Uh, sorry. We'll talk later."

Bonnie lets go of Logan's hand, and tells them, "I'll get Ralph right now." Bonnie exits the concession stand and heads to Ralph's office to go look for him.

Logan snaps out of his love trance for a minute, and tells Mark, "So, how do you know this guy?"

Mark tells Logan, "Around." Linda and Logan look at Mark, and Mark explains to them, "He and I have known each other since juvenile hall. After we got out, and I made it big, I invested in his bowling alley, and he owes me big. He used to be a drug dealer, and he still has connections with some drug dealers, but he keeps them out of trouble. He even runs a community service program to get them straight. He even gets them to spill the beans about who they work for, and who they used to deal with. And also, he has connections to the DOJ office, since his uncle is an associate district attorney there. He gives him anything he needs."

Logan and Linda tell Mark, "That explains a lot."

Ralph comes over to the counter at the concession stand and sees Mark, and tells him, "Mark? Is that you? Hey man, it's great to see you. It's been a while since we saw each other. Man, I owe you everything."

Mark tells Ralph, "Man, it's really great to see you too. I also need to thank your uncle for getting us both out of juvenile hall."

Ralph tells Mark, "Hey, no problem." Both of them let go of each other and Ralph tells Mark, "Man, I really loved your *Nitro* movies, they were awesome." Ralph even recognizes Logan, and tells him, "Oh my god! You're Logan Myers, you were one of the members of M-D-L Hey, a lot of people think you are dead."

Logan tells Ralph, "No Ralph, I'm not dead, I just switched careers." Logan and Linda show him their LAPD badges, and Logan tells Ralph, "Yeah, we're cops. Right after the band split, Mark helped me to get into the academy, and helped me study for the detective exam, and the rest is history, so here I am."

Linda tells Ralph, "And you still couldn't help him get his record expunged, with the help of your uncle?"

Ralph tells Linda, "My uncle and the governor had a falling out, so we could never expunge his record back then. So, Mark, what brings you here?"

Mark tells Ralph, "Well, I'm a private investigator and I am working as a private consultant with the LAPD. I'm helping them investigate a case to look for a mysterious drug kingpin. That's why I'm here, I need your help with something."

Ralph tells Mark, "Sure what is it?"

Mark tells Ralph, "Well, um, let's not talk here. We'll talk in your office. We don't want anybody to listen to this, besides we could be bugged."

Ralph tells Mark, "Good idea, besides somebody might be listening in." Mark and Ralph move towards Ralph's office, but before they leave Ralph tells Logan and Linda, "Hey why don't you guys bowl a game here, besides the beer, the food, and the game is on me. I am a die-hard M-D-L fan."

Logan tells Ralph, "Well if you have one of our CDs, we'll autograph it for you."

Ralph tells Logan, "That'd be great."

Mark and Ralph enter Ralph's office, and Logan sees Bonnie at the counter and she has bowling shoes out on the counter for them, and she knows their sizes. Logan tells Bonnie, "Hey, how do you know our sizes?"

Bonnie tells Logan, "I read about you online. You know, Logan, I still get off at 4, I'd just like to know if you would like to come have a drink with me?"

Logan tells Bonnie, "I'll be happy to, but right now I'm working a case, but maybe we could meet tonight at 7, here in the alley?"

Bonnie tells Logan, "Sure, it's a date, you're lane 12."

Both Bonnie and Logan smile at each other, and Logan and Linda grab their shoes, and head to lane 12.

Linda tells Logan, "You are one weird guy, big bro."

Logan tells Linda, "Tell me about it."

Inside Ralph's office, where Ralph and Mark are meeting, Ralph is on his laptop, and he presses the enter button. Ralph tells Mark, "Okay, we're officially sound proof, so no one can listen in on our conversation. So, tell me about this case."

Mark tells Ralph, "Okay, here's the favor, I think I found out who this mysterious drug kingpin is, and his name is John Steel."

Ralph tells Mark, "Yeah, I heard about that guy. I heard his father owned a million dollar steel industry that he founded in Boston. He died about five years ago and left the company to his son John. He also put a lot of money in a trust fund for his younger son Bruce, because deep down he always cared about the kid, even though he'd always seen him as a disappointment."

Mark tells Ralph, "Both of the sons run a steel company now."

Ralph tells Mark, "Yeah, I read about that in the Wall Street Journal."

Mark tells Ralph, "Bruce is nothing like his father, you know mostly because he's an honest businessman and he works hard for his money. Guys like John and his father steal, plunder, and walk over anybody to get ahead. But, I found out that Steel has been running a heroin business on the side to make some extra money. Both he and Bruce are competing for a Navy contract to build some new battleships, and they're willing to a pay a few hundred million dollars for one company."

Ralph tells Mark, "Man, if one of them get the contract, those stocks are going to hit the roof, they're going to make a fortune."

Mark tells Ralph, "You think?"

Ralph tells Mark, "What makes you think that John Steel might be our mysterious drug lord?"

Mark tells Ralph, "I read the police files that Logan provided. I figured out that Steel Industries may be involved. One of the guys Logan arrested for heroin dealing, his name is Marvin Keltner, I think he was framed for dealing because one of Steel's guys planted all the heroin inside Keltner's place, and they busted him for it. But luckily for us, the search warrant didn't really come through, it was forged."

Ralph tells Mark, "The only way you can authorize a search warrant is through a DA or a judge."

Mark tells Ralph, "An assistant DA, Eugene Medford, signed the search warrant, but it was actually forged. They thought it was actually a prank or something, because Medford never knew that Keltner was a drug dealer."

Ralph tells Mark, "I think I remember Marvin Keltner, he was ex-drug dealer, but he was trying to go straight. He had a job working for Steel Industries."

Mark tells Ralph, "Yeah, you're right, he did get a job in Steel Industries, but not by John. He got hired by Bruce as a corporate spy, to spy on John and figure out what he was up to. I think he figured out that Steel was running a drug business, and I think he was trying to figure out who his client was, because he was killed last night."

Ralph tells Mark, "If he was killed last night, I bet he was planning on spilling the beans to Bruce, or the police, about what was going on. I bet that's why Steel's men wanted to plant the heroin on him. Besides if they read about his record, they'd know he's the perfect target for this arrest, and he thought he could actually lead them to the mysterious drug lord. And I bet Bruce was the anonymous tipster when they found out the search warrant was fake, and Keltner walked."

Mark tells Ralph, "I think I figured out he was gonna tell his brother, and Bruce was going to tell the police. But Bruce isn't aware that it is actually his brother. If Keltner got arrested, they would have found out about Keltner's corporate spy work for Bruce, and then they'd think he was the mysterious drug lord, and then he'd go to jail with Keltner."

Ralph tells Mark, "That explains a lot about why Bruce would make that tip, because he wanted to protect his company. Too bad Keltner got killed for it."

Mark tells Ralph, "That's one reason why we need this place soundproofed, Logan and Linda are working for Internal Affairs. I think Steel has some cops on his payroll, working to cover his tracks, and I think we may have figured out who they are."

Ralph tells Mark, "Who do you think it is?"

Mark tells Ralph, "I think it is Captain Matthew Smithson, and my brother Ben. I think they may be connected. I know me and my brother haven't spoken since he transferred to L.A. from Boston."

Ralph tells Mark, "How come you two guys never kept in touch?"

Mark tells Ralph, "You know, he was my Dad's favorite. He was the big shot. We never hung out a lot. Plus, he always picked on me and Donnie when we were kids. Besides, my dad was happy that Ben became the big shot, and Donnie and I were disappointments. He always figured we'd end up at dead end jobs, or out on the streets, but boy was he wrong. That was before he died, after we went into juvenile hall. So that's why I need a favor. I'm trying to find Steel's drug operation, and where his deal is going to be. And, I'm trying to figure out anything about who he is selling this heroin too."

Ralph tells Mark, "Well, Mark, you've been there for me a lot of times, so I owe you. And I'd love to help you and Logan out, since I was a fan of yours. It will take me a day to contact my uncle, but I will give you a call when I'm done."

Mark takes out a calling card for Donnie from his left pants pocket, and puts it on Ralph's desk, and tells Ralph, "This is my brother, Donnie's, number. Give him a call after your uncle gets you the information."

Ralph tells Mark, "No problem. Oh and don't forget you, Donnie, and Logan have to sign my album before you guys go."

Mark tells Ralph, "Sure, no problem."

Ralph tells Mark, "Hey, I hope you stay and bowl a game with me."

Mark tells Ralph, "Well, we do have to go, but I guess I could bowl one game."

Ralph takes out an album from out of his desk drawer, the album is the M-D-L CD, and he hands it to Mark.

Mark takes the album and observes it for a minute. Mark tells Ralph, "Do you have a pen?" Ralph gives Mark a pen that's on the desk, and Mark takes the pen and signs the album, and tells Ralph, "I'll get Logan to sign it, and we'll leave it in the concession stand tomorrow. It's nice talking to you Ralph."

Ralph tells Mark, "It was nice seeing you too Mark." Mark heads to the door and exits Ralph's office. Ralph picks up the phone, and makes a call to his uncle, and Ralph tells him, "Hey Uncle Steve, listen I need a favor."

Back in the bowling alley, Mark sees Logan and Linda bowling a game, and both of them are drinking Bud Light, and having a couple of hot dogs. Mark goes over to Logan and Linda to talk to them. Mark is also carrying the M-D-L CD and a pen for Logan to sign it with.

Logan tells Mark, "Hey man, so can Ralph help us out?"

Mark tells Logan, "Yup, he's calling his uncle right now, and he's going to call Donnie tomorrow."

Logan tells Mark, "So, hey, do you want to stay and bowl, or should we head back to the library?"

Mark tells Logan, "Let's bowl one frame, and then we can go."

Logan tells Mark, "Alright, you go first."

Mark grabs a bowling ball, and rolls the ball down the alley, and gets a strike. Mark tells Logan, "It's a good thing I'm a two-time celebrity bowling champion."

Logan tells Mark, "Try not to show off, will ya?"

Back at the library, Donnie is speaking to Bruce Steel in the computer room. Donnie tells Bruce, "Thanks for the information Bruce, I really appreciate it."

Bruce tells Donnie, "Well here's all the information I have. Do you think my brother is really trying to put me out of business?"

Donnie tells Bruce, "Well, Bruce, the guy you hired, Keltner, was killed last night. We know you hired him to try and figure out what John was after, and what he was running. I think John figured out that he was your corporate spy, and he must have planted the heroin in his place."

Bruce tells Donnie, "Man, I knew that guy would do anything to put me out of business. I knew my Dad always saw disappoint in me, he and I were never all that close since my mom died, but I was only five. He always told me I didn't have a killer instinct."

Donnie tells Bruce, "Hey, I know how you feel, you know. It was really rough when our mom died. She always favored us, but her and my dad never got along. Sometimes I wondered why she even stayed with that guy, why she didn't just leave and take us with her. Maybe she was scared, or didn't have anywhere to go. Besides, I always saw how my dad just stayed away most of the time."

Bruce tells Mark, "Well, I looked over the files. It's kind of weird, but I think my father knew your dad."

Donnie tells Bruce, "Yeah, when I looked at your father's name, I knew it looked familiar, and I knew he ran a steel company in Boston. I think I figured it out. You know, I really didn't hear anything specific, but I think I heard my dad talking to Mr. Steel once, when he visited us in our home. And I think he was actually bribing my dad. I think my dad was actually on your dad's payroll, and now my brother Ben is on your brother's payroll."

Bruce tells Donnie, "Wow, I guess I never knew your father was crooked."

Donnie tells Bruce, "I kind of figured it out myself too. So, I found out my brother Ben transferred to the police force about a week ago, he and I don't really talk, I know he was my Dad's favorite, so does Mark. He always told us that we had no business being cops, because deep-down these guys were tough, by-the-book cops, and we had no business being cops because we were weak and nice."

Bruce tells Donnie, "Tell me about it. You know, it was really great to meet you Donnie. You know, I am a great fan of M-D-L, and I always wanted to meet you guys. I wish I had one of my CDs so that you guys could sign it, but since I have a notepad in my briefcase, do you think you could just sign it for me?" Bruce takes the notepad out of his briefcase that was laying on top of a table, and gives it to Donnie.

Donnie has a pen that's on the table and he signs it. Donnie tells Bruce, "Here you go. Hey, it's really great to meet a fan."

Bruce grabs the notepad, and was totally thrilled when he saw Donnie's signature.

Donnie tells Bruce, "I would've gotten my brother Mark and Logan here but they're kind of busy working on the case."

Bruce tells Donnie, "Oh, no problem. Besides you and Mark were always my favorites, and so was Logan, but I don't want to pick favorites, but you were always one of my favorite stars."

Donnie tells Bruce, "Hey, I appreciate that."

Bruce tells Donnie, "So when is your *LA Beat* movie going to start. I always wanted to see that movie, I heard it was really good."

Donnie tells Bruce, "Actually, we're taking two weeks off from production right now, because we're working on this case. That's why we opened this P.I. business, to get into character, to learn how to eat, breathe, and be detectives."

Bruce tells Donnie, "Well, I guess running a detective agency is a really great idea. To tell the truth you're doing a really good job. Just let me know when the movie will be out so I can get a front row seat."

Donnie tells Bruce, "Tell you what, once the movie's finished, I'll send you a premier ticket, and get you into the after party."

Bruce is a little bit excited, and tells Donnie, "Thanks, I really appreciate that." Bruce puts his notepad in the briefcase, and closes it. They get up from their chairs and Bruce shakes Donnie's hand and tells him, "Thanks for your help, I really appreciate it, and I hope you get justice for my man, Keltner, he was a really good guy."

Donnie tells Bruce, "Hey, no problem." Donnie lets go of Bruce's hand, and Bruce grabs his briefcase from the table and exits the computer room. Donnie sits down in his chair and looks at the file.

Mark, Logan, and Linda enter the computer the room and go over to talk to Donnie. Donnie tells them, "Hey guys, how'd it go?"

Mark tells Donnie, "Well, big bro, I think Steel didn't suspect anything, not right now but soon. We've got to be careful, I think he might send some guys to come after us."

Donnie tells Mark, "Mark I've watched a lot of cop movies, I doubt they would send guys to come after us, they might call us first, or send us death threats, but I doubt anybody is going to come after us."

Logan tells Donnie, "I think it might happen. I think Steel might send a couple guys to come after us, I've got to agree with Mark on this one. And if that's the case we have to keep a look-out."

Mark, Logan, and Linda sit down in their chairs and Linda tells them, "We still have to figure out where Steel's operation is, and where he is going to make the deal at."

Mark tells them, "We still have to figure out who Steel is going to sell his heroin to."

Donnie tells them, "Well Bruce came over a few minutes ago, and he also got some of the notes that Keltner gave him while he was spying on his brother."

Mark tells Donnie, "What did you find out?"

Donnie tells them, "Keltner said that John was talking to a couple of Chinese guys, these guys looked pretty scary. Keltner said he saw a tattoo in the middle of one of the guy's left arms because he was wearing a short sleeved shirt." Donnie takes the file that Bruce gave him and shows it to Mark, Logan, and Linda.

Linda tells them, "This was two days ago, before he died."

Logan tells them, "If it was two days ago, Keltner got arrested after that day."

Donnie tells Logan, "The phony search warrant that the assistant DA gave you to search Keltner's place? I think that explains a lot about why Steel planted those drugs in Keltner's place in the first place."

Mark tells them, "Because Keltner was listening in on the conversation. He figured out those two Chinese guys that Steel was talking to were his clients, and his clients were the ones that Steel was selling heroin too."

Linda tells Donnie, "Donnie, what was the tattoo of that was on one of the Chinese guy's arms, was that in Bruce's report?"

Donnie tells them, "Simple, it was a red dragon."

Logan and Mark figure out something. Logan tells Donnie, "I think I know what that red dragon means. The Red Dragons were the street gang that me and Mark fell into before we started our singing group."

Mark tells them, "That's before I went to juvenile hall, and the crowd that we fell into. We never knew who the leader was, we were just following the guys. One of the guys we listened to, his name was Chang."

Donnie tells Mark, "Was there a last name?"

Mark tells Donnie, "That was it, his name was Chang. He was like a middle guy. Mostly he tells us the boss wanted us to do something. He wanted us to vandalize some store that was next door. That's how I got arrested, and got caught, because Chang told us to vandalize the area. I always felt like somebody tipped us anyway, when we broke into that store and vandalized it."

Logan tells them, "You think maybe Ben? Besides he really did hate us back then. He would have done anything to bar us from the police force. Mark really helped me out when he saved my butt."

Mark tells them, "I don't think it would've been Ben, it would've had to have been someone higher up who knew about that store."

Linda tells them, "What was the name of the store that you guys broke in to?"

Mark tells Linda, "Chang never said what we were breaking into, he just wanted us to vandalize it. But I did see a lot of coffee cups, and a coffee maker. I think it looked more like a Chinese restaurant. I saw a lot of Chinese food on the tables when we got caught."

Donnie tells them, "Wait, did you say it was a Chinese restaurant?"

Mark tells Donnie, "Yeah."

Donnie tells them, "You guys never mentioned about what you were breaking into, you told me you got in trouble for vandalism, but you never told me what you were vandalizing or what was inside."

Mark tells Donnie, "Well, you never asked. Besides, I try to forget about that day, and besides Chang never told me what was the name of that restaurant."

Donnie tells Mark, "This Chinese restaurant, was it in Chinatown?"

Mark tells Donnie, "Yeah, of course."

Donnie looks up in the computer for a minute, and looks for Chinese restaurants in Chinatown in Boston. Donnie tells them, "Well there's about 10 restaurants, but one of them looks familiar to me. Got it!"

Donnie taps the computer screen, "It's the Mandura Restaurant. They have a symbol on their sign that has a red dragon on it. I saw them every time I visited Chinatown."

Logan snaps his fingers, "I think that Mandura Restaurant may be a front to the Chinese triads, but we never knew who owned it. It's going to take us a couple of minutes to figure that out."

Linda tells Logan, "Are you saying the Mandura Restaurant is owned by the triads?"

Logan tells Linda, "Yeah of course, but I don't know the name of the guy who owns that restaurant."

Mark tells them, "I think Ralph knows. I think he might figure out who Steel is selling his heroin too."

Donnie tells them, "Ralph won't call until tomorrow. So, until then why don't we eat first and we'll figure out what our strategy will be tomorrow."

Mark tells Donnie, "Yeah, I'm really hungry, we haven't had the chance to eat yet."

Donnie tells them, "Don't worry I already made the arrangements. Our food is outside the computer room, on the table."

Mark tells Donnie, "Hey. I saw 5 pizzas from Pizza Hut and 8 bottle of Diet Pepsi, and 5 Bud Light bottles."

Donnie tells them, "Yeah, I ordered in before you guys got here. I figured you guys would be hungry. So why don't we bring it in and eat. And we can play a couple video games on the computer."

Mark tells Donnie, "Man, you sure now how to read our minds. Our candy bars, Reese's Peanut Butter cups, are they outside too? Because I didn't see those."

Donnie tells Mark, "They're behind the pizza boxes."

Mark, Logan, and Linda tell Donnie, "Alright!"

Mark tells them, "I'll get the pizzas, Linda you get the sodas and beers, and Logan you get the candy bars."

Logan and Linda tell Mark, "Okay."

Mark, Linda, and Logan get up from their chairs and go outside the computer room and get the food.

Back at the warehouse manager's office, Smithson and Steel were waiting for the results. Both of them are sitting down in their chairs, and Smithson tells Steel, "Mr. Steel, is there anything I can get you before my guy calls?"

Steel tells Smithson, "No, I'm good."

The phone rings and Smithson answers it, and he tells the person on the other line, "Hey Roy, you got it? Alright, thank you, just e-mail me the information. Alright, bye." Smithson hangs up the phone, and checks his e-mail and he starts printing the information that Roy found. Smithson tells Steel, "Mr. Steel, we found the information on those two guys who were speaking to you in your office."

Steel tells Smithson, "That sounds great, who are these guys anyway?"

Smithson tells Steel, "Well, the information that Roy sent is printing out now."

Steel tells Smithson, "Alright, let's go take a look."

Smithson and Steel get up from their chairs and go over to the printer and Smithson grabs the information.

Steel tells Smithson, "Who are these idiots, and how did they know about my drug operation?"

Smithson tells Steel, "Man, you're not going to believe this, and I can't believe it either."

Steel tells Smithson, "Well, who are they?"

Smithson tells Steel, "They're cops, they're LAPD, I knew I recognized these two."

Steel tells Smithson, "Are you saying that there are two LAPD cops running around my operation trying to shut it down. I thought you kept all of your cop buddies out of my operation and my deal with the Red Dragons."

Smithson tells Steel, "One of the cops that spoke to you worked for me, his name is Sergeant Logan Myers. I suspended him for a week with no pay. I told him to stay off this case. Turns out that he is working for Captain Jake Johnson from Internal Affairs. I can't believe it, he's got IA running around. And I thought I kept those guys at bay, but not this guy."

Steel tells Smithson, "And the other guy? Who was he?"

Smithson tells Steel, "I knew I recognized this guy. This is Mark Wahlberg. You know, he was a successful singer. He and Logan were in a successful group called M-D-L. They went their separate ways, and Mark went into the movie industry with Donnie. He was an actor and a box office champ. They made those six *Nitro* movies that made him a box office star."

Steel tells Smithson, "Yeah, I've seen those movies, I think Wahlberg is a terrible actor, and now he's out there playing cop."

Smithson tells Steel, "He's actually a PI. He has a new place called Wahlberg PI. Internal Affairs hired Wahlberg to track us down, so he's working with Myers on tracking us down."

Steel tells Smithson, "You think I'm threatened by some wannabe box office champ and a washed-up singing group? No way."

Smithson tells Steel, "Well the guy is a total loser. You know if you want to get this guy off our backs, why don't we just alert the paparazzi? Then they'll be in his face 24/7, and they'll put lots of tabloid crap out about him, and he won't be able to touch us."

Steel goes over to Smithson, and tells him, "Smithson, get over here for a minute." Steel grabs him by the nose and knees him in the stomach. Smithson is hurting for a minute, and Steel tells him, "You don't think I know that? Because I know that. But it would be too easy to just alert the paparazzi, and that way Wahlberg would just stay out of my face, and so would Myers." Steel lets go of Smithson's nose, and tells him, "Smithson, tell me, who took over Lincoln's spot after he was killed by John Wilkes Booth?"

Smithson tells Steel, "I don't know, I'm in too much pain to figure that out."

Steel tells Smithson, "I'll tell you. Andrew." Steel kicks Smithson in the balls, and he tells Smithson, "Johnson. If we alerted the paparazzi, they might tell everybody about us, even though nobody would believe them. But I have a better idea to get rid of these two, because we need to keep this private. Because if he grants one of those tabloids an interview and he tells them about us, it will be hard to cover our tracks with the tabloids in our face. We need to keep a low profile."

Smithson is feeling a little better and tells Steel, "What's your plan?"

Steel tells Smithson, "Simple, if your buddy Myers is working with Wahlberg, all we have to do is find Myers and figure out where he's going and we can kill him, but we need a private area. I'll get some of my men to tail him, and you'll be going with them. Once you see him with Wahlberg, I want you to follow them and take them out. And I want to make sure you keep a low profile, because I don't want any witnesses running around, and if there are any kill them too."

Smithson tells Steel, "Well, don't worry. You forgot I'm LAPD, I know how to cover people's tracks. And besides, I can keep my posse at bay. And besides, I've got the mayor, the police commissioner, and even the DA eating out of my hand, we've got nothing to worry about."

Steel tells Smithson, "Smithson, I want you to call Warren, and tell him to be ready tomorrow morning, 8 AM. I want you to stake out Myers' place and start tailing him. Once you see him with Wahlberg, it'll be your job to take them out."

Smithson tells Steel, "Yes sir."

Inside the computer room at the library, Mark, Linda, Logan, and Donnie are eating their dinner and also playing poker on the table in the computer room. Mark tells them, "It's a good thing, the head librarian had some poker chips inside the closet."

Linda tells them, "I got to hand it to you, Mark, it's a good idea to play poker while we're eating. It relieves our stress and all."

Donnie tells them, "There's a question that I wanted to ask, if I had to pick any author who wanted me to adapt their book into a movie, who do you want meet to pick? Like, if John Grisham, Stephen King, and Nicholas Sparks wanted me to adapt one of their books into a movie, who would you want me to pick?"

Linda tells Donnie, "If I had to pick, I'd pick Anne Rice, because I am an Anne Rice fan."

Mark tells Linda, "Well, I don't think I would've picked Anne Rice, her last movie, *Queen of the Damned*, wasn't even that good, besides the only big hit she ever had was the movie *Interview with the Vampire*."

Logan tells them, "Well I wouldn't pick John Grisham to develop a movie with. He's had a couple of bad movies. *The Firm, The Pelican Brief,* and *Time to Kill* were the only big hits he had."

Donnie tells them, "Yeah, but they were big hits."

Mark is drinking his beer, and he tells Donnie, "Well, big bro, I'm going to say Nicholas Sparks. Even though he's not a part of our genre. He's had a few big hits, like *A Walk to Remember, The Notebook, The Last Song,* and *Dear John.*"

Linda tells Mark, "Hey don't forget Zac Efron's movie, *The Lucky One* that was a big hit too."

Mark tells Linda, "Sorry, my mistake."

Donnie tells them, "I guess it is official. Nicholas Sparks. Besides I would've picked Stephen King, but horror is way out of my genre. But if Stephen King begged me, I would've said yes. But, Nicholas Sparks it is. Because if he also asked me I would've said yes too."

Linda tells Mark, "You know, Mark, I read somewhere that you hated a lot of models. I wondered if that was true or not, because, man, you're like James Bond or something."

Mark tells Linda, "No, I'm not James Bond. Besides I've barely even dated. All of that tabloid stuff was just rumors. I'm always so busy, so I don't exactly get a lot of dates."

Linda tells Mark, "Really, even a good looking guy like you who is easily worth one or two-hundred million dollars?"

Mark tells Linda, "Actually it's more like three-hundred million."

Linda tells Logan, "You know, Logan, I never did understand. You made so much money, and you could never lend a sister a dime?"

Logan tells Linda, "Sis, you've been sponging off me for a long time."

Linda tells Logan, "Sorry, my mistake. Besides, I was testing you to see if you could remember. I wanted to see the look on your face."

Logan tells Linda, "Huh, cute, but funny."

Donnie tells them, "Well, the library is about to close. Oh I forgot, I have keys to the place so we can stay all night. Huh, my mistake."

Logan tells Donnie, "Well, Donnie it's getting late, besides we have a lot of work to do for tomorrow. We have to wait for Ralph's call, and besides, I've got a date, and I promised I'd meet her at the bowling alley."

Donnie tells Logan, "With who?"

Logan tells Donnie, "Someone you don't know."

Donnie tells Logan, "Who is it?"

Logan tells Donnie, "It's actually Bonnie Carter. She's the manager at Ralph's bowling alley."

Donnie tells Logan, "Hey, I know who she is. Me and Mark have bowled a few games there."

Logan tells Donnie, "Well, I better hurry. I don't want to keep her waiting. Good night guys."

Donnie tells Logan, "Yeah, good night to you too, I have to head home."

Logan and Donnie get up from their chairs and exit the computer room. Mark and Linda are still sitting in their chairs. Linda is a little bit shy, seeing Mark, and she tries to tell him something, but she's a little gun shy. So Mark tells Linda, "You know Linda, I wanted to ask you something. I know you're way out of my league, and you're a cop and I'm a private investigator, but I was going to ask you-"

Linda interrupted Mark for a minute, and tells him, "Yes. I want to say yes. I would definitely love to go out with you."

Linda kisses Mark, and Mark kisses her back, but then they both stop.

Mark tells Linda, "I actually was going to ask you if you would like to be my date to the premier party after we finish *LA Beat*."

Linda tells Mark, "Oh, man, I'm really sorry, I guess it was a misunderstanding. I guess it wasn't a date after all. Of course, I'd love to, you know I've always wanted to see what those movie premiers are like. I wish I could've gone to the *Nitro* movies but I wasn't...?"

Mark tells Linda, "Actually, it was a date, I really wanted to ask you out, and I really like you, and I just wanted to know if you wanted to come with me, and you can go stag if you want, and all of us are going, but I really could use a date."

Linda is a little bit excited, and tells Mark, "Of course." Linda starts making out with Mark for a few minutes.

Back at Mark and Donnie's house, Donnie is watching TV in the living room, and he hears Mark enter. He gets up from the couch and goes to talk to Mark, "Hey Mark."

Mark tells Donnie, "Hey big bro."

Donnie tells Mark, "Hey, you came home really late, I bet you were really looking over those files, working really hard in the library."

Mark tells Donnie, "Nah, of course not. Actually I had to stay after at the library because I had a date."

Donnie tells Mark, sarcastically, "Let me guess Kristen Stewart actually returned your calls, and you asked her to come to the library, and you had a little make-out session with her?"

Mark sarcastically tells Donnie, "No, actually, I had a make-out session with Rebel Wilson. I think her Australian accent kind of turned me on a bit."

Donnie tells Mark, "Well, they always do."

Mark tells Donnie, "It was Linda, you know Logan's sister?"

Donnie is a little bit excited and tells Mark, "Man, I can't believe it. She's really hot, and she's a cop. I didn't figure she'd date guys like you or me, I always figured that she'd date her own kind, you know cops, DA agents, and feds."

Mark tells Donnie, "You also forgot they have to be good looking, and six-pack abs have to come with the package too."

Donnie tells Mark, sarcastically, "My mistake."

Mark tells Donnie, "You know, I really like her a lot, she's amazing. She's beautiful, she's nice, and she really likes me for who I am. And she understands what I go through."

Donnie laughs for a minute, and tells Mark, "Relax man, I was only joking. She is really beautiful, and she's amazing. Besides, she's the only one who ever liked us for who we were. So, how far did you go? First base, second base? Or did you hit a home run?"

Mark tells Donnie, "I only got to first base, and that's how far it's going to go. Right now we're just dating, and we're going to take it slow."

Donnie tells Mark, "She wanted to take it slow, or you did?"

Mark tells Donnie, "Actually I did."

Donnie tells Mark, "Hey, I've got all the Mel Gibson *Lethal Weapon* movies on DVD, you wanna watch?"

Mark tells Donnie, "Sure no problem, you know I'm a dire Mel Gibson fan. But how about instead of Mel Gibson, why don't we watch the *Rocky* series with Sylvester Stallone?"

Donnie tells Mark, "Yeah, sure you no problemo man. C'mon Robert Mark Wahlberg, let's watch Sly knock out a few people."

Mark tells Donnie, "Sure thing Donnie Wahlberg, first let me get some beer and we'll watch away."

Donnie tells Mark, "Hey don't forget the pretzels. We need them too."

Mark tells Donnie, "No problem."

Mark heads to the kitchen to get the beer and pretzels, and Donnie sits back on the couch, putting in the *Rocky* DVDs that were on the coffee table.

Outside of Logan and Linda's apartment building, the doorman opens the door, and Logan and Linda exit the building. They see the valet opening the door to Logan's car, a 2014 Grand Jeep Cherokee. Logan and Linda get inside the car, and Logan starts the car. Right across the street, a black SUV is parked outside Logan and Linda's apartment building. Smithson and Warren are in the front seat, and four of Steel's men are in the back. Smithson is using his binoculars, and sees Logan and Linda exiting their apartment building.

Inside the SUV, Smithson tells Warren, "Alright, they're on the move, let's go."

Warren tells Smithson, "It's a good thing you're good at tailing people, Smithson."

Smithson tells Warren, "Yeah, lucky for me, I excelled in that part of the academy. Steel is going to be really proud of me when I take these bozos out."

Inside Logan and Linda's Jeep, they are driving to downtown LA to meet Donnie and Mark in the public library. Linda looks in the back, and she doesn't see anything. Linda tells Logan, "You know, I have a strange feeling that we're being watched. Like somebody is following us."

Logan tells Linda, "Relax, Sis, I highly doubt anyone is going to follow us. Besides, if somebody is following us, we'll be ready for them. You forget, we are cops, we are highly trained for anything."

Linda tells Logan, "Well we better be prepared, just in case somebody tries to follow us."

Logan tells Linda, "If you want to keep your mind off it, here why don't we play some music."

Linda tells Logan, "You want me to put in Taylor Swift or Hillary Duff?"

Logan tells Linda, "I think I'll go for Hillary Duff."

Linda tells Logan, "Good selection."

Linda turns on the CD player and puts on Hillary Duff. The traffic light turns green, and Linda and Logan exit the street, but one car behind them is Smithson's car, and they are following them. Logan and Linda are unaware that they are being followed. In the parking lot outside of the Los Angeles Public Library, Mark is waiting for Logan and Linda to get there. He promised to unlock the library and take them inside early, because they have to keep their privacy really low, because they may have spies looking for them. Logan and Linda's car arrives at the parking lot, and they park their car. Linda and Logan exit the car, and go over to see Mark.

Mark tells them, "Hey guys."

Linda and Logan tell Mark, "Hey."

A couple blocks from the parking lot, the black SUV is parked. Smithson, Warren, and four of Steel's men exit the car. Before they enter the parking lot, Warren tells Smithson, "Hey boss, you sure there is nobody there?"

Smithson tells Warren, "Nobody in sight, we can make a clean get away."

Warren tells Smithson, "Whatever we do, we have to keep a low profile. You know what Mr. Steel said."

Smithson tells Warren, "I know what he said. 'No witnesses.' We'll have to sneak in really quietly if we want to make it a clean hit."

Smithson, Warren and four of Steel's men take out their Smith & Wesson 4506s from their holsters and aim them at Mark, Linda, and Logan. Mark sees them and is a little bit frightened, but Linda and Logan aren't, but they don't have their guns on them. Smithson tells them, "You know Myers, I told you to keep off this case. And you Wahlberg? Sticking your nose in other people's business? I'm kind of glad they have a law that bans ex-cons from joining the police force, and here you are some big box-office champ, playing cop."

Warren tells Mark, "Ha! Robert Mark Wahlberg thinks he's Dirty Harry. Man, I've seen the movie *The Hard Way*, Michael J Fox's character, Nick Link thinks he can play cop rolling with the fuzz, and play hero. But that was a movie, this is real life. And in real life, guys like you end up dead."

Mark, who is frightened, tells them, "Let me guess, Steel sent you? I guess he found out about us. All this was just a simple low-key case. I thought we could find Mr. Steel's drug operation, and bust his deal with the leader of the triads. And I thought it was going to just be a simple bust, but I guess you guys find us out and now we're the targets. I know you can't tell anybody, because you don't like witnesses, so I think it's better off that you just kill us."

Smithson tells Logan and Linda, "You two, drop your guns!"

Logan tells Smithson, "I don't have a gun, Captain. This explains why you took us off the case. Besides, we're not running this case, we're just here. All that stuff Mark just said is all lies. Me and Linda are here to just to visit our old friend Mark. We're really busy. You suspended me without pay. I said I'd stay off this case, and I did."

Smithson tells them, "Don't lie to me, you assface. I know a bluff when I see one. I know Captain Johnson from IA sent you to investigate me. I've made IA look stupid for that last few years. They could have never found Steel, or me, because I knew how to cover my tracks really well. And I know you guys brought guns here. And I would shoot you myself, but I know you will duck, or take cover, and I know you brought some guns, so I want to see them."

Linda, who was totally frightened, tells Smithson, "We don't have any guns, you can come search us if you want, but we didn't bring any here."

Warren tells Mark, "What about you Wahlberg? Did you bring a gun? Besides, I know a big shot like you wouldn't go anywhere without a gun. But we would arrest you for carrying one if it wasn't registered."

Mark tells them, "I don't have a gun. Mostly, I'm anti-gun. I don't even like carrying one. You can search me too, if you want, but I don't have one. I'm just a private investigator, here to investigate a case. I usually stay out of the action."

Smithson tells Mark, "I know you're bluffing. But, if we want to search one of you, we'll search you. Warren, search Linda, check to see if she has a gun. And if she doesn't, we'll kill them all."

Warren goes over to Linda and tells her, "Turn around, and hands up." Warren searches Linda to see if she has a gun, and finds that there is no gun, not on her back, not in her coat, nowhere. Warren tells Smithson, "She's clean."

Smithson tells Warren, "Before you search the others, shoot her."

Warren tells Smithson, "Yes sir." Warren aims his gun on Linda, and Logan and Mark give Linda a nod. Warren is about to pull the trigger, and Linda knots on herself, and stomps on Warren's left foot really hard. Smithson and the four guys are distracted for a minute, and Mark takes out his Beretta 92F out of the back of his pants, aims his gun on Warren. Warren turns around and Mark fires his gun. Three bullets come out of Mark's gun, and hit Warren in the chest and he dies. Logan takes out two guns from the back of his pants, and tosses one to Linda, and she catches it, and Linda fires her gun, and two bullets fire out of her gun and hit Steel man one in the chest, and he dies.

Logan tells them, "Get down!" Everyone dives down to the ground, Smithson and the three remaining men are distracted now, but they fire their guns. Six bullets come out of their guns, three from Smithson's gun, and one from each of the other's guns. They all hit the ground near Logan, and he dives out of the way. Three more bullets come out

86

of nowhere, and Logan, Linda, and Mark roll to one of the cars and take cover. Linda fires her gun, and four bullets come out, and hit one of the reflectors on the cars, but miss Smithson. Logan fires his gun, and hits the windshield of a second car that's near Steel man four, but misses him. Five other bullets hit the car, but miss Linda, Logan, and Mark. Logan fires his gun again, and five other bullets come out of his gun, and hit the ground near Steel man two, but miss him. Mark fires his gun, but hits the road near Steel man three and misses him. Steel man three jumps a little. Smithson fires his gun, five bullets come out, and hit the trunk and hood of the car near Mark, Logan, and Linda, but miss them.

Mark tells Linda and Logan, "Cover me, I'm going in."

Logan tells Mark, "Got it." Logan aims his gun on Steel man one and one bullet comes out of his gun, hitting the road near Steel man one, but missing him. Mark leaps out from behind the car, and dives down to the road again, but he fires his gun, and two bullets hit Steel man one in the stomach, killing him. Logan gets a good shot on Steel man three, Mark dives down on the ground, and rolls away while five other bullets come out of nowhere. He hides behind the other car across from them.

When he rolls over there, Linda asks Logan, "Got a good shot?"

Logan tells Linda, "I'm not getting the target, I need a little more room to shoot him."

Linda tells Logan, "Leave that to me." Linda takes six quarters out of her right pants pocket, and throws them in the air. It distracts Steel man two and three, and Smithson. Logan has a good shot, and hits Steel man three in the head, killing him. Linda stalls Smithson and Steel man two, she fires her gun, and two bullets come out of her gun, and hit the road near Steel man two, missing him. Mark comes out of cover, and charges over to Smithson, tackling him onto the road, and

Mark drops his gun. But Smithson gets the lead on the fight, when he knees Mark in the stomach, and gets up from the road and kicks him in the stomach. Steel man two was a little bit distracted when he sees Smithson beating up Mark. Smithson punches Mark in the face, and picks him up from the ground and punches him in the stomach three times, and again in the face. Smithson also drops his gun, and Logan sees that Steel man two is distracted, but when he turns around and sees Logan, he aims his gun on him. Logan fires his gun, and three bullets come out of his gun, hitting Steel man two in the stomach, killing him.

Smithson kicks Mark in the stomach again, and he sends him to the ground. Smithson sees his gun on the road where he dropped it. Smithson grabs his gun and aims it on Mark, and tells Mark, "You know Wahlberg? I got to hand it to you, you've got some guts coming out here. You know you're *Nitro* movies? They stink, because they needed better actors. And I'm sure with some great acting lessons, maybe you could do great, but it's a little late for that. Like in the movies, it's time to fade to black and roll the credits."

Mark sees Logan, and he nods at him. Smithson aims his gun on Mark, and he's about to fire, until Logan sees Smithson, and one bullet comes out of his gun, and hits the road near Smithson to distract him. Smithson turns around, and Logan tells Smithson, "Hey, Captain Smithson, consider yourself suspended. Or, should I say, you've just been thrown off the force?" Logan fires his gun, and three bullets hit Smithson in the chest, and he dies. Mark, Linda, and Logan get up from the ground. Logan and Linda go over to Mark to see if he is okay. Logan tells Mark, "Hey, are you okay man?"

Mark tells Logan, "Yeah, I'm good. I always knew that would work."

Linda tells them, "What would work?"

Logan tells Linda, "It was when we played paint ball, to distract the enemy, we needed something. So we call this 'Duck for Cover.'"

Mark tells Linda, "When you're surrounded by the enemy you need someone to distract the enemy, so one person distracts him while the other aims his paint on him. That's why we call it 'Duck for Cover.'"

Linda tells them, "Does that ever actually work?"

Mark tells Linda, "We're three time paint ball champs. We always win."

Logan tells them, "Here I better call this in, before we go inside."

Mark tells Logan, "I always knew Steel would send his goons to take us out. Guess he figured out where we are."

Linda tells them, "You think Steel is going to send some more guys out to come after us?"

Mark tells Linda, "I don't know, but I doubt it. But if Steel does come after us again, we'll be ready for him."

Logan takes out his cell phone, and makes a call to the department to call this in, and get the department here. Back in the computer room, Donnie is playing a baseball video game on the screen until he hears his phone ring. Donnie picks up his phone, and says, "Hello? Hey Ralph. Oh, you got it? Alright, hang on a second." Donnie has a post-it and a pen, and he grabs them. Donnie continues, "Okay Ralph, tell me what you have."

Outside the computer room, the elevator door opens, and Mark, Logan, and Linda enter the space outside the computer room. Linda tells them, "Hey it's a good thing Captain Johnson cleared them out. At least he doesn't have to worry about the leaks since we took down Captain Smithson, and Johnson got a call that Ben was killed too, mostly he was declared missing, but I think they declared him dead after 24 hours, and I think Steel killed him too. So they're both dead. But we still need to find Steel and his operation."

Mark tells them, "Just hope Ralph called. He said he was going to get us the information today. I just hope he hurries up before Steel finds out what happened, and sends another couple guys to come after us."

Logan tells Mark, "Yeah me too."

Inside the computer room, Donnie is still talking to Ralph on the phone, and he finishes filling out all the information that Ralph gave him. Donnie tells Ralph, "Alright thanks Ralph. Okay, I'll see you tonight. Trust me, I'm going to go for the perfect score this time. Bye." Donnie hangs up his phone, and lays it down on the table. Mark, Logan, and Linda enter the computer room, and Donnie tells them, "Hey guys, where'd you go? I've been waiting for nearly half an hour."

Mark sarcastically tells Donnie, "LA traffic, you know how it is. You could be stuck there all day, you couldn't get in and out of that place."

Donnie tells Mark, "Funny Mark, cute, but funny."

Mark tells Donnie, "Steel sent some of his men after us while we were trying to come into the library."

Donnie tells them, "Man, are you guys okay."

Logan tells Donnie, "Yeah, well we took them out before they took us out. I guess Steel found out about us, and he sent Smithson and his buddies to come after us. At least it'll make Captain Johnson happy, since they're gone. But we still have to find Steel and his drug deal and his clients."

Donnie tells them, "Well, we have nothing to worry about. Ralph called. He found Steel's operation, and the leader of the triads."

Mark, Logan, and Linda sit down in their chairs, and Linda tells Donnie, "So, where are they?"

Donnie tells them, "Steel owns a building on 112 West Avenue. Mostly it's an abandoned building, they never asked what he was planning on using it for, but he just went out and bought it. Mostly it looked like it was a storage unit, like for storing old equipment from the steel plant or something."

Mark says, "But I highly doubt he's storing old equipment. I think I know what he was storing."

Logan tells them, "Heroin. That's where his drug lab is. I think he's hiding all that heroin inside of some molten steel."

Linda tells them, "Mostly if you hide heroin inside of melted steel, it'll take the scent off. It explains a lot why they never found Steel's drugs in there."

Mark tells them, "I know my dad covered his father's tracks back then. He also must've helped him store all that heroin inside of melted steel. And I bet IA already questioned him about it, and I bet they figured out my dad was working for him." Donnie tells them, "Well, he was already killed before he said anything or he got caught."

Logan tells them, "That explains about what happened to Ben. That explains why Steel killed them. He got too close to the fire when IA questioned him."

Donnie tells them, "Or he was trying to squeeze into the business. You know, steal a little money or drugs and try to run his own business behind their backs, that's another reason why Steel might have killed him. I also found out who the leader of the triads is."

Mark tells them, "Who is he? Who is this leader?"

Donnie tells them, "It was Chang's father. He also worked with our dad. His name is Louis Chang Sr."

Logan tells them, "Chang's full name is Louis Chang Jr.? Man I read about that guy, no one has ever been able to bust him. The FBI has been after him for ten years, but they could never pin anything on him. He really knows how to cover his tracks. They quit trying to get him after he was acquitted on accusations of drug trafficking, since they could never find his operation or his business contacts."

Donnie tells them, "Well, at least we know who his business contact is, it's John Steel. So we know who Steel's client is, and where his operation is at, but that won't be enough to put him behind bars."

Mark tells them, "The only way we can find Chang, Steel, and the heroin, is to find the drug deal itself. Donnie do you have any idea where the drug deal is?"

Donnie tells them, "It could be anywhere. It could be any of the properties that Steel could buy, but it will probably be unlisted because he doesn't want anyone to find out where it is."

Linda tells them, "So, I guess Steel could have his deal anywhere. I wish we could find out where it is. Besides, even if we get a search warrant, he'll just have someone inside the department to bail him out. Remember, he has a lot of people on the inside, so he knows when we make a move."

Donnie looks at all his notes on the post-it from Ralph, and he tells them, "I may not know where the drug deal is, but I think I know when it might be. Steel's last drug deal with Chang was last month on Friday night around 10. He usually makes these deals once a month, on the second Friday. I think his deal might be in two days."

Mark snaps his fingers, and has an idea, "At least we know when the deal is going to be, in two days, on Friday night at 10. I have an idea, what we need is a tracking device, or a cell phone."

Logan tells Mark, "What are you talking about?"

Donnie gets what Mark is thinking too, and tells Logan, "Logan we know when the operation is at. If he's going to be making the deal at 10 PM, he's not going to be leaving until 9 PM. I hacked into the DMV and found out that he has a limo right outside his office, and he's not going to leave without the limo. All we have to do is tape one of our cell phones to the limo, and once he leaves, we just track the GPS on the phone. And we've got him."

Logan tells them, "That sound brilliant. Well, we have two days to get everything ready, but what happens if that deal doesn't work out?"

Donnie tells them, "That would be Plan B. Plan A is that we have to find one of his guys to tell us where the deal is, and I think I might know who. His name is Rogan Hersch, he's Steel's right hand man. He owns a nightclub called Club Car, and he comes to the club around 9 PM on Friday nights. We go over there, and ask him where the deal is, and if he doesn't talk we haul his ass into jail and make him talk, or beat the snot out of him, whichever comes first."

Mark tells them, "Well, we have a lot of work to do. Logan, Donnie, you come with me to Club Car, we're going to talk to Hersch, and ask him where the deal is. And if he doesn't talk we'll beat the snot out of him. But if that doesn't work, we'll go to Plan B. Linda, you go attach your cell phone to the back of Steel's limo. Once he leaves, make the call, and find out where he's going. Then call us and let us know where he's going to be."

Linda tells Mark, "Sure thing."

Mark tells them, "Okay, we have a lot of work to do. Donnie installed two rooms, one of them is a training room, where we can practice our fighting skills, and a video game gun to practice our shooting. That way we can get ourselves prepared. Alright we have a lot of work to do, is everyone on board? Because our asses are on the line here. Not just you, Logan and Linda, but us too, because our movie, *LA Beat*, is depending on us to make sure this movie doesn't fail. That's the main reason we started this agency in the first place."

Donnie tells Mark, "You had us at when do we start?"

Logan tells Mark, "I'm in. I've got a job to finish."

Linda tells Mark, "So am I."

All of them put their hands together, and Mark says, "Guys, welcome to Wahlberg PI."

Back at the warehouse manager's office, Steel is working in the office until Hersch enters his office and talks to Steel. He tells Steel, "Mr. Steel, we have a problem."

Steel tells him, "What is it Hersch?"

Hersch tells Steel, "It's about Smithson, sir, and the troops."

Steel tells Hersch, "What about them? Did they take out those meddlesome cocks?"

Hersch tells Steel, "Actually, sir, they're dead. Wahlberg and his men took them out."

Steel seizes his desk lamp, and breaks it. Steel yells really loud to himself, "That son of a bitch! I'm going to kill that moron. That son of a bitch is going to be tasting steel in three seconds when I get my hands on him."

Hersch tells Steel, "So, do you want us to send out some other troops to take him out?"

Steel tells Hersch, "We don't have time. We've got a lot of work to do in two days. Chang is going to be here with a lot of cash, and we need to get this heroin ready. Once we're finished, we'll find Wahlberg and his posse, and once we get them they'll be tasting lead in three seconds."

Hersch tells Steel, "Sir, we've got to be careful. If he took out Smithson and our troops, he could take one of us out too."

Steel gets up from his chair and goes over to Hersch. Steel knees Hersch in the stomach and grabs him by the nose, and tells him, "I don't like it when people doubt my authority, or question it. Am I right Hersch?"

Hersch is scared and tells Steel, "No sir, no sir, I'd never question your authority."

Steel tells Hersch, "You know, I don't like when people make negative comments about my drug deal. Or about me killing Wahlberg's guys. And right now, I'd do anything it takes to kill these guys. I'd steamroll them right here if they were here. I'm thinking about steamrolling you, but I need you to run my deal. There's a lot of money on the line, you catching my drift?"

Hersch is still frightened, "Yes sir, yes sir, I catch your drift."

Steel tells Hersch, "I'm glad we understand each other. Oh, by the way I forgot something." Steel lets go of Hersch's nose, and gives him a roundhouse kick to the face. Hersch falls to the floor, still hurting, and Steel tells him, "Get up and walk it off, we have a lot of work to do. I know you have to be at the club at 9, but just meet me at the deal around 9:30 and get everything ready."

Hersch is still sore, but tells Steel, "Yes sir."

As Hersch gets up from the floor, Steel tells him, "C'mon, let's go check out our operation before you get ready."

Hersch tells him, "Yes sir." Hersch and Steel exit the manager's office and see the operation. Everybody who works in the drug lab is putting plastic bags of heroin inside a box of melted steel, and they're loading the boxes into a truck.

Steel tells Hersch, "Make sure you get everything ready. I'll be in my office."

Hersch tells Steel, "Yes sir."

Steel heads back to his office.

Back in the library, Logan and Linda are working in the training room. Linda flips Logan, and kicks him in the stomach. Linda tries to kick him again, but he blocks it and brings her down. Mark and Donnie are doing target practice on the live action video game. Right now the bad guys are in the harbor, and they shoot six bad guys with their video game guns. Linda is punching hard on the punching bag, and Logan is pumping iron with some dumbbells. Donnie is flipping Mark on the mat. They're also boxing for a minute. Linda is also doing target practice, she's shooting six bad guys in a warehouse with her video game gun. Mark is doing some boxing style with his punching bag, and also practicing his kicking too.

Back at the warehouse, Hersch is supervising the drug operation. He is seeing two of Steel's men loading the boxes of heroin inside the truck.

Back at the library, Mark is practicing martial arts with Linda, and Linda flips Mark really hard. Mark sees Linda for a minute, and smiles at her. Logan is practicing his shooting on the video game, and he shoots five bad guys on the roof. Donnie is in the computer room. He's typing up his script. Mark is still finishing his target practice, and he has one last bad guy to take out, and it was the last guy in the harbor, and he takes him out. Mark tells himself, "I think I'm ready. And so is everybody else."

It is now Friday, and Outside of Club Car, at 9 PM, Mark, Logan, and Donnie exit the Grand Jeep Cherokee that is parked right across from the club. Logan tells them, "Alright guys, all we have to do is go inside, find Hersch, talk to him about where the deal is, and get out. Just hope we can stay alive for this one."

Donnie tells Logan, "Hey relax man, we're going to get in and out. Besides, what could go wrong?"

Logan tells Donnie, "You know, I always hated when you say that."

Mark tells them, "Well, just remember guys, this ain't the movies. So whatever happens out there, this is the real thing."

Donnie tells them, "Yeah, at least in the movies the good guys always win. Here, nobody wins, because I think we'll all be dead in three seconds once we get inside."

Mark tells Donnie, "Don't worry big bro, we've got this."

Donnie and Mark go inside the club, and Logan watches them for a minute, and he tells himself, "I hate it when he says that." They go inside the club, and they see a waitress, and ask her where Hersch is.

Mark tells the waitress, "Excuse me."

The waitress tells Mark, "Hi, can I help you?"

Mark tells the waitress, "Yeah we're looking for Rogan Hersch. We kind of owe him some money, and he told us to give him his money right here in his club."

The waitress tells Mark, "Is Mr. Hersch expecting you? He didn't tell me that you were coming."

Mark tells the waitress, "He called us last minute. I guess he didn't have time to tell you, since he's busy running this club."

The waitress tells Mark, "Okay. He's in the VIP room on the right."

Mark tells the waitress, "Thank you." Mark, Logan, and Donnie head to the VIP room to talk to Hersch. Inside the VIP room, Hersch and five of Steel's men are talking. Hersch is looking at his watch to make sure he gets ready for the deal. Mark, Logan, and Donnie enter the VIP room and see Hersch, and go over to talk to him.

Donnie tells Hersch, "Hey Hersch, I hope we made it to the party on time."

Hersch sees Logan, Donnie, and Mark in the VIP room and recognizes him, and he tells his men, "It's them. Shoot these morons!" Hersch and five of Steel's men take out their SIG-Sauer P226s from behind their jackets, and aims their guns on Logan, Donnie and Mark.

Mark says, "Oh shit." Mark, Logan, and Donnie take out their Beretta 92Fs from the back of their pants. Donnie fires his gun, and two bullets come out of his gun, and hit Steel man five in the chest and he dies. Eight bullets come out of nowhere, and Logan, Mark, and Donnie dive down to the floor, and roll over to one of the booths, hiding behind the table. Hersch fires his gun, three bullets come out of his gun and hit the VIP mat, but misses them. Mark sees Hersch, and he fires his gun. Three bullets come out of his gun, and hit the floor near Hersch but miss him. Steel man two fires his gun, two bullets come out of his gun, and hit the table. Mark fires his gun again, two bullets come out of his gun, hitting Steel man two in the chest, and he dies. Logan fires his gun, and three bullets hit the wall near Hersch. Hersch and Steel man one are still firing their guns. Five bullets hit the wall, missing Logan. Logan pulls his trigger, but he's out of ammo. He takes out the clip, and grabs a new one from the back of his pants, and he reloads, and fires. Three bullets come out of his gun, hitting Steel man three in the chest, killing him. Everybody outside in the club is panicking when they hear the gunshots, and they frantically exit the club. Mark tells Logan and Donnie, "We need to get out of here now!"

Logan tells Mark, "Why?"

Mark tells Logan, "There's too many people around here. We can't start a panic right now. There's just too many people."

Donnie tells them, "We need to stall them."

Logan tells them, "Leave that to me." Logan aims at the floor near Hersch, and Logan fires his gun. One bullet fires out of his gun and hits the floor near Hersch. Hersch jumps a little, and it distracts Steel man one and four. Mark, Logan, and Donnie get out of the VIP booth, and exit the club.

Hersch sees them leaving, and tells his men, "Come on, hurry! They're getting away!" Outside the club, Mark, Logan, and Donnie are getting in their car, and everyone is panicking. Logan is driving the Grand Jeep Cherokee, and Mark and Donnie are the passengers. All three of them are inside the car, and Logan turns over the ignition and drives away from the club, and they head to the freeway. Hersch and Steel men one and four see them driving away from the club, and Hersch is upset, and tells them, "Man, they got away!"

Steel man one tells Hersch, "So Hersch, what do we do? Let them go?"

Hersch slaps Steel man one, and tells him, "No, we're not letting them get away. I'm not going to let those wimps run around my city. I know exactly where to go, follow me."

Back on the LA freeway, where Mark, Logan, and Donnie are driving the Grand Jeep Cherokee, Donnie tells them, "Do you think we lost them?"

Logan tells Donnie, "I really doubt it. They were too busy getting out of there. Luckily the freeway isn't jam-packed today."

Mark tells them, "Well, I guess Plan A hasn't worked out, guess we'll have to go to Plan B." All three of them hear a gunshot out of nowhere. Hersch and Steel man one and four are riding in a black SUV, and Hersch is firing his Franchi SPAS 12 out the window. Hersch fires his gun again, and hits the back the reflector with one bullet. He fires three more times and hits the trunk of the Jeep Cherokee. Inside the Grand Jeep Cherokee all three men are panicking. Mark tells Logan, "We have got to lose them now!"

Logan tells Mark, "We need something to stall them so I can lose them."

Mark tells Logan, "Hang on." Mark sees an extra Beretta 92F gun, and he has five ordinary looking pens that are 1.2 pound grenades.

Logan tells Mark, "What are you carrying a lot of pens for in the glove compartment?"

Mark remembers something, and tells Logan, "Oh, I forgot. The guy in the prop department used to work for the CIA R&D department. He let me borrow a few pens, just in case of an emergency. I think I could use this. But right now we need to lose them."

Logan tells Mark, "We need to stall them first!" Mark grabs his gun, opens the window, and turns around a bit to see the black SUV. Hersch is still firing his gun, and five bullets come out of his gun hitting the road and the bumper of Logan's jeep. Mark fires his gun, hitting the SUV's hood. Mark keeps firing his gun, and five bullets come out, hitting the left headlight of the van. Mark distracts Hersch for a minute, while he fires one bullet at the hood. It also distracts Hersch's guys for a minute. Logan sees that the road is closed on the right side of the highway. Logan tells them, "Hang on!" Logan turns right, and hits the road closed sign, crashing through it. Hersch's men follow them, still firing their guns. Hersch's men are going closer, and they almost touch Logan's bumper, but Logan is driving fast.

Mark turns back around and yells at Logan, "Of all the god damn highways in the world, did you have to pick this one!"

Logan yells back at Mark, "Hey I need to distract them for a bit! There's a flare gun in the glove compartment. I have an idea."

Mark yells at Logan, "What the hell do we need a flare gun for!?"

Logan yells back to Mark, "Just aim it in the air and trust me, and throw the pens!"

Donnie yells at them, "Will you two shut the hell up! Mark, fire and throw!"

Mark yells at them, "If I die, I'm going to shoot both of you in the head!" Mark aims the flare gun at the air to distract Hersch, and fires one of the flares. As the flare goes up it distracts Hersch for a minute. Mark clicks on five of the pens, and throws them at Hersch's car. Mark tells Logan, "Stop!" Logan stops the car, and Hersch can see better now that the flare is gone.

He sees the pens, and Hersch yells, "Oh shit!" The pens explode, blowing up the car with Hersch and the two Steel men. Logan parks the car, and Logan, Donnie, and Mark exit the car, seeing the remains of the explosion. Hersch gets out of the car, but Steel's men are dead. Hersch is bloodied and battered, but aims his gun on Mark. Mark has another gun in the back of his pants, and he takes it out, aiming it at

Hersch. Mark fires his gun, three bullets come out of his gun, hitting Hersch in the chest, killing him.

Logan tells them, "I guess he didn't make it to the barbeque this time."

Mark sarcastically tells them, "I guess his invitation was lost in the mail."

Logan tells them, "I guess Plan A didn't work, I just pray Plan B works."

Mark and Donnie tell Logan, "Yeah, me too."

Outside of Steel's warehouse, Linda is using Mark's 2015 black Porsche. She turns on her laptop, and uses one of her cell phones. She sees the limousine parked right outside the warehouse, and is waiting for him. Linda exits the car with scotch tape and a cell phone. She tapes the cell phone to the back bumper of the limo, and heads back to the car, just as people begin exiting the warehouse. Linda gets back inside the Porsche, and ducks down, listening to the people exiting the warehouse. Linda gets back up, and sees Steel's limo, a truck, and four SUVs leaving the warehouse. Linda gets on the computer, and dials the cell phone number, and the cell phone rings inside her car. Linda starts the GPS tracking system, following the cell phone on Steel's bumper. Linda tells herself that she's in.

Back on the highway, Mark, Logan, and Donnie are about to get back in Logan's Jeep. Mark's cell phone rings, and he tells the guys, "It's mine." Mark picks up the phone, and answers it, "Hello?"

Linda's voiceover tells Mark, "Mark, good news. I turned the cell phone on, the GPS is on. Steel is leaving 112 West. I'll tell you the rest of the directions."

Mark tells Linda on the phone, "Okay, sure thing Linda. Alright, I'll give you a call." Mark tells Logan and Donnie, "Good news, Linda taped the cell phone to Steel's car. He's leaving 112 West. Donnie get on your phone and track Linda's directions."

Donnie tells Mark, "Sure thing little bro."

Back on the LA highway, Steel's men are driving to their deal. Linda tells the directions to Donnie on the cell phone, still outside of Steel's warehouse, in Mark's car, "Okay, make a left, and head to 13th South."

Back on the LA Highway, Donnie tells Logan, "Left on 13th South."

Linda looks at the laptop, "Alright, go west on I-22."

Donnie tells them, "West on I-22."

Linda tells Donnie, "Okay, make a right, and go to Krenshaw Avenue."

Donnie tells them in the car, "Okay, right on Krenshaw Avenue."

Linda tells Donnie on the cell phone, "Okay, I think I found the deal. It is six miles from an abandoned warehouse. It's at 123 South Street."

Donnie tells them, in the car, "Okay, 123 South Street. It is in six miles. That's where it is."

Mark tells Donnie, "Tell Linda to call in for backup."

Donnie tells Mark, "Sure thing."

Inside the 123 South Street warehouse, Steel and eight of his men are waiting for Louis Chang. Linda is driving Mark's Porsche down the LA Highway, and calling Captain Johnson on the cell phone. She tells him, "Alright, sir. Call in two squad vans and one helicopter and five squad cars. Tell them to hurry up, it's going to be going on soon. The deal is at 123 South Street. Hurry up."

Outside the warehouse where the deal is at, Logan's Jeep is parked right outside. Mark's car is also parked outside the warehouse when Linda arrived. Mark, Logan, Donnie, and Linda exit their cars. Mark opens the trunk for a minute, and takes out a few guns, handing them out to the others. Mark asks Linda, "Alright, is help coming?"

Linda tells Mark, "I called them, they'll be here in a few minutes."

Donnie tells them, "Well, we don't have a few minutes. The deal will be done before they get here."

Logan tells them, "Without a search warrant, those guys will be gone before they get here. You guys are right about that."

Mark tells them, "We'll have to stall them until they arrive. I have an idea. Logan, you go first."

Logan tells them, "Why do I have to go first?"

Mark tells Logan, "Because, it's my idea. And plus, deep down, we drew straws in my head, and we chose you."

Logan tells them, "I hate when you guys do that."

Inside the warehouse, Chang and five of his men from the triads have just arrived. Two of Chang's men put their briefcases down on the table, and open them. They see five million dollars each in the briefcases, and Steel smiles for a minute, really happy about seeing his payday. The box from the melted steel is open, and Steel takes out the bag of heroin from inside the box, and wipes the melted steel off the bag for Chang's men to see it. Chang is really impressed when he sees the heroin. The two men are about to close the deal, until Logan enters the warehouse, since the door is open. Logan tells them, "Hey guys, hope I'm not interrupting something. I kind of got lost. I'm looking for Universal Studios, but I'm so lost. Could you tell me where it is? You know LA is a big city, and you could get lost here. I'm kind of old-fashioned and I don't use GPS, so could you guys give me the directions?" Steel and his men, and Chang and his men, take out their guns, all aiming at Logan. Logan tells them, "Did I catch you guys at a bad time?" Logan dives down on the floor as five bullets come from nowhere, hitting the floor behind him. Logan rolls around behind some boxes to hide. Logan gets up a little, taking his gun from the back of his pants. Logan fires his gun, and three bullets come out of his gun, hitting Chang in the chest, and he dies. Mark, Logan, and Linda enter, and Mark fires his gun. Two bullets come out of his gun, hitting Steel man 2 in the chest, killing him. They see a huge pillar on the right, and they hide. Donnie fires his gun, and three bullets come out of his gun, but they don't hit anyone. Mark dives down on the floor, and three bullets come out of his gun and hit Steel man eight in the stomach, and he dies. He rolls around on the floor, and six bullets fire at him, but miss. He rolls behind the boxes next to Logan. Linda fires her gun, and three bullets hit Steel man one in the chest and he dies. Chang man two fires his gun, and two bullets hit the wall missing them. Linda fires her gun, three bullets come out of her gun, and hit Chang man one in the chest, killing him. Logan fires his gun, and three bullets hit Chang man five in the chest, and he dies. Donnie fires his gun, and three bullets kill Steel man three. Steel fires his gun, and hits a barrel near Donnie with three bullets, but misses him. Mark fires his gun, two bullets hit Chang man four in the stomach, and he dies. Steel is really upset, and sees Mark's foot. He fires two bullets, but they hit the floor and miss Mark. Mark gets upset. Logan fires his gun, one bullet comes out of his gun and just misses Chang man two. Linda fires her gun, and three bullets hit Steel man five in the chest, killing him. Donnie fires his gun, but he's out. He loads a new clip from the back of his pants, and fires three bullets, hitting Steel man four in the forehead.

Mark tells Logan, "Cover me, I'm going in." Logan sees Steel's foot, and he fires his gun, missing Steel. Mark comes out from behind the boxes, and charges Steel. Six bullets come out of nowhere and hit the floor near Mark, but miss him. Mark tackles Steel on to the table, both of them dropping their guns. Steel has the upper hand, kicking Mark in the stomach. He grabs Mark by the shirt, and punches him in the stomach three times. He tosses him to the floor on the other side of the warehouse like a rag doll. Linda fires her gun, and three bullets hit Steel man six in the chest, and he dies. Mark gets up from the floor, but Steel gives him a roundhouse kick to face, and Mark falls back down. Steel picks him up and punches him in the face three times, and knees him in the stomach. Steel again kicks him in the face, and Mark falls down on the floor. Chang's remaining men try to leave through the back door of the warehouse. Three SWAT guys carrying Franchi SPAS 12s stop the two Chang men, firing six bullets at them. Three of the bullets hit each of them, killing them both. Steel man seven fires his gun, and three bullets come out of his gun, but hit the wall, missing Linda. Logan nods at Linda, and Linda fires her gun near Steel man seven, hitting the ground near his foot. Linda comes out of cover, and aims her gun on Steel man seven, Linda fires her gun, but she's out of ammo. Steel man seven is still loaded, and he aims his gun on her. Linda is about to put her hands up, but takes a couple quarters out of her pocket, throwing them up in the air. Steel man seven is a bit distracted, and Linda pulls a spare clip from the back of her pants. She reloads, and shoots Steel man 7 in the chest, killing him.

Logan tells them, "I'm going to go check on Mark." Steel kicks Mark in the stomach. Mark is battered and beaten. Steel tries to kick him in the stomach again, but Mark blocks the kick, and punches Steel in the groin. He knees him in the stomach, and punches him in the face twice, flipping him to the floor. Steel tries to get up, and Mark gives him a roundhouse kick to the face. Steel falls to the ground. Mark punches him in the face five times. Mark grabs him by the shirt, knees him in the stomach, and gives him another roundhouse kick to the face. Mark grabs him by the shirt again, and goes to punch him in the face, but Steel blocks the punch and knees Mark in the stomach. Steel kicks Mark in the face again, and punches him six times in the face. Steel sees his gun on the floor and grabs it. Mark gets up from the floor, and Steel fires his gun. One bullet hits Mark in the left arm. Mark falls back down, wounded.

Steel aims his gun on Mark, as he goes over to him. Steel tells Mark, "I gotta hand it to you Wahlberg. You come here, ruin my deal, and cost me millions of dollars, and not only that, you took out my clientele. I should kill you for this, and to tell you the truth I am going to enjoy it. I always loved playing this game, because in the end, I always win. What can I say Mr. Movie Star, you came this close, and your movie just bombed, right in front of me. And guess who lit up the ignition? Me. And here's what they say in the movies. Time to drop the curtains."

Logan sees Steel, and he fires his gun. One bullet hits near the heel, but misses Steel. Steel turns, but doesn't see anybody. Mark sees his gun, rolls over to it, grabs it, and aims it on Steel. Mark tells Steel, "Sorry, Steel, my box office didn't bomb, it just became a smash." Mark fires his gun, three bullets come out of his gun and hit Steel in the chest and he dies. Mark falls on the floor, a little bit weak. Logan sees him, and helps pick him up. Outside the warehouse, a lot of LAPD squads and SWAT and an ambulance are waiting.

Logan grabs Mark by the shoulder to see if he's okay. Logan tells Mark, "Well, is this the ending you were looking for Mark?"

Mark tells Logan, "I don't know. I think it is."

Outside the warehouse, the movie turns into a silver screen, with Mark, carried by a different actor, being taken to the ambulance van. The actor tells Mark, "You are one god damn son of a bitch." Everybody in the audience is watching, as the credits of *LA Beat* roll. All the audience is clapping, and they love the movie.

Back at the computer room, Linda, Logan, and Donnie are sitting down waiting for Mark. Mark enters the computer room, and Logan tells Mark, "Hey, did you read the news? *LA Beat*? It's box office gold. It's opened with 90 million on the first weekend."

Mark tells Logan, "I know about that. Me and Donnie got a lot of offers to do more movies. We've also got the next *LA Beat* movie scripted, so I think we'll have another one out next year."

Donnie tells them, "Yeah, don't worry. It's almost finished, and it's gonna be better than ever. Right now, I'm still blocked on it, so I'm figuring it out. Meanwhile, I heard from Bruce, and he's got the Navy contract signed and sealed. His company is going through the roof, thanks to those contracts."

Logan tells them, "I got a call from the chief, he wanted to thank us for taking down Steel and dismantling his empire. He's awarding all of us a medal of honor, and he wanted to thank you and Donnie personally. Hey Linda, why don't you tell them the news."

Linda tells them, "Me and Logan got promoted to detective lieutenants in IA, so we're going to be working there full time."

Donnie tells them, "Hey that's great!"

Logan tells them, "We also got bigger news, the chief wants to thank you and for helping us. And if you still wanted to join the LA reserves, Mark, they'll let you. The chief pulled some strings."

Mark tells Logan, "Thanks for the offer Logan, but I think I'm going to stay where I am. If it's okay with you, I'd like to stay as a consultant for the LAPD, and you could hire us. You know, hunt down some more crooked cops or other bad guys. You know, if the job is still open for us."

Linda tells Mark, "Well, I already talked to Captain Johnson, and he said the jobs yours. You can stay on as full-time police consultants. We'll hire you case-by-case, when we need you guys."

Donnie tells them, "Sounds great. We'll take the deal."

Logan tells them, "We've got another case we're working on. Maybe it can help your sequel to *LA Beat*."

"What's the case?" asks Mark.

"I heard there's a cop taking bribes and working for some arms dealers. We don't know who it is, but we need to find him. I was wondering if you guys could help us?" said Logan.

Donnie tells Logan, "When do we start?"

Logan tells them, "We need to go see Captain Johnson, he'll give us the file so we can get started. We have to report to him in a few minutes."

Donnie tells Logan, "Well, we better get going."

Donnie and Logan are about to exit the computer room, and Mark tells them, "Hey, we'll catch up to you guys, I need to speak to Linda for a minute."

Donnie tells Mark, "Okay, guys, but we need to be at the station in a few minutes."

Logan and Donnie exit the computer room. Linda gets up from her chair and goes over to Mark. Mark tells Linda, "Hey before we report to Captain Johnson, I wanted to ask. Where do you think we should go on our date tonight?"

Linda tells Mark, "You know, I was thinking we should go to that new miniature golf place, I've been wanting to go there. Besides, I hear they have great pizza, I was wondering if you wanted to go."

Mark tells Linda, "Heh, not for all the money in the world would I miss that new pizza bar."

Linda tells Mark, "Maybe we can get there a little faster."

Mark tells Linda, "I've still got some time left." Mark and Linda start making out, before they report to Captain Johnson.

THE END

NOCOMO

By: Bobby Cinema

Synopsis

Detective Nathan Devers of the Kansas City Police Department is on a case to track down an Arms Dealer. He is trying to find this guy, but has no details. Nathan is partnered up with Natalie Xalatan to find this arms dealer. Nathan works on Robberies and he was also working on this case. Natalie and Nathan had troubles trying to find a lead on this case. But Nathan knows somebody that can help him. Natalie asked who can help them find this arms dealer. Nathan's friend Jason Boswell. He is mildly autistic and he works in NOCOMO industries. Natalie asks how his autistic friend could help them. Nathan tells Natalie that his friend is highly intelligent. He helped him out on an armed robbery case and he was a big help catching those robbers. Natalie was stunned, but she gave him a chance to get Nathan's friend's help. So, they both went to NOCOMO for their help.

nside the Kansas City National Bank, there are five guys dressed in clown masks. Nobody is suspecting them. Nathan is at the table, filling out a deposit slip. He is wearing Ray-Ban sunglasses, a ball cap, and a black leather jacket, so no one would suspect him. Nobody in this bank has any idea that this place is going to get robbed. Not until one of the robbers, who is wearing a clown mask, tosses a smoke bomb to the floor. All the men in masks throw smoke bombs down to distract everybody in the bank. The five robbers take out their 92F Beretta guns from the back of their long jackets. Clown Robber One fires his gun up in the air, and a bullet hits the ceiling. While the smoke clears, everyone is panicking, while the five robbers aim their guns on the bank tellers. Clown Robber One tells the people in the bank, "Don't move! Everybody, stand still now! You guys, behind the cage, don't even think about pulling that alarm! You pull that alarm, and I'm going to put a bullet in your damn heads!"

Clown Robber Three takes a look at Nathan standing at the table where he was filling out a deposit slip. Clown Robber Three tells his boss, "Hey boss, I think this guy looks a bit suspicious. I think he might be a cop."

Clown Robber One tells Clown Robber Three, "Search him."

Clown Robber Three goes over to Nathan and tries to search him, telling him, "Turn around, hands up, and spread 'em."

Nathan turns around and puts his hands up, and tells Clown Robber Three, "Look, I don't know what's going on. But I heard what you were saying just now, that I'm a cop. I'm not a cop, I swear."

Clown Robber Three tells Nathan, "I'll be the judge of that." Clown Robber Three searches Nathan for a minute and sees he's clean. He even checks his wallet and cell phone, and Clown Robber Three takes a look at him and realizes he's just an ordinary guy, "You're clean."

Clown Robber One tells Nathan, "Too bad you're not a cop, because if you were, I would've shot you. But even though you're not, we'd still kill you. But since we're in a hurry, we have to leave."

"Excuse me, see that green button on my phone?" says Nathan, "Can you turn it on for a minute, I just wanted to check my messages."

Clown Robber Three tells Nathan, "Well we don't have any time to turn on that green button, because we're going to be going pretty soon, once we empty out the cash."

Nathan begs Clown Robber Three, "Please press the green button, I really need to check my messages, please. Look, just press the green button and you can leave. I know you're in a hurry and the rest of your guys are taking all the money out of the bank."

Robbers Two, Four, and Five are collecting all the money that the bank tellers are giving to them at gunpoint. Clown Robber Three tells Nathan, "Okay, I'll press the green button, but only because it will shut you up and we're in a hurry. Plus, I think someone will trigger the alarm pretty soon."

Nathan tells Clown Robber Three, "Before you press the green button, I don't get it. Why go for the small bills behind the counter? The big payday is in that safe over there."

Clown Robber Three puts Nathan's wallet on the table, and tells Nathan, "First of all, why don't you shut the hell up. I would put a bullet in your head right now if we weren't in a god damn hurry." Clown Robber Three presses the green button on the cell phone, and an alarm goes off, and there are sounds going off.

Nathan tells Clown Robber Three, "Next time you want to search me, you should also check the front." Nathan turns around, and takes out his Beretta 92F from the front of his jacket, where it was taped to his chest, and fires his gun. Three bullets hit Clown Robber Three in the chest killing him. The rest of the cops arrive. Three SWAT teams are already surrounding the bank.

SWAT team member one says, "Hands up! It's over!"

SWAT member two tells the bank robbers, "It's over guys, get your hands up now!"

Clown Robber One tells the SWAT and everybody else, "Oh, yeah, before we get our hands up, you forgot to mention one thing."

SWAT member one tells the robber, "I think I remember what we said, just drop it."

Clown Robber One tells the SWAT team, "Good thing you forgot to tell us to drop our weapons first. I bet you guys are practically new on this site. But we'll drop them, and we'll come quietly, but first we have to wind our watches. Let us wind our watches and we'll come quietly."

SWAT member two tells SWAT one, "It might be a trick, but since they say they'll come quietly, I guess we don't have a choice."

SWAT member one tells the robbers, "Okay, wind you watches, and then come quietly."

Clown Robber One tells the SWAT, "I knew you'd see it my way." Four of the bank robbers wind their watches. They get their hands up, but one thing they forgot to mention is that their watches have an explosive. While the robbers put their hands up, their watches explode, and so do they. All four of them are dead.

SWAT member one tells them, "Man, that's what I call winding your watch. Even though I really stink at telling jokes."

Nathan goes over to the SWAT team. Nathan's boss, Captain Ben Warner, and his partner Natalie Xalatan, enter the bank and go over to talk to Nathan. Captain Warner talks to Nathan, "Man this is the third bank they heisted, but this time they actually killed themselves for it."

Nathan tells Captain Warner, "They robbed a lot of money in three banks. We know they heisted this one because it's an easy target. They were about to give themselves up when SWAT arrived, and then they killed themselves. It's like they gave themselves up quietly, like it was a suicide mission."

Natalie tells them, "The three banks they heisted were in the dark. They just had to break in, steal the money, and get out. Now they're robbing in daylight. It's like they changed their pattern. And once SWAT arrives they 'come quietly'?"

Ben tells them, "And kill themselves. Just like a suicide mission. It's like they wanted to die here."

Nathan tells them, "You know, Ben, the way I look at those watches? Those explosives had to be military grade. I think these guys were hired to rob these banks. It's like it was staged. Oh my God, I think I figured something out. They never robbed the big bills from the safe, but what if they did? They would just need someone on the inside to do it."

"We better go take a look at that safe," said Ben. They go inside the safe to see all the big bills that were stored. There were 20 million dollars stored inside the safe, but it was all gone.

Nathan tells them, "Man, I knew it, I knew they were just stalling us. Those guys out there robbing this place? It was all staged, it's like they were distracting us from one thing. It's the money from this bank."

Natalie tells them, "We need to speak to the bank manager and see how much was in there. And we better go check the back."

Nathan tells them, "Natalie, you go talk to the bank manager and see how much money was in this safe. Sir, you and I can go check the back, I think they may have had a getaway car."

Ben tells Nathan, "Let's go check it out."

Outside the bank, the door opens, and it's Ben and Nathan. Nathan tells Ben, "Sir, I checked everything around this bank. There were three armored trucks here. I knew it was a distraction. I had three bullets in the gun. I looked over this heist a million times. I knew these guys were going to rob this place. I guess I didn't look at the back. This was all staged."

Ben tells Nathan, "We'll worry about that later, right now I think the chief is going to want to talk to me. He's in the bank and he's probably going to be really upset about what happened."

Nathan tells Ben, "Whatever happens, sir, I have your back."

Ben tells Nathan, "Well, I'll meet you back at the station."

Back in the meeting room in the Kansas City Police Department, Nathan and Natalie are sitting down in their chairs waiting for Ben. Ben enters the meeting room, and goes over to talk to Nathan and Natalie. Ben sits down in his chair, and tells them, "Well, I spoke to the chief. He is really upset that we let this heist happen. We lost a lot of money, and he is already chewing me out for messing this up. You two were working this robbery case for a year, and you still haven't found anything. You finally get those guys on the suicide mission, but we find out that they were just hired help to distract us while the real robbers stole money from the back!"

Nathan tells Ben, "Look, Captain, I'm really sorry about what happened. I thought I had a great instinct about this case. They were all related. There were three bank heists over the year. It's like they knew the place. And all of the security cameras were destroyed? It's like we've got some blackhat hacker who destroyed all the footage before we could track it down."

Natalie tells Ben, "I found out how much they stole."

Ben tells Natalie, "How much?"

Natalie tells Ben, "There was about 20 million dollars inside that safe. But there was something weird about that money. All that money was marked. All those bills were practically stolen. That's what the bank examiner told me, that all those bills were practically useless to spend, since they were all marked."

Ben tells them, "If those bills are marked that's good news. It means we can track down the numbers."

Nathan tells them, "Sir, before you jump into anything, I don't think we can find them. If those bills were marked, I think this might be a money laundering operation. When they steal from places like banks, they know all those bills are marked. What they need to do is change those bills into newer ones so that they won't be tracked down."

Ben tells them, "Well Sergeant Devers, are you telling me that this might be a money laundering operation?"

Nathan tells Ben, "Well, Ben, if this wasn't a money laundering operation, why would they steal bills that are so obviously marked. It had to be somebody owned by the mob, but the mob would never just deposit marked bills, they would have somebody take it out."

Natalie tells them, "I think I agree with Nathan. Nobody is stupid enough to steal a bunch of marked bills from a bank and use it, unless they were using it for a money laundering operation. They'll use it to change those bills into something they want to sell."

Ben tells them, "Like what?"

"I don't know, probably drug dealing. What if we're dealing with a drug lord on this one? You know these guys launder a lot of money for drugs."

Ben tells them, "Those are excellent hunches. I don't think this is anything to do with drugs. We're going to have to figure this out. It's going to take a lot more than marked bills to figure this one out. We have to find that money, and crack down. Whatever you're going to do, do it quick, because the chief is breathing down our necks on this one. He's given us one week to close this case, or he's bringing the FBI on board."

Nathan tells Ben, "Don't worry sir, you can count on me and Natalie, we'll get this case done in no time."

Ben tells them, "Well I hope so, because our asses are on the line for this one." Ben exits the meeting room.

Nathan and Natalie look at the case file. Natalie tells Nathan, "You think we can find these guys?"

Nathan tells Natalie, "Well whatever we do Natalie, we better do it now. Because deep down, I think it's going to take more than a week to solve this case."

Jason Boswell is working at NOCOMO industries, a workshop for people with disabilities, in the workshop. He tears out rolls of paper while sitting down in his chair. His job was to tear rolls of paper and put them inside a barrel. It's for a recycling job that NOCOMO is being paid for. While Jason is tearing out paper, one of his coworkers tells him, "Hey, Jace, you think its quitting time yet?"

Jason tells his co-worker, "Not yet, Luke."

Luke tells Jason, "When is quitting time anyway?"

Jason tells Luke, "2:30 PM." Jason looks at the clock, sees that it's 2:29, and tells himself one more minute.

The clock strikes 2:30, Nicki is working at her desk, and picks up her phone that is a speaker, and tells the crew, "Have a good night." Everybody gets up from their chairs. Jason and Luke and all the workers head to the cafeteria and locker room that they called "the lounge." Jason and Luke take off their gloves and put them in their respective lockers. They grab their wallets, and house keys, and cell phones, and are about to head out. Jason sees Nicki Samson waiting for them. Nicki is the general manager of NOCOMO. Nicki goes over to Jason and Luke, and tells Jason, "Hey Jace. How's the job?"

Jason tells Nicki, "It's good."

Nicki tells Jason, "By the way, I'd like to ask, is your mom going to make another endowment for the place?"

Jason tells Nicki, "No, not yet."

Nicki tells Jason, "Well, I hope she hurries. We need another grant if we want to stay open."

Jason tells Nicki, "Well my mom is the president of Northwest Missouri State University, about a few miles from Shawnee County. I'll talk to her, and see if she wants to put another endowment in. I always have to remind her when to put another check in."

Nicki tells Jason, "Well tell her we expect her check this week. Besides the only way to keep NOCOMO open is through her check. Your family's company, Boswell Battery, has always been good to Kansas City."

Jason tells Nicki, "You don't have to remind me. You forgot, my grandfather founded Boswell Battery Company and turned it into a national product. We have 40 battery companies around the country, and one in China."

Luke tells Jason, "Actually, it's 55 battery factories, because there's also small towns from each state that have one. Especially China."

Jason tells Luke, "Sorry, my mistake."

Nicki tells Jason, "Well, I hope you talk to your mom and make sure she gets the check. You know, besides, the bank is expecting me to mail them a check this week."

Jason tells Nicki, "Well, my mom may be the donor, and also president of this company, but she always goes by my word. Besides my dad died when I was 10, and he left the company to my mom. He was planning on leaving the company to me, but I'm only 30 years old, and I don't think I'm old enough to run the company."

Luke tells Jason, "Or sane enough to do it. Since you are mildly autistic."

Jason tells Luke, "Hey, you're also dyslexic too Luke."

Luke tells Jason, "Try not to rub it in."

Outside NOCOMO the bus is waiting for them. Jason is on his cell phone with his mom. Jason tells her, "Hey Mom, I just wanted to remind you to send in the check for NOCOMO, they need the endowment, and the bank is waiting on the check. Oh you've already sent it in? Okay, I was just checking. Okay, I'll meet you at home after bowling. Bye!"

Luke tells Jason, "Is today our bowling night?"

Jason tells Luke, "Of course, it's Tuesday. The bus always takes us to Bearcat Lanes on Tuesday, plus my ride will show up after we're done." NOCOMO was actually in Shawnee County in a town called Maryville, it's a section of Kansas City, Missouri.

Nathan is at his apartment, in his living room watching a game on TV. It's a football game, and he's drinking a beer. Nathan tells himself, "You got to love Superbowl '96. I better get the WrestleManias on DVD. I don't know if I want to watch WrestleMania 1 or 5 or 3. No I think I'll just watch WrestleMania 3, and go all the way through WrestleMania 10 tonight." The phone rings, and Nathan answers it. Nathan tells the person on the other line, "Hello? Hey Jason. You guys

121

are bowling? How come you didn't invite me, I wanted to go bowling with you guys. Oh, I guess it was kind of last minute. Plus, I forgot it was Tuesday, and I was supposed to go with you guys. I'm kinda busy with this case I'm working on. Uh, what is it? Well I don't think I can tell you right now, it's confidential. And besides, I don't think you could solve it anyways. This is a tough case, way beyond your alley anyway."

Jason's voiceover on the phone tells Nathan, "Okay, man, I was just checking. But if you need anything, just give me a call alright?"

Nathan tells Jason, "Alright bye man." Nathan hangs up his phone, and puts his beer down on the coffee table, and looks at the file. He thinks, "I wonder if Jason could help me on this one, but it's probably too complicated for a guy like him." Nathan is still looking at the file.

Inside of Bearcat Lanes, Jason is bowling in alley 3. It is Jason's turn to bowl, and he rolls the ball down the lane but he misses it. Jason goes back to his seat, and Luke tells Jason, "Man, I always hate it when they put our balls in the gutter."

Jason tells Luke, "Well, it takes a lot of hard work to release the ball. Besides, my average is usually 60 and yours is 80."

Luke tells Jason, "Well, it's an improvement."

Jason tells Luke, "Alright, Luke, you're up man." Jason sits down, and Luke gets up from his chair. He grabs a ball, and bowls down the lane. This time, Luke rolls his ball down the lane, and hits a 7-10 split. Jason is upset, and tells Luke, "Aw man, you got a 7-10 split."

Luke tells Jason, "Man, I always hate when I hit those, that's why my bowling average is way down."

Jason tells Luke, "Maybe this time you can pick up a spare." Jason sees his beer bottle on the table, it's a Bud Light. Jason grabs his beer and drinks it. Luke grabs another ball. Luke focuses, but doesn't know where to hit the ball. Jason has a gift, not only does he have a photographic memory, but he also has keen eyesight. Jason tells Luke, "Aim at the pin to the left."

Luke tells Jason, "Are you crazy? If I aim the ball to the left, it'll hit the gutter, or I'll only get one."

Jason tells Luke, "Just roll the ball. Trust me on this one."

Luke tells Jason, "Okay, I'll try it your way. If I don't make this spare, you're buying me another beer."

Jason tells Luke, "Fair enough." Luke rolls the ball, and he hits the pen on the left, and it flings over and hits the right pin, and it's a spare. Jason tells Luke, "Told ya so."

Luke tells Jason, "Alright! I got a spare! I never get a spare! Hey, how'd you know if I hit the pin on the left it would get the right one?"

Jason tells Luke, "I've got good eyesight. Plus, I never had the chance to use my eyesight before, until now."

Luke tells Jason, "Maybe you should try it. Besides the only time you're blind is because you haven't used it. Maybe you should try it sometime."

Jason tells Luke, "I don't know man."

Luke tells Jason, "Well, you're bowling average is 60. Besides, who knows, maybe it'll change, and maybe I'm wrong. It wouldn't hurt to give it a shot."

Jason tells Luke, "Alright, that was my last beer, so I'll pay for a new game, and we'll try it out." After Jason pays for a new game, Jason bowls another frame. This time he looks at the pins from the alley, and he observes it, and he looks at the angles. Jason rolls his ball down the lane, and this time hits a strike. Jason hits three more strikes as they play. Luke is astonished, and Jason bowls another strike, followed by four more. Jason bowls two more, and Luke was really astonished. He sees the bowling score and it's 300.

Luke tells Jason, "Man, 300? Nobody could do that. Not even a record guy could do that."

Jason tells Luke, "Well, you owe me a beer."

Luke tells Jason, "How did you do that?"

Jason tells Luke, "Like I said, I have good eyesight." Jason rubs his forehead for a minute, and closes his eyes. Jason tells Luke, while stuttering, "M-m-man I never thought I could do that. Man, rolling 60, and now with my new eyesight I get a 300? Man, I haven't done that for years, not since I graduated college."

Luke tells Jason, "Well you always had this photographic memory. There are times in my life that I think you should be working at NASA or should've gone to Harvard or MIT. You've always been this super genius, but you never actually use it."

Jason tells Luke, "Because nobody asked me. And besides, I'm not just going to persuade people to get what I want, I'm a terrible salesmen. Besides I choked on my Harvard interview, so I chose Northwest to be close to my mom."

Luke tells Jason, "You know, Jace, don't take this the wrong way, but I always feel like you're wasting your potential. Because I always thought you could do anything you wanted to do."

Jason tells Luke, "You may be right, Luke, but the truth is, I don't know what my potential is, or what I want to do. I used to coast through life because I'm wealthy. But I've always envied Nathan. We've always known each other, since we were kids. And he always knew what he wanted to do and where he wanted to go."

Luke tells Jason, "You're the one who helped him get into the academy."

Jason tells Luke, "My mom is the one who got him into the academy. She donated a lot of money to the mayor's election. I'm just the one who helped him study for the exams, with my eyesight. Every time I blinked my eyes, I knew my sense would start. It's like my very own superpower that I never used."

Luke tells Jason, "Well he's been on the force for 9 years. He's always been busy."

Jason tells Luke, "Yeah, I know. You know, ever since he graduated from the academy and got appointed as a detective in robbery, he's always been busy. You know, sometimes, I'd wish he'd ask for help. I could really help him on some of those cases. He's always backlogged. You know, I talked to him earlier and it sounded like he was busy with a case from a year ago. Man, I wish I could help him, but it sounds like he doesn't want my help."

Luke tells Jason, "I'm sure he wants your help. Maybe we just need to give him some time or something."

Jason tells Luke, "I'm sure he will, Luke."

Back in the police department in the meeting room, Nathan and Natalie are still working on their case. They're reading the file, and they still can't find anything. Natalie tells Nathan, "Do you have any idea who these robbers are?"

Nathan tells Natalie, "Natalie, we've been tracking these robbers for the last year. They robbed the three banks that are in this area, but it was all staged. All they had to do was break into it at night and steal it, but now they're doing an armed robbery in the day, and making it look like a suicide mission."

Natalie tells Nathan, "What about the watches the robbers were carrying. There were explosives inside those watches, and they blew themselves up just like that. And you told me they were mercenaries. So if mercenaries were hired, who do you think hired them?"

Nathan tells Natalie, "You know I checked the files on these guys. All their files said they were dead already. Like they were ghosts. The only way you can make yourselves dead in the files is through the NSA. I know how the NSA works, they make themselves look dead on paper, so no one can track them down and they can work."

Natalie tells Nathan, "Are you thinking the NSA may be involved in this?"

Nathan tells Natalie, "I really doubt it. These guys must have a blackhat hacker on their payroll. Or these guys are blackhat hackers. They'd have to be computer geniuses to do something like this."

Natalie tells Nathan, "Well Nate, the million dollar question is who hired these guys?"

Nathan tells Natalie, "We have no idea who hired them, because when they destroyed themselves, they destroyed their cell phones with them. I even checked the backlog. Even the security data, and all the calls they made had disappeared. I think those phones were untraceable."

Natalie tells Nathan, "Well, we've got to find out who hired these guys, and the real robbers who stole that 20 million dollars in all marked bills. I know they're going to use that money for money laundering, so I know this is going to be a money laundering case."

Nathan tells Natalie, "Well, like I said, the one thing about money launders is what are they laundering money for? You know drugs? Guns? What are they laundering for? Besides, all those bills are marked, and I know they're going to change it pretty soon."

Natalie tells Nathan, "I've looked at the list of money launders from the DOJ's office, but none of them really fit the description. Besides, none of them are really in Kansas City."

Nathan tells Natalie, "We have to find a money launderer that nobody would suspect, and that nobody has caught yet. This mysterious money launderer is probably mysterious because nobody suspects him, and nobody is going to find him, or know who he is, or where his operation is at."

Natalie tells Nathan, "Look I know we never ask for help, but I think maybe we should. Besides, our sources are practically dried up. I think we may have to go outside the box for this one."

Nathan tells Natalie, "I've been telling you that for a year, but you wouldn't listen to me."

Natalie tells Nathan, "You think we should hire a private investigator to help with this one?"

Nathan tells Natalie, "Private investigators are really expensive, and I really doubt the Captain or the Chief want us to spend any more money on this guy."

Natalie tells Nathan, "Well I wish we could find a private investigator that's really good and cheap to work with, but I highly doubt we can find one."

Nathan is thinking for a minute, and snaps his fingers. Nathan tells Natalie, "I think I know somebody who could help us. Besides, I kind of owe him. I've never used him before, but I think he's our only hope to catch this guy."

Natalie tells Nathan, "Who is he?"

Nathan tells Natalie, "I'll tell you tomorrow, I think we can meet him at 12:30 PM, because that's when his lunch hour starts."

Natalie tells Nathan, "Well, whoever he is, we really need him to find this guy."

Back at NOCOMO, Jason and Luke are doing their jobs, tearing out paper, and putting it in barrels. Nicki is at her desk working, and she is looking at the clock. Nicki picks up her phone, and tells the workers, "Lunchtime." Everybody gets up from their chairs and heads to lunch.

Outside NOCOMO, at the main entrance, Nathan and Natalie are about to go inside. Natalie tells Nathan, "NOCOMO? What is this place anyway?"

Nathan tells Natalie, "This is like a factory and workshop where mentally retarded or handicapped people can work."

Natalie tells Nathan, "So, uh, the person who is going to help? Is he the manager, or the owner, or one of the staff members working here?"

Nathan tells Natalie, "Uh, not quite."

Nathan and Natalie go inside the building. Luke and Jason are eating their lunch. Jason is eating a bologna and cheese sandwich, and drinking a can of Diet Pepsi, and so is Luke. Nathan and Natalie enter the building and they see Jason eating his food. Jason turns around and sees them entering the building. One of the workers from NOCOMO asks them, "Excuse me, who are you?"

Nathan takes out his police badge, and shows it to the worker, telling them, "Hi, I'm Sergeant Nathan Devers, from Kansas City PD, and this is my partner Sergeant Natalie Xalatan. We're here to speak to Jason Boswell."

The employee says, "Hi, I'm Nicki Strokes. I work here. Is Mr. Boswell in any trouble, I'm practically new here, and I don't know his background, but he hasn't done anything. He's a good kid, he didn't touch or break anything. You know, his mother is the president of Northwest Missouri State University, and she's friends with the mayor. Whatever he did, I'm sure she can straighten it out."

Nathan tells Nicki, "Oh no, nothing like that. Jason's not in trouble. He's a friend of mine, and we just came to see him. It's nothing bad."

Nicki tells Nathan, "Okay, normally you'd need a visitor's pass, but you're not visiting the entire place, and you are a cop. So you can just go see him, he's right over there."

Nathan tells Nicki, "Thanks Nicki." Nathan puts his police badge back inside his left pants pocket. Nathan tells Natalie, "Okay, I'm going to go speak to Jason for a minute. You know, you can ask Nicki to sign you in for one of those visitor's passes, and she can show you around. That way you don't get bored."

Natalie tells Nathan, "Well, actually Nate, I don't need to see the whole place. Besides, if you're gonna talk to him, I'm gonna talk to him too."

Nathan tells Natalie, "Okay, but you know how I told you this place is a mentally handicapped workshop? Well, my friend Jason? He is mildly autistic, but he's a really good guy."

Natalie tells Nathan, "Well, don't worry, I don't have to talk to him or anything. Besides, if he's autistic it's okay, he's just a normal guy like anyone else. Look, you do all the talking, and I'll chime in whenever you need me."

Nathan tells Natalie, "Okay, I'll tell you when to chime in."

Natalie tells Nathan, "Okay." Nathan and Natalie go over to Jason's table, and he sees his friend Luke eating with him.

Jason and Luke see Nathan, and get up from the table to greet him. They shake hands, and Jason says, "Hey Nate! Man, it's great to see you. It's been a while since you came down here."

Nathan tells Jason, "Well, I'm sorry, I've been really busy with work. Since I made detective, I've had a lot of cases. I'm on the robbery division right now."

Jason tells Nathan, "Nathan, I read your site. You're in the MCU, you know the Major Crimes Unit? You handle big and major cases." Jason looks at Natalie for a minute, and has a crush on her, and he tells Nathan, "Hey Nate, who's your friend? Is she your girlfriend or something?"

Nathan tells Jason, "Uh, no. She's my partner from the police force. This is Natalie Xalatan."

Nathan nods his head to Natalie, signaling her that it's okay to talk. Natalie tells Jason, "Pleased to meet you Jason. You know, Nathan told me a lot about you. I'm sure he's told you a lot about me."

Jason tells Natalie, "Well, pleased to meet you too Natalie." They shake hands, and Jason continues, "Well, Nathan never told me about you, we haven't seen each other in three years, since he made detective."

Natalie lets go of Jason's hand, and tells Nathan, "Man, you should see this guy more often."

Nathan tells Natalie, "Yeah, well sorry, my mistake. I've had a busy career. Didn't have time to see my friends."

Jason tells them, "Hey Nathan, you remember Luke Mosby? He went to school with us, remember?"

Nathan says, "Oh man, hey Luke! Man, we haven't seen each other since graduation! How's it been?"

Luke tells Nathan, "Hey, I'm doing fine. After graduation, I stayed with my parents, and I've been working here full time, so the rest is history."

Jason tells Nathan, "So, what brings you here buddy? I don't think you just came here to talk old times."

Nathan tells Jason, "Look, I'm sorry if this is a bad moment, but I need your help on something."

Jason tells Nathan, "Is it a case? Because I heard you were working on a real big case right now."

Luke asks, "Is it about the mysterious money launderers? They robbed the Kansas City National Bank two days ago, but it was a suicide mission. Mercenaries were hired to rob the bank, but they killed themselves before they stole anything, but they were just a distraction while the real robbers robbed the back and got away. Sounded like an inside job."

Natalie tells them, "Whoa whoa whoa, makes you think this was an inside job? And how do you guys know all this?"

Jason tells them, "We surf the net all day. And we read." Nathan and Natalie look at Jason for a minute. Jason tells them, "My mom's friends with the mayor, he can give me any information I need. You know, my mom donated a lot of money to his campaign, so he owes her a lot."

Natalie tells them, "Well, since you guys know so much about this case, that's the reason why we're here."

Luke tells them, "Well, let's have a seat, and we can talk about it."

Natalie and Nathan and Jason and Luke sit down, and discuss about why they're here. Nathan tells them, "You're right about one thing, I think it might be an inside job. I've been over the files a couple of times. Somebody had to be inside to get past all of the security codes and locks. I think it has to be a money laundering operation because all of those stolen bills…?"

Jason interrupts Nathan, "Cause those bills are marked. If those bills were marked, that means that they're going to be using it to launder. I read that a bank examiner would be examining those numbers, and if they can track them, it would lead back to the guy who stole it. All the money would have to be connected to a drug lord or an arms dealer."

Nathan tells them, "How do you know all that stuff anyway? Oh, let me guess, the mayor told you?"

Jason tells Nathan, "I kind of figured it out when he gave me some of the information about the stolen money. And I think I know why you guys are here, and like I said, I really doubt it was to visit an old buddy."

Nathan tells them, "You're right Jace, I didn't just come here to visit an old friend. We need your help, you know so much about this case, and you do have some great detective skills. Plus, I kind of owe you for helping me to pass the detective exam. I haven't been really successful on cases lately, so maybe you can help me out with this one."

Jason sarcastically tells Nathan, "I don't know Nate. I'm actually kind of busy right now, and we haven't seen each other in three years, and now you suddenly need my help? I don't know. Plus, I'd probably be bad, and lead you on a wild goose chase, or to the wrong guy. Besides, I have horrible detective skills. Sorry, man, I don't think I can help ya."

Natalie tells them, "Well I guess we're back at square one. Guess we'll have to solve this case ourselves."

Jason laughs, and says, "I'm only kidding. Of course I'll help you guys. I just wanted to see ya squirm for a minute."

Nathan tells Jason, "Funny man, cute, but funny."

Jason tells Nathan, "Besides, I have a P.I. badge. I applied for it last year and got one. So I can work with you on this case as a police consultant. So here are the conditions: You hire me and Luke as police consultants, give us authorizations for anything, you know badge, guns, everything, and we'll help you with the case."

Nathan tells Jason, "Okay, but no guns. Because, no offense Jason, but you do realize that you're...?"

Jason interrupts him again and says, "That I'm mildly autistic. And plus, I don't have good skills for shooting. Here, I want to show you something, I still have a few minutes left in my break. This is a secret area that people have never used before. Follow me."

Nathan tells Jason, "What secret area?"

Jason says, "I'll show you." Nathan, Luke, Natalie, and Jason all get up from their chairs, and they see an elevator right next door to the cafeteria. Jason presses the elevator button, and the doors open. Jason says, "There's an elevator button out here, but it only works with a key." Jason takes out a key, and opens it, and the elevator door closes, taking them down. The elevator descends, stopping at the basement. After the elevator door opens, the basement leads to a tunnel. Jason flips the light switch outside of the elevator, revealing the huge tunnel. Jason tells them, "Follow me." Jason and the others walk down the tunnel. They make a right, and there is a door that is locked. Jason opens the door with his key, and shows it to them. Once they go inside the secret room,

Jason turns a light switch on. This secret room is a computer room, a meeting hall, a firing range, and a lounge with vending machines and a refrigerator. There is also another elevator lift. Jason tells them, "Welcome to Jason's Secret Room."

Natalie tells them, "So, how did you build this place?"

Jason tells Natalie, "I built this two years ago. This was a top secret room that I built for the university. I have a trust fund, and put in a 10 million dollar grant for the university to build a top secret room here that only elite members can use. The elevator goes up to the university library. You know, I found this room a couple of years ago when I saw an elevator key lying around the elevator door. It was opened. Nobody had used that elevator in years. This area was built in the 1950s as like a fallout shelter or something. When I went inside it was just an abandoned space, so I went to the university and put the grant in, and built it as a top secret room. You know, when I helped Nathan pass his detective exam, I always thought he would hire me as a private investigator, and so I had this place to work as a police consultant from."

Luke tells them, "Yeah, Jason showed me this place after it was finished a couple years ago. Even after Nathan passed his detective exam, we thought about using this as our own detective agency. We had just been using it as a private lounge with a couple of friends, but then we gave up on it."

Natalie tells them, "Man, this is a great setup here. I can't believe you were planning to use this as a detective agency."

Nathan tells them, "If I had known about this place, I definitely would have helped you out. What were you going to call this place anyways?"

Jason tells Nathan, "Well Nate I was going to call this place NOCOMO Detective Agency. That's right. Any problem you have, anything you've lost, or anything you've found. If anybody was cheating you, or something was stolen, we'd help you retrieve it. That's our motto."

Nathan told Jason, "Well, Jace, you told me yourself that with your disease you couldn't fire a gun, or even use one."

Jason told Nathan, "You're right I couldn't, until now. I started practicing." Jason, Nathan, Natalie, and Luke head to the firing range. Jason presses a red button, "You know I could just use some targets, but I have to be smart. And you know I don't have a good judgment so I have to be really smart. So watch this."

Jason sees the headphones and shooting glasses, and puts them on, right after he takes off his eyeglasses. Jason sees the Beretta 92F gun on the table, and sees the cardboard cutout of a robber holding a hostage. Jason fires his gun, hitting the robber in the head. Another robber cutout comes from a second story window, and he fires two bullets, hitting him. An innocent bystander cutout comes from behind a car, but he doesn't fire. Another car comes from the left of the cityscape, and three bullets leave Jason's gun, hitting the robber that comes out of the car.

Nathan tells Jason, "Wow, that's really good, you have excellent judgment."

Jason tells them, "Yeah, but this is easy. Just cardboard cutouts. But, I have to be fast and smart. So I built something else on this computer. Because I have to be smart and quick if this was a life and death situation."

Jason, Nathan, Luke, and Natalie head to the computer. Jason turns on the computer screen. Right behind the computer is a flat screen TV with a video game stand on it. Jason starts the game. He sees the video game gun handle on the floor. He grabs it, and the game starts. Three robbers on the harbor come out to attack Jason, and he fires killing them. An innocent bystander comes out, but Jason doesn't shoot.

Another robber comes out holding a hostage, and Jason hits the robber in the head, and the hostage gets away. After he fires eight bullets, it shows his high score. The game shows that he's number one. Jason tells Nathan, "Well, Nate, got any questions?"

Nathan tells Jason, "I'm kind of glad I have you on my team. Why didn't you tell me about this place? I would have loved to come down here."

Jason tells Nathan, "Like I said, you never asked. And we lost touch three years ago, remember?"

Nathan tells Jason, "Sorry, my mistake."

Natalie looks for her file, but she had left it upstairs in NOCOMO. Jason tells Natalie, "You looking for this?" Jason takes out the file from the back of his pants, and shows it to Natalie. He tells Natalie, "I forgot to tell you, I have quick hands. Not for stealing, or shoplifting, I can just move things really fast."

Natalie tells Jason, "Wow, I'm really impressed."

Jason tells them, "Okay, let's get started. By the way, if you guys want something to drink, I have some beer and soda in here. I also have some candy bars in the fridge. I always keep cool."

Natalie tells Jason, "Well we're on duty, but since we're really busy, we'll just settle for a soda."

Nathan tells Jason, "Besides, the captain would chew us out if he catches us drinking on the job."

Jason tells them, "Okay, fair enough. I've got some Pepsi, Diet Pepsi, Dr. Pepper, and Diet Dr. Pepper. Which would you guys like to have?"

Nathan tells Jason, "Diet Pepsi."

Natalie and Luke tell him, "The same."

Jason tells them, "Okay."

After a couple of minutes, they're drinking their sodas and sitting down at the meeting table looking at the file. Nathan tells them, "What about the bank president? Do you think he'd be involved in this?"

Jason tells Nathan, "Well, he does have a lot of access to get in and out of the bank in a minute. But he'd be, like, the easiest person to suspect. You need someone lower down, someone they would never look at."

Luke tells them, "Yeah, like Clark Kent being Superman. You know the glasses, him being a mild mannered reporter. Him being a nerd. No one would suspect him in a million years."

Nathan tells them, "Or Bruce Wayne being Batman. No one would suspect him of being Batman. Besides they always suspected that Batman was a DA or a fed, since he knew the ins and outs of crime areas."

Jason tells them, "Yup, all of that's true. So like I said, we're looking for like a Security Guard or a Janitor. Do you have a list of any of janitors or security guards who worked at that bank?"

Nathan tells them, "Yeah, it's in the file right there."

Jason looks at the file, and observes it. Jason tells them, "Some of these guys are easy marks to pass as bank robbers, some of these guys even have rap sheets. This looks like it could be an open and shut case. I think there's one person that nobody ever looks at."

Luke tells Jason, "What's that Jace?"

Jason tells them, "Hang on a second." Jason sees his laptop on the table, and turns it on. He types out the list of everybody he might suspect at the bank. Then Jason tells them, "It has to be an accountant, or a bank clerk. But I would go with a bank clerk, because they're the ones no one will suspect. They make good money, but they're not rich or anything. Not unless they're at the executive level. Here's a list of the bank clerks in the file."

Nathan tells them, "You think any of them are involved with the bank robbery."

Jason tells them, "Well, I think the robbers might have been disguised as one. You forget these guys are mercenaries, masters of disguise. How do you think they get in and out of places?"

Natalie tells them, "We have got to find these guys, they could be anywhere. Besides, we've been after them for a year."

Luke is looking over the files, and tells them, "You might be right about one thing Jace. That these bank clerks are the last people that anyone would look at. Most people would look at the bank presidents or the bank reps, but these guys are the last guys that anyone would look at."

Jason tells Luke, "Did you find anyone in that list yet?"

Luke is looking over the file for a minute, and sees someone, and tells them, "You know it's kind of weird but I think I might have found somebody. His name is Roderick Carter, I saw his bio pic, and it looks like its fake. None of the bank clerks have military records, but this Roderick Carter looks kind of familiar to me."

Nathan tells Luke, "Why is he familiar to you?"

"You know I saw all these pictures of these guys. They look like average Joe types, just like average bank clerks. And we're not looking at their figures, just their faces, their eyes. And there is one thing I figured out. That there is a tattoo of a small dragon on his left hand. But since there are no military records in bank files, I'm going to have do something a little extreme. But, I've got to warn you, what I'm about to do isn't exactly legal, so whatever happens we never saw anything."

Jason tells them, "Guys, whatever Luke is doing, it's don't ask, don't tell, okay?"

Nathan and Natalie tell them, "Okay."

Luke is looking up a file in a military database, it takes him a few minutes to get in, but when he clicks enter, Roderick's file is there. Luke tells them, "I think I found his file, but I remind you guys, what

I hacked into was illegal, and we could get in serious trouble for this. We didn't see anything, we don't know anything."

Natalie tells Luke, "How did you get into that system anyways?"

Luke tells Natalie, "Hey, I'm pretty smart, and I have excellent hacking skills." Natalie and Nathan look at Luke for a minute, and Luke tells them, "My Uncle Steve is a major in the army, he works at Fort Dexter. He runs all the high tech stuff in the military, he also has friends in the DOJ and the FBI, he can get me anything I need."

Natalie tells him, "Okay."

Nathan tells them, "Just tell us what you found out. The less we know, the better."

Luke tells them, "Okay, his real name is Jackson Lucas, he was a major in the green berets, and he traveled around Afghanistan and Iraq. There were a lot of rumors that he was working with Al-Qaeda. But the biggest rumor was that he was in cahoots with this Jordanian war lord, named General Ashuk Kabob. He was a freedom fighter from Jordan, who hated the royalty. He was part of a movement to overthrow the royal family. But Lucas was never officially connected to Ashuk, just suspected of selling weapons. Also, people call the guy General Ashuk, because he hates his last name so much that he insists on it."

Jason tells them, "You know, I read somewhere in the news that there were reports that some Jordanian war lord had been seen in Kansas City, and that some guys from the military are selling weapons for 20 million dollars."

Nathan says, "We know that money was laundered, so it's dirty money. We know those bills are marked, so we know he had to use it to launder it, that's why it was inside that bank."

Jason tells them, "You know I read somewhere in the Wall Street Journal that a defense company just got an army contract good for over

20 million dollars, but when they signed the contract they never saw the money, it was just deposited in a bank."

Nathan tells him, "Let me guess, the Kansas City National Bank, that's the one right?"

Luke tells them, "Yes, that's the one."

Natalie tells them, "What was the name of that defense company that just got the 20 million dollar deal?"

Jason tells Natalie, "It was Lucas Weapons."

Luke tells them, "And guess what? Our pal Jackson Lucas' uncle owns the company. It's a family company, his uncle and his father built it, and Jackson is the VP. You know, it's kind of weird, what if his uncle is the one involved in this? Besides Jackson has a military background, and I'm sure he did jobs for the CIA or NSA, because I read somewhere that he did some missions for the NSA once."

Natalie tells them, "Well the NSA can find anything in three seconds, they have high-tech gear all around the world. You think his uncle could be the mastermind behind all this?"

Luke tells Natalie, "I think so. His uncle's name is Thomas Lucas, you know he's the guy who owns the company. Besides, nobody is ever going to look at him, or suspect that he is the one selling weapons to Ashuk."

Nathan tells them, "What if he was the mastermind planning the robbery? Besides, that 20 million dollars was stolen. He knows those bills are marked, so he needs that money laundered so he can steal that dirty money from his safe and use his money laundering equipment to clean it up, and give the 20 million dollars to pay for new weapons from General Ashuk. That's what he's doing. It's simple, he owes Ashuk 20 million dollars, and he's going to trade in the weapons and the 20 million dollars for an even bigger paycheck. That's what this is about."

Jason tells them, "It's simple, Lucas owes Ashuk money, and he knew getting that weapons deal could pay him off and get him the weapons, and he can also trade him for more money, all Lucas needs is to give him the 20 million dollars and new weapons and he'll get a bigger trade, which means bigger money, and the bigger money is his reward."

Luke tells them, "If he's going to store all that laundered money and the weapons, he needs someplace big. You know, he did make all the weapons he promised the army, but I think he's going to stiff the army and give them to Ashuk."

Nathan tells them, "And Ashuk can use the weapons to overthrow the Jordanian government, while the military gets stiffed on the 20 million dollars, because you know there's a clause in their contract that says that they're not responsible if the weapons are unaccounted for or not on time. They can't sue if they don't get them. I think Lucas' uncle must've put that in there."

Jason tells them, "If Ashuk made a deal with Lucas, I don't think his uncle was there because he was at a military conference in DC speaking to General Colin Author. He's the guy that's paying him 20 million dollars. I don't think Lucas' uncle has anything to do with it. I don't think he is even aware of it. I think Lucas is the one who stole the 20 million dollars and the weapons. If anything happens General Author is going to hold Lucas' uncle responsible, because it's his name on the contracts. He's the scapegoat. I think you're grasping at straws, Nathan."

Nathan tells him, "My mistake."

Luke looks at the computer, "Well, I know General Author is in town, he's in Fort Dexter, you know overseeing the contract. He's waiting for the weapons delivery that should be shipped to him in a week. And good news too, even Lucas is in town this week."

Natalie tells them, "Why don't we just go over and arrest him. We can interrogate him to find out where the weapons and the money are."

Jason tells them, "It's a bad idea to go over to Lucas' company and arrest him, he'll just get his high-priced attorney to bail him out and get the case dropped, you forget he has like a million workers. Plus, I doubt you'll get a search warrant to find the weapons, the place is huge, and Lucas has guys on the inside who could just move them. The best bet is to figure out where he's going to sell the weapons and the laundered money to General Ashuk."

Luke tells them, "What are we going to do?"

Jason tells them, "Luke I want you to look up more information about Ashuk and Lucas, find out some locations for where they might have the deal. Natalie, you work with him. Nathan, you and I can go pay a visit to Lucas, we can start talking to him about what he knows about those weapons, but we won't arrest him or interrogate him, because than he won't talk to us."

Nathan tells them, "We're going to go in disguise. Besides, if Lucas can go in disguise and order his posse to kill themselves to steal the 20 million dollars of laundered money, he's also going to suspect that we're cops and never talk to us. Even without interrogation, his lawyers will bury us in mountains of paperwork and we'll never get to him. Going in disguise is an awesome idea, Jason, how are we going to do this?"

Jason tells him, "Simple, we're going to go home and change. He'd never talk to us looking like this, so we're going to go dress up like business men, that's the only way he'll talk to us."

Nathan tells them, "Luke, Natalie, call Lucas' uncle, and tell him to meet us here, because we want to tell them what's going on."

Luke and Natalie tells him, "Okay."

Natalie also tells Jason and Luke, "Hey, don't you guys need to get back to work? Won't your boss be mad?"

Jason tells Natalie, "Don't worry Nicki's our friend, and besides this place is an excellent working environment. Besides, my mom put a lot of money in this place, so I can come and go anytime I please, but I am a very loyal guy, so I'll tell Nicki that Luke and I are going to need a couple weeks off to work with you guys. We've never cashed in any vacation time before, so now is a good time to use it, besides she owes us."

Natalie tells them, "Okay."

Jason tells them, "I'll go talk to Nicki before we leave, so we better get back upstairs. I'll tell them we're working on a police matter. Nate, I may need your help so that I can convince her to give me the two weeks off anyway."

Nathan tells them, "Hey I thought you said she owes ya?"

Jason tells Nathan, "She does, but she won't believe me. She can take a look right at me and tell I'm lying. So I need your help to prove that I'm not lying."

Nathan tells Jason, "Okay, I'll do that talking."

Jason tells him, "Okay, let's get to work." All four of them do their fist bumps.

Back in Nicki's office, Nathan is finished talking to her about getting Jason and Luke two weeks off, and Nicki tells Nathan and Jason, "Okay, well just give me a call if you guys need anything, I'll be right by."

Jason tells her, "Thanks for giving me the two weeks off, it really means a lot to us, besides I really want to help Nathan out on this case, and I really owe it to him."

Nicki tells Jason, "Relax, Jason, it's only going to take you one or two days to solve this case, you are a great detective. If anyone could solve it, it would be you."

Jason tells Nicki, "Yeah, thanks Nicki, I owe ya. Alright, we have to get going. Bye Nicki!"

Nathan tells Nicki bye too, and Nicki tells them, "See you guys, and good luck." Both of them say thanks. Jason and Nathan exit the office, and they close the door.

Outside NOCOMO, Jason is on the phone with Natalie, "Hey Natalie, alright remind Luke to call Mr. Lucas to meet with you guys, because we have to tell them what his nephew is up too, because trust me, this guy is bad news."

Natalie's voiceover tells Jason, "Okay, good luck."

Jason hangs up his phone, and Nathan tells him, "So which car should we take, your car or mine, since you don't drive?"

Jason tells Nathan, "We'll take mine, because my driver is showing up, and plus we can go to my house, because your room is still unoccupied, so all your clothes are in there. That's where you used to crash."

Nathan tells Jason, "Okay. I keep forgetting about that."

Back in Jason's house, inside Jason's room, Jason is undressed, wearing his boxer shorts, and he puts on his suit pants, and dresses in a suit, and looks in the mirror. Nathan comes in and puts on his suit too. Nathan tells Jason, "Do you think Lucas will buy it?'

Jason tells him, "I hope so, don't worry I got Tom to help us out. He'll introduce us, that way he can tell them we belong to a top finance company when we're inside."

Nathan tells Jason, "Sometimes, I think about how we first met. How did I end up in Special Ed class anyway?"

Jason tells him, "You were dyslexic, you always had trouble remembering things and words all the time. We met when we were nine, and you're parents died in that car crash when you were 15 and you came to live with us. We both wanted to get into the force, but I couldn't but you could because deep down you weren't mentally incompetent. Besides, my mom helped get you in, and I helped you study for the detective test. I always wanted to join you, and that's why I tried to do the P.I. work. You know, it's a good thing my mom was friends with the mayor. If it wasn't for my mom you never would have gotten in."

Nathan tells Jason, "Yeah, I really do owe her a lot. Is she here today?"

Jason tells Nathan, "No, I think she's at work, besides I haven't told her that I'm working with you yet. I think she'd get kinda worried."

Nathan tells Jason, "Yeah, I guess I can see why she's always been worried about you. She was worried about me when I joined the force. But you're going to be okay."

Jason tells Nathan, "Yeah, I'm sure Nate." After they finish dressing up, they head to the front door, and they see Mary waiting for them outside. Jason tells his mom, "Hey Mom, what are you doing home?"

Mary tells Jason, "Well, it's 2 o'clock, it's my lunch hour, and I thought I'd eat at home today."

Jason tells his mom, "Okay."

Before Jason leaves, Mary tells him, "So, what are you doing home at this hour, aren't you supposed to be at work?"

Jason tells his mom, "Actually, Nicki gave me the day off. 'Cause you know, I've been working really hard and she thinks I need some time off, so that's that."

Mary looks a little bit suspicious, but she doesn't ask questions, and tells Jason, "Okay."

Jason tells his mom, "Hey, Mom, I'm going to be spending the day with Nathan. He has the day off from work too, so we're going to cruise around for a bit."

Mary tells Nathan, even though she didn't notice he was here until now, "Hey, Nate. I didn't see you there. I've been so busy I haven't had time to see you."

"That's okay, Mary," said Nathan.

Mary tells Nathan, "So, how's the job? You know I really worry about you. You ever think about getting a desk job?"

Nathan laughs a little, and tells Mary, "Mary, I'm going to be fine. Besides, I'm a cop, I love being in the field, I love the action. I'm not exactly a desk guy."

Mary tells Nathan, "Okay, I'm just worried about you. Would you like to come to dinner tonight? We're having spaghetti with meatballs."

Nathan tells Mary, "Well, I'd love to, but I'm going to be really busy the whole week on a big case, so I won't have any time."

Jason tells his mom, "Actually, I have to tell you, I got a couple weeks off from work. I earned it, so I'm going to spend some time in the library. It's a community service project that I'm working on. I promised Joe I'd help him out."

Mary tells him, "Okay. Just be careful out there."

Jason and Nathan exit the house, and Mary looks at them. Mary kind of knew that they were lying, and she tells herself, "You know, I never ask questions. I just let them make their own choices. I just hope Jason stays alive out there, I do worry about the guy."

Outside of Lucas Weapons, Jason's black SUV parks in the lot. Tom, Jason's security guard, exits the car, and opens the door for Jason and Nathan in the backseat. Tom is wearing a suit with Ray Ban sunglasses. Nathan and Jason are wearing suits and sunglasses too. Jason is carrying a briefcase. Jason tells Tom, "Hey, thanks for doing this Tom. I know my mom worries about me a lot, but thanks for helping me out."

Tom tells Jason, "Hey, no problem. I always love looking out for you guys. Besides, it's the most exciting thing I'll get to do today. You've been living a pretty mundane life, this is the most exciting thing I've gotten to do since I left the force."

Nathan tells Tom, "Well, you've got me to thank for that. Besides, I'm the one that pulled the strings with his mom to let you bodyguard Jason."

Tom tells Nathan, "Well, you don't have to rub it in. Besides, I was partners with you before Natalie came in."

Nathan tells them, "Okay, guys, let's get started."

Jason tells Tom, "Okay, Tom, I need you to introduce us. Tell the secretary that we're here, and who we are, and see if you can get us in. Besides, you were a master interrogator."

Tom tells Jason, "Of course I was. How else would you get any suspect to admit the robberies they committed?"

Inside the lobby of Lucas Weapons, Tom enters and sees the secretary and goes over to talk to her. The secretary tells Tom, "Hi, can I help you?"

Tom tells the secretary, "Hi, my name is Thomas Mason. I represent Mr. Nathan Devers, he's from Devers Investments. He's planning on investing a lot of stock in Lucas Weapons, because he heard that they closed a great deal with the US Army for 20 million dollars, and they want to invest in that too."

The secretary tells Tom, "I'm sorry, do you guys have an appointment? Mr. Lucas doesn't see anybody without an appointment."

Tom tells the secretary, "Well, no, we don't have an appointment. Is he in today? Because we're planning on investing a lot of money in stock for this. I guess we could take our 300 million somewhere else, but if this project is successful, not only is your stock going to go through the roof, it will make Mr. Devers a lot richer."

The secretary tells Tom, "Okay, I'll call Mr. Lucas, and see if I can get you in, and tell him the news."

The secretary picks up the phone, and makes a call to Lucas, "Hello, Mr. Lucas?"

Jason and Nathan are outside the lobby, and Nathan tells Jason, "You think they bought it?"

Jason tells Nathan, "I hope so, because we need to get in that building. It's a good thing Tom helped us out, besides my mom hired him a year ago with your recommendation. And he did teach me how to be a great detective, and how to fight, and how to use a gun to defend myself. Even though I hate guns, and I never carry one, only Tom can carry one. If I ever use one it will be a life and death situation, I think I might need to use one pretty soon."

Nathan tells Jason, "Well, it's a good thing you called Tom a few minutes ago to help us out."

Jason tells Nathan, "Yeah, Tom got shot in the line of fire, on that huge robbery bust you guys had. They shot him in the leg, and it took him a few weeks to walk, but your boss couldn't put him back in the field, and he didn't want to take desk duty, he wanted to do something else with his life. It's a good thing my mom gave him the job. Besides, he'd be dying to work on a case with us. It's like he's back in the field again."

Tom looks at the secretary, and the secretary finishes talking on the phone to Lucas, "Thank you, Mr. Lucas. Bye." The secretary hangs up the phone, and tells Tom, "Well, I talked to Mr. Lucas, and he'd be happy to see you right now. He wanted me to ask if you guys were serious about investing 300 million dollars in his company."

Tom tells the secretary, "Yeah, we're really serious."

The secretary tells Tom, "His office is on the 23rd floor. When you reach that floor, make a right, and you'll find his office there."

Tom tells the secretary, "Okay, thank you. I appreciate this." Tom turns around a minute, and nods his head.

Nathan and Jason look at Tom, and Jason tells Nathan, "Well, alright. We're in. Let's go." Jason, Nathan, and Tom head to the elevator, and they summon the elevator, and the doors slide open. They all enter, and head to the 23rd floor. When the doors slide open again, Tom, Jason, and Nathan exit into the lobby, and head to Lucas' office on the right. Jason tells them, "Okay, Tom you wait outside, me and Nathan will do the talking. We're going to see what we can find out."

Tom tells them, "I hope you guys will be okay, because if he tries to pull a gun on you, I think your mother will have my head."

Jason tells Tom, "Relax, we've got nothing to worry about. Besides, I doubt he's going to pull a gun on us anytime soon. Right now we're just going to ask him questions, and we're going to keep it low-key. Besides, if anything does happens, I have a beeper on my phone. If anything happens, I'll turn it on and you can come inside and save our asses."

Tom tells Jason, "Sure thing Jace. Good luck."

Inside Lucas' office, he's working at his desk until he hears the intercom button come on. Lucas presses the button and asks who it is, telling the person on the intercom, "Hello?"

The secretary comes over the intercom telling Lucas, "Mr. Lucas, Mr. Devers and associates are here to see you."

Lucas tells his secretary, "Okay, send them in Kathy." Lucas turns off the intercom, and the door opens. Jason and Nathan enter the room, as Lucas gets up from his chair. Jason is carrying his briefcase, and he and Nathan go over to greet Lucas.

Nathan tells Lucas, "Hello Mr. Lucas. I'm Mr. Devers, and this is my associate Mr. Boswell." Nathan shakes Lucas' hand for a minute, and Nathan looks a little skeptical, because the guy who he's been after for a year is right there in front of him.

Lucas tells Nathan, "Well it's a pleasure to meet you Mr. Devers." After he shakes Nathan's hand, he shakes Jason's hand, "And it's a pleasure to meet you Mr. Boswell."

"It's a pleasure to meet you Mr. Lucas," Jason says.

After they shake, Mr. Lucas says, "So, gentlemen, can I get you anything? Coffee, wine? Anything?"

Jason sarcastically tells him, "Hey, how about a hooker? Can you call one up?" All three of them start laughing for a minute, and Jason tells Lucas, "Sorry about that Mr. Lucas. It was a bad joke."

Lucas tells Jason, "Well it was funny. Cute, but funny."

Jason tells Lucas, "No we're good."

Lucas tells them, "Okay gentlemen, why don't you have a seat."

Jason tells Lucas, "Well, Mr. Lucas, I've been pitching the idea to Mr. Devers about investing 300 million dollars in your stock. He's been hesitant, because investing in the stock market is risky, and we know how bad it is in the financial market right now. But, I convinced him to take this risk. Besides, if we invest 300 million dollars in your account, your stock is going to go through the roof, because every time somebody makes weapons for our military defense, they're going to make us rich. But you sir, are the best, and you always hit a home run, and I hope you hit a home run for us too when you invest with us. And besides like I said, we're not buying stock, we're buying the person. Isn't that what our sales motto is?"

Lucas tells Jason, "Of course, I know the sales motto. We're not buying the product, we're buying you."

Jason tells them, "We have something to show you. I know we're taking a big risk doing this, but if you look at our financial portfolio, I know you'll be our biggest investment ever." Jason sees his briefcase on the floor where he put it down after he took a seat. Jason grabs his briefcase, and takes out the financial portfolio from his briefcase, and hands it to Lucas. Lucas grabs the portfolio, and takes a look at it. Jason tells Lucas, "Trust me, sir. We are a number one investment company. Besides, when we invest, we invest in the best, and that's what you are."

Lucas tells Jason, "Well, I don't have to read the rest of your financial portfolio, because I'm happy that you guys want to invest in us. That's one of the reasons I called you guys over, is to invest in me."

Jason tells Lucas, "Yeah, I know you don't take appointments, that's what your secretary said to my associate, but you took a chance to see us, and we are a big investment. Well, anyway, we'll send in your check tomorrow morning. We don't actually do express mail anymore, I'll let my associate Thomas Mason give you the check in person."

Lucas tells them, "Well, I'm happy that you guys are choosing to invest in my company."

Jason tells Lucas, "You know before we go and send you that check tomorrow. You ever read the news? You know, about a bank heist that happened a few days ago? It was at the Kansas City National Bank."

Nathan tells Lucas, "Yeah, I heard they stole about 20 million dollars. You know the lead robbers who were about to rob that bank? They just told people to keep their hands up. They didn't take any of their money, they just held them hostage. And then they killed themselves. They had all these grenades in their pockets, and they just blew themselves up. From the look of those guys, they were mercenaries."

Jason tells Lucas, "Why would these guys blow themselves up? They had the guns, they could have just stolen the money and gotten away. They didn't have to do that. It's like they were hired as a distraction. They were independents, it's like they were hired to just hold up the bank and distract the police. It makes you wonder if they figured out that the police were right there in front of them. But they didn't worry, because they knew they were setting them up. Because they were hiding the real prize."

Nathan tells Lucas, "Yeah, something like nearly 20 million dollars in a safe that was really worth stealing."

Lucas tells them, "You don't say? Man, I can't hardly believe that. That some nutbag bank robbers had to do a suicide mission and not steal any money. And they just blow themselves up right in front of everyone, and not take the 20 million dollars. But you told me yourself it was a setup."

Jason tells Lucas, "Of course it was a setup, because those mercenaries were a distraction so that the real robbers could steal the real money from the back. And they got in and out of that safe within a few seconds without being spotted. No way could they do that, not unless they have a blackhat hacker working for them. And some of those hackers were ex-military and into high-tech in the military."

Nathan tells Lucas, "You know what was really weird? That 20 million dollars was dirty money, because those bills were all marked. When you steal money from a bank, any cop or fed could track down those bills in a minute. But if you are a robber, and you have marked bills, you just use a big machine to launder it and make it unmarked. But for what? What would you need a clean 20 million dollars for?"

Lucas is a little suspicious about these guys, and tells them, "Beats me."

And Jason tells Lucas, "You know I heard once that you were actually ex-military too. Man, I can't imagine what it would be like if you associated with those guys. You're uncle runs this company, he and your father built this company. Isn't it kind of weird that there were rumors that your dad was selling weapons to the Middle East, and that he passed it on to his kids. You know it's funny, because a guy who had a deal to make some weapons for 20 million dollars of clean money, and he thinks he could get away with it without his uncle finding out. And he thinks he could sell it to some Jordanian war lord like, I don't know, General Ashuk, a crazy dictator who is trying to overthrow the Jordanian royal family."

Nathan tells Lucas, "Yeah, he thought those weapons would bail him out. But the army will be really pissed off that they didn't get those weapons they paid for, and they'll be out 20 million dollars. But I bet they won't press charges, or have anyone court marshalled, because they aren't exactly military, even though they build guns for the military."

Jason tells him, "Yeah, but it wouldn't be the guy who built those weapons and stole them. And the 20 million dollars. Because if the military presses charges, his uncle will go to jail instead of him, because, it's simple, his uncle's signatures were on the papers, and so he would go to jail, and he would be able to take over the company. I'm sure that was the plan all along. But hey, those were just rumors, I'm sure they had nothing to do with this company or with you."

Nathan tells him, "Yeah, I'm sure it doesn't."

Lucas laughs for a minute, "Man, I can't believe some other weapons company has a kid trying to take over his uncle's company, overthrow him, and sell stuff to some Middle East warlord, so that he could make a fortune off it. Well like you said, it was just a rumor."

Jason tells Lucas, "Well, we have to get going, but it was great meeting you, and don't worry, I'll make sure Tom delivers your check tomorrow morning."

Lucas tells them, "Hey, sure, no problem." All three of them get up from their chairs, and Nathan and Jason shake Lucas' hand, "Goodbye gentlemen, and good luck. And don't worry, you're going to make a fortune once you invest with us."

Nathan tells Lucas, "Sure, no problem." Jason grabs his briefcase from the floor and they exit the office.

Lucas sits down in his chair for a minute, and he doesn't buy all that stuff that they said. Lucas grabs his phone, and makes a call to his secretary, "Hey Kathy? Transfer me to security. Tell them I need a DVD of the security footage of my office for the last few minutes."

Outside Lucas' office, Jason and Nathan see Tom sitting down in a chair. Tom gets up from the chair and goes over to talk to them, "Hey, you guys okay? How did it go?"

Jason tells Tom, "Well, I think he bought it for now, but the look on his face, I think he's suspicious. So like I said, I need you to watch my back in case he sends his guys after us. Not just mine but Nathan's too, because we need both of us alive."

Tom tells them, "Sure. Hey don't worry, I want to make sure both of you guys are staying in great shape. Besides, Nate, you used to be my partner, and I always had your back, and I still do."

Nathan tells Tom, "Thank you buddy."

Outside of Lucas Weapons, Tom, Jason, and Nathan head to their car. Nathan tells Jason, "You know every time I think of Lucas and Luke, it's kind of weird to confuse their names. I never noticed it before, but I can't believe both of them have the same names."

Jason tells them, "Well, maybe we should just call Lucas Jackson that way we don't have to confuse them."

Tom tells Jason, "I kind of agree with him Nate. That way we won't confuse their names all the time."

Nathan tells them, "I think you've got a point on that one. Anyway, we still have to find Jackson's operation. It could be anywhere right now. Besides, we know he stole the 20 million dollars out of that bank to launder it, and give it to General Ashuk, and especially those weapons that they finished designing for the military, that they're giving to Ashuk to start a plot to destroy the Jordanian royal family."

Jason tells them, "Well, Jackson does have the 20 million dollars laundered, but he still needs those weapons. I think they're inside a hidden safe, but we need to know what those weapons were, what they were designing, but that information is top secret, it's not in the military database. It's not even in the company's database. We need the password to get in. We need the password to open the safe and see the weapons that they were designing. But I think Jackson is the only one who can open it."

Nathan tells them, "What if the weapons are not exactly in Kansas City, what if they're somewhere else? Besides, he wouldn't just build the weapons and store them in a safe in Kansas City, it has to be somewhere out of town that the military is never going to use."

Jason tells them, "I think you've got a point, Nate. I think it's in a military hangar. And I think that's where the deal is going to be, but there's a million hangars around here, and we don't know which one it is. I think it's going to take one or two days until Jackson gets the password to open up the safe, because the safe is electronic, and so only a password can open it."

Tom tells them, "I think Jackson knows where he's going to make the deal at, he only needs the password. I don't think it will take him one or two days though, it's his father's company, so he and his uncle were the only ones who knew the password. Maybe he's already figured it out. He just needs to wait until the deal starts to get Ashuk."

Jason tells Tom, "I think you're right."

Nathan tells them, "Well, we've got to find out where his operation is and where the deal's at. We also have to find out if Jackson is working for anybody, because he seems like the middleman. He may also be the second-in-command, but I think he's the one who robbed that 20 million dollars from that bank."

Tom tells them, "Hey Nathan, do you have any sources that could help you find Jackson's operation, or his deal, or his boss? Because if we could find Jackson's deal, we could pin Jackson, Ashuk, the weapons, and the money, and it'll be more than enough to bust them."

Nathan tells them, "Sorry, guys, my sources are practically dried up. I don't even know where to look, or who I could get to help me."

Jason tells them, "Hey, you forgot Luke's uncle. He's the one who gave Luke the access to the military files and the DOJ computers. He could find any guy in 3 seconds, and get any information you want to know. Besides, he is a major in the army."

Nathan tells them, "Hey, isn't he with Luke already, in the library? I thought he was speaking to him about what was going on."

Jason tells them, "I'll call Luke and see if his uncle is with him." Jason takes out a cell phone from his right pants pocket, and sets his briefcase down. They all stop for Jason to make the call. Jason starts dialing, and tells Luke, "Hello? Hey Luke! Hey listen, I just want to ask, is your uncle with you today? Okay, thanks a lot. Because we need to see him. I think he can help us out. Alright bye." Jason hangs up his phone and tells them, "Luke's uncle is not with him, and he's not in his office right now, but he tells me he knows where he is because he always goes to this place to unwind every day when he's not working at Fort Dexter. But the good news is, he got ahold of Jackson's uncle Thomas, and he's over there talking to him right now."

Tom tells them, "Man, it's kind of weird, that he and I have the same names. Man, talk about weird."

Nathan sarcastically tells Tom, "At least now we can call him Thomas, and we can call you Tom, or idiot, or balloon head, and that way we won't confuse anybody."

Tom tells Nathan, "Funny Nate. Cute, but funny. How about I call you drumstick head, because I think that'll fit your personality in no time."

Nathan laughs a little, and tells Tom, "Aha, very funny."

Jason tells them, "Okay guys, enough. You guys can rip each other later. Let's go talk to Luke's Uncle Steve." All of them get inside of the car, where Nathan is driving.

Inside the officer's club, Luke's Uncle Steve is drinking beer at the bar, where all the other officers are. Jason, Nathan, and Tom are inside the officer's club, and see Steve drinking at the bar, and Nathan tells Jason, "Hey, how did we get in here anyway? I thought this place was restricted, and none of us have a pass. Not even my police badge could get me in here."

Jason tells Nathan, "I have an army pass here, me and Luke hang out with Steve all the time here, just to shoot the breeze. We visit him sometimes, when he's not working."

Tom tells them, "Well, let's go talk to him, maybe he can help us out."

Jason tells them, "Let me do that. I'll go talk to him. You guys sit down, and get some beers, it's on me." Jason takes out his wallet, and hands each of them 50 dollars. Both of them take it, and buy a beer.

Nathan and Tom tell him, "Thanks man." Nathan and Tom see some empty seats, and sit down. They see a waitress, and Nathan tells her, "Hey!"

The waitress is very attractive and goes over to see Nathan, and the waitress tells Nathan, "Hi, I'm Helena, and I'll be your server today. Can I get you guys anything?"

Nathan sarcastically tells her, "Yeah, we'd like to have two grenades and five machine guns, and also your phone number."

Helena laughs a little, "Funny, cute but funny."

Nathan tells Helena, "Hey I'm really sorry about that, I was just playing around. I don't get out that much. I'm not good at being funny."

Helena tells him, "No, you're not."

Nathan tells Helena, "We'll take two Miller Lights in mugs please. And I'll have mine in a dirty glass."

Helena tells Nathan, "You've really gotta lay of the jokes once in a while, Nathan."

Nathan tells Helena, "Hey, how did you know my name."

Helena says, "Um, around. Besides, I know you're friend Jason. He told me a lot about you."

Nathan tells Helena, "Wow, really? Um, how do you know Jason?"

Helena tells Nathan, "Cause Luke is my cousin, and the guy talking to Jason is my dad."

Nathan tells Helena, "Uhh sorry, my mistake. Pray you don't sick your father on me. I'm really terrible about the jokes, and I didn't know he was your father. But besides, I am a cop, and I'm not scared of him or anything, he may be an army guy, but I'm a cop, even when I don't carry a badge."

Helena laughs a little, "You know, you really are cute. I'll get your beers."

Helena leaves, and Tom slaps Nathan's arm, "Real smooth, Romeo."

Nathan tells Tom, "Actually, it's 007, because I am like James Bond, except I always strike out."

Tom tells Nathan, "Yeah, even when we worked as partners, you always kept striking out with girls like Helena."

Back at the bar, Jason goes over to talk to Steve. Jason taps him on the shoulder, and Steve turns around, "Hey Steve."

Steve tells Jason, "Hey Jace. Hey how's it going buddy?" Steve hugs Jason for a minute when he gets up from his barstool. They stop hugging, and Steve tells Jason, "Hey, I'm sorry I didn't have any time to see Luke right now. I was really busy with work, and right now I think he's talking to my buyer. Luke already filled me in when he called me. So, what's the favor?"

Jason tells Steve, "Here, let me have a seat for a minute." Jason sits down at the barstool with Steve, and tells the bartender, "I'll take a Miller Light." The bartender gives Jason a Miller Light beer bottle that's opened, and Steve sits back down. Jason takes a drink of the beer and tells him this favor, "Listen, I need a favor. I think the guy who worked with Jackson? I think he might be the guy involved with stealing all the money. If we find him, we might be able to pin Jackson. And Jackson has a hangar that the military is using, and I think that's where he's hiding the weapons that his uncle designed. He already has 20 million dollars that was laundered when he stole it. And we already know he's going to sell those weapons to a Jordanian warlord named Ashuk Kabob. So we need to find out where that military hangar is, because that's where he's going to store those weapons at. I thought you, or Jackson's uncle might know where it is, or could find out where he's storing the weapons."

Steve tells Jason, "Look, I'd love to help you out man, but I'm not in charge of the manufacturing. Only General Colin Author knows, since he's the one who's in charge of it. Besides, he's the one who gave out one of our hangars that they're using to store the weapons. But he's pretty forgetful, so the only ones who would know where that is are Jackson or his uncle. Besides, only Jackson or his uncle have the combinations to open that electronic safe where the weapons are stored."

Jason tells Steve, "So there's nothing you can do about it? Since you can't find the hangar where they're storing the weapons. Because if we could find that hangar, we'd know where Jackson and Ashuk were at, and he's gonna use that money to fund his war against the Jordanian royal family, and also the weapons that he's going to use, in exchange for a lot of money. I know they made a deal before, and he made 50 million dollars from the last deal, now he's going to get that same amount when they're done."

Steve tells Jason, "On the contrary, hey I have no idea where the hangar is, but I may know where Jackson's middle guy is. Since his uncle is unaware about what Jackson is up to in his company, nor where his operation is out. But it's going to take me a day to figure out where it is. One of them may help lead you to where the hangar is at."

Jason tells Steve, "Hey thanks man, I appreciate that. Besides if we can find one of them, it might lead us to where the deal is at. We're looking at the stolen money, and that's the Kansas City PD's turf, and that's why we need your help. I just wanted to ask if JAG knows anything about this arms deal gone wrong."

Steve tells them, "I don't think so. I never got a call from JAG about that. No one in the military reported any missing weapons involved. You know it's weird that they're not investigating this case too."

Jason tells Steve, "What if one of the JAG guys is maybe involved? Besides Jackson may have a friend who is on the JAG's military police payroll."

Steve tells Jason, "I'll take a look into it. What if this guy who stole that 20 million dollars actually works for JAG?"

Jason tells Steve, "He might be the guy who is working for Jackson."

Steve tells Jason, "I'll go take a look into this. I'll give you a call tomorrow when I find out."

Jason tells Steve, "Hey, no problem. You have your nephew's phone number, just give him a call when you find anything out."

Steve tells Jason, "Okay, no problem. Hey, since you're here, why don't you stay and finish your drink, and have another one on me."

Jason tells Steve, "Hey, don't you have to get back to work?"

Steve tells Jason, "Jace, I'm off duty. Besides, this is where I come when I'm off-duty."

Jason tell Steve, "I keep forgetting about that."

Helena comes back and gives Nathan and Tom their beers. Helena tells Nathan, "You know, Nate. You really should work on your flirting a bit. If you wanted to take me out, all you had to do was ask."

Nathan tells Helena, "Well, I was going to tell you, would you like to go out with me tomorrow? Maybe we could hang out here, it's a good place to meet. And if you're not working…or even if you are working I could just hang out. Hey, if you want to say no I understand, I'm not the kind of guy girls usually date."

Helena laughs a little, and tells Nathan, "I get off work at 6 PM tonight, you can meet me then."

Nathan tells Helena, "Sure, no problem."

Back at the NWMSU library, Luke is talking to Jackson's uncle, Thomas Lucas. Also, Natalie is there. They are at the computer room. Luke tells Thomas, "Hey, thanks for the information about your weapons deal. I'm really sorry about your nephew."

Thomas tells Luke, "Yeah, I'm really sorry about my nephew too. You know he gets this from my father's side of the family. I always hated that guy. You know, I already watched my brother push me around, and I already watched my dad pushed me around because I didn't have enough sense or raw power to make it in business. Now they pass it on to my nephew. I would have fired the guy, but then I would have insulted my family. Since they're both dead, and their will says I can't fire him."

Luke tells Thomas, "So Mr. Lucas if you can't fire the guy, couldn't you turn him into the police or JAG about what he's doing?"

Thomas tells Luke, "You know, Luke, I'd love to. But I can't because I don't have any proof that he's connected to this, or who he's selling the weapons too. And besides, the guy owns 80% of my company, so he overrules me on a lot of decisions. And the board members favor him, so I can't make any decisions without their say-so. Plus, he's also on the board with them."

Luke tells them, "If we can prove your nephew is selling weapons to Ashuk, we may have enough evidence to put him away. I think with enough evidence that would be enough for the board to have him removed. He may still get some shares of the money while he's in jail, but he'll lose his share of the company, and it'll revert back to you."

Thomas tells Luke, "Well, I appreciate you doing that for me Luke."

Natalie tells Thomas, "So, Mr. Lucas, any idea what these weapons are that you built for the military?"

Thomas tells them, "I have no idea what they are. Jackson is the one who is in charge of the deal. It was his idea to make the deal in the first place, he has full control and authorization."

Natalie tells Thomas, "Well, don't worry, we're going to do whatever we can to find this guy. But, I have to warn you, if this deal is successful, and JAG or the FBI figures out this arms deal, all of your names are ruined, and I think you might go to jail. It seems he picked you as a scapegoat, by having your name on all those contracts."

Thomas tells them, "What are you talking about? I never signed anything. This was Jackson's idea in the first place, he was the one who made the authorizations. I didn't know anything about it. Are you saying if this goes wrong, I could end up in jail and he gets to run off with 20 million dollars *and* the stolen weapons?"

Natalie tells Thomas, "Well, Mr. Lucas, it won't be 20 million. It would more likely be 40 or 50 million. The 20 million dollars in laundered money if for him to give to Ashuk to pay for his terrorism against the Jordanian royal family. But Ashuk is going to pay Jackson for the laundered money and the weapons. So it's true, you could go to jail. And I wish we could help you out, but there's nothing we can do. If this deal goes through, it's out of our hands. But one thing we can do is prevent this. If we can find your nephew's arms deal, we'll have enough evidence to book him. All of the blame will go on him, and you'll get off scot-free."

Thomas tells them, "That sounds great. I'm not going to take the rap for my nephew's mistakes. Sometimes I wish I could fire that guy, but like I said, he's well-connected."

Luke tells Thomas, "Well don't worry Mr. Lucas, you can count on us."

Mr. Lucas gets up from his chair, and shakes their hands. Mr. Lucas tells them, "Well, thanks for helping me out on this one. I really owe you guys. I want to run an honest company, and I'm not going to let guys like Jackson ruin that."

Natalie tells Mr. Lucas, "Well, don't worry sir, we'll handle this. And thanks for the files that you gave us on this deal."

Mr. Lucas tells them, "I'm glad I could help, but I'm not sure how much they're worth. They don't tell you what the weapons are, or where they're held, or where this deal is going to be."

Natalie tells Mr. Lucas, "We'll see what we can do."

Mr. Lucas leaves the computer room, and both Natalie and Luke sit back down. Both are sighing because they have had a long day. Luke looks at the file, "Well, there's not a lot of info we can get on this weapons deal. But, one thing we can do is stop this deal and maybe the army can actually get the weapons they need from Lucas Weapons, and he can keep the 20 million dollars. I just hope Jason and Nathan can help us on this one, because there's not much help this file can give us. It's a shame we don't have Jackson's files, because we could figure out where it is and who he's working with." Natalie blushes a little when he mentions Jason. Luke tells Natalie, "Hey, Natalie you okay?"

Luke snaps his fingers in front of her face, because she looks like she's in shock, but it's actually love shock when he mentions Jason's name. Natalie tells Luke, "Oh, uh, sorry. I was just out of it for a minute. Luke, can I ask you something?"

Luke tells Natalie, "Sure, what is it Natalie?"

Natalie tells Luke, "I know Jason is mildly autistic, but he could still get married or have kids right? He could still date right?"

Luke sarcastically tells her, "Yes, autistics can get married and have children. They also can pee on their pants for five seconds. Why do you ask?" Luke looks at Natalie for a minute, and tells her, "Oh my god, you really have a crush on Jason? I know he may not be a catch, but he has always had a way to attract women."

Natalie tells Luke, "No, no of course not."

Luke tells Natalie, "Look, I know Jason is a little bit different. Yes, he may be mildly autistic, but he does date. I mean not a lot, because he's always been cautious. And Jason does really like you a lot. I mean he can't drive a car or take care of himself sometimes, but he can date. Sometimes he can barely lift things without breaking his back, but he's fine."

Natalie tells Luke, "Look, I'm sure there's nothing bad about him. Besides, lots of people are a little mentally handicapped."

Luke tells Natalie, "Well, me and Nathan are dyslexic, but one thing you should know about Jason is that he didn't know how to read until when he was nine. He was a mute until he was 5 or 6, that's what he always told me. He still has a few social problems, but he's a good guy. He's really the kind of guys that girls want to have as a husband. Look, I know you're going to have doubts, because he's mildly autistic, but he's really just a guy, like everyone else. But Natalie, I do have one question. Do you really like him? And please don't tell me 'as a friend,' because Jason really hates being in the friend zone. Like, he'll be okay with it, he'll just sulk alone in private, but you can tell me, to my face."

Natalie tells Luke, "You know, I really do like him a lot. He's amazing. I just hope sometime I can ask him out."

Luke tells Natalie, "Well, I'm sure you will. Maybe if you tell him."

Natalie tells Luke, "I hope so."

Luke tells Natalie, "Until Nathan and Jason arrive, why don't we play the NBA game on the computer? The library got us the video game package on this computer."

Natalie tells Luke, "Alright, I've got the package right here, but I'm playing for the Lakers. I'm a dire Lakers fan."

Luke tells Natalie, "Okay, I'm the Knicks, I'm a huge Knicks fan." Luke turns on the computer, and they start the game.

Inside Jackson's warehouse, a limo enters when the garage door opens. The limo parks from inside the warehouse, and the driver exits and opens the back door. The person who exits is Jackson, and he heads upstairs, to the manager's floor. He sees some of his workers are storing the rest of the weapons inside of a safe to be ready for their deal with Ashuk. Jackson's right hand man, the manager of this warehouse, is working in his office until he hears a knock at the door. The manager tells the person at the door, "Come in." The door opens, and Jackson enters the manager's office, and the manager tells Jackson, "Mr. Lucas! It's great to see you sir, what can I do for you?"

Jackson tells the manager, "Roderick, listen, I need a favor."

Roderick tells Jackson, "Anything you want sir."

Jackson is carrying his briefcase in his left hand, and sets it on Roderick's desk. He opens the briefcase and takes out a DVD and shows it to Roderick. Jackson tells Roderick, "Roderick, I want you to come here for a minute. There's something that I want to show you."

Roderick tells Jackson, "Sure, what is it sir?"

Jackson tells Roderick, "By the way, can you bring two of your men in here, because I want to see them right now."

Roderick tells him, "Uh, yes sir." Roderick picks up his phone, and turns on the speaker, "Gable, Norville. Come to the manager's office right now, the boss wants to see you."

Gable and Norville enter the manager's office and see Lucas and Roderick. Gable tells them, "You wanted to talk to us Roderick? Hey, Mr. Lucas! It's great to see you, what brings you here?"

Jackson tells Gable, "Well, actually I thought I'd make a little surprise visit, because I wanted to see how you guys were doing, and how my business was doing too. Because you know there was a rumor out there that somebody was trying to horn in on my weapons deal. And somebody must've ratted out to the police that I was running an arms deal with my client, General Ashuk Kabob. Do you know who General Kabob is gentlemen?"

Gable tells Jackson, "No, Mr. Lucas. Who is he?"

"He's my important clientele. You know, this guy is giving me a lot of money for the weapons that I designed and built for him to help his country. You know, his country is having a lot of invaders right now, and he wants to use my weapons to protect his country, and protect his turf. And somebody must've ratted on me that the military was paying me 20 million dollars to build weapons for the army, but I was building those weapons for Ashuk, and I had even found a way to screw the military out of it. But I didn't even have to worry about that, because they would've gone after my uncle. But somebody must've told my uncle what I was doing too. Does anybody know who could've done that? Anybody? I'll give you a hint, he's right in front of me, and I don't think he should be here when I'm not in a good mood."

All three of them are worried, until Jackson takes out his Beretta 92F from the back of his jacket. He aims his gun on the three of them, but doesn't know who to target, until he found the guy who ratted on him. And the target was Roderick. Jackson fires his gun, three bullets come out of his gun, hitting Roderick in the chest, and killing him. Jackson says, "I hate it when people think they can muscle into my business. And I hate it when people think an undercover cop or a fed can rat on me. And he was my right hand man too. Go check him out, see if he was the informant. See who he's working for."

Gable tells Jackson, "Yes sir." Gable heads over to Roderick's dead body, and checks him out for a minute. He finds his wallet, and tells Jackson, "No, he's clean. He's not a cop, a fed, or anything. Not even an informant. I really doubt he's working for anybody, except you. Besides, if he was an informant or a cop, he would've ducked from that gunshot, or he wouldn't be that frightened."

"My mistake, but I never liked him anyway, because I think he was trying to steal millions of dollars from me. And besides, somewhere down the line I always thought he was my informant, because I don't like it when people steal from me or try to overthrow me, but there's a reason that I called you two here."

Norville tells Jackson, "What is it Mr. Lucas?"

"I wanted to ask. Did anyone else know about my deal with General Ashuk that could have cost me a lot of money?"

Gable tells him, "No, sir. We didn't tell anyone. No one knows that you stole the 20 million dollars, and laundered the dirty money from that safe to give to General Ashuk, and also take the weapons and store them in a safe in a top secret military hangar that we're using to make a deal with Ashuk."

Jackson tells them, "I want to show you two men something." Jackson grabs the laptop, turns it around, and turns it on. He places the DVD into the laptop, and he sees a security monitor of Jason and Nathan talking him in the office. "Now, why are there two gentlemen asking me questions about my arms deal? Since I don't have an informant on my team, I just want to know how these two men figured this out."

Gable tells Jackson, "I have no idea, sir. I am a member of the Judge Advocate Generals sir. I have helped you cover your tracks. I am also a well-respected military general, and I went to Harvard Law to get this job. Because your father is the one who put me through law school, since he is our dad."

Jackson tells him, "Try not to rub it in. You are my half-brother. And he did knock up your mother, who was his secretary, while having an affair on my mom. One good thing he did for both of them was sending a hit man to take both of them out, so they didn't go public, so that he could save his business, and he took us in too."

Gable tells Jackson, "Well, Jackson, I know you don't want to play the charade of me being your half-brother, and besides you are my older brother. And we did get Roderick to take out our moms for us, so we could save our father from scandal. So we do owe him, to make sure this deal goes through. Last year, he had a heart attack. The stress was too much for him, so we're going to pick up where he left off."

Jackson tells Gable, "Yeah, I'm sure we do. Anyway, back to business, I want to find out who these two men are, and why they're asking questions. And call someone to have this body removed. Put him a furnace and burn him to ashes. I can't look at his face right now."

Norville tells Jackson, "Yes sir."

Jackson tells Gable, "Oh by the way little bro, there's something I want to show you. Come here for a minute."

Gable tells Jackson, "What is it Jackson?"

Jackson knees Gable in the stomach and gives him a roundhouse kick to the face. Gable falls down on the floor, and he's hurting really badly. Jackson lifts him up by the shirt, and grabs Gable by the nose, "First of all, it's not Jackson, its Mr. Lucas. I need you to keep my cover, so it doesn't look like I'm giving special treatment to anyone who is related to me."

Gable tells Jackson, "Yes sir."

Jackson lets go of Gable's nose, and tells him, "Oh, by the way, Gable, I was going to ask you, who was the NBA finals MVP in 1980?"

Gable is too hurt to answer that question, and tells Jackson, "Uh, I don't know Mr. Lucas."

Jackson tells Gable, "Magic. Johnson." Jackson punches Gable in the groin, and Gable is hurting right now, and Jackson tells Gable, "Call your guy, and find out who these two are. I don't want these two losers running around my arms deal. If these two screw up my deal, I'm holding you two responsible. It's going to be your asses on the line, when I put a couple holes in your foreheads."

Gable tells Jackson, "Yes sir."

Jackson tells Gable, "Go make the call."

Gable sees the phone on the desk, he grabs it, and makes a call to his guy, "Hello, Ryan? Listen I need a favor."

Back at the college library, Jason, Nathan, and Tom enter the library. Luke and Natalie are playing video games on the computer, and turn around and see them heading to the computer room. Natalie and Luke get up from their chairs, and go over to talk to them. Luke tells them, "Hey guys, how'd it go?"

Natalie tells them, "You think he bought it?"

Nathan tells them, "Well, right now he does, but I think we might have to beware. He might come after us if he figures out who we are."

Tom tells them, "Right now, we have to figure out what to do with finding Jackson's operation and deal."

Jason tells them, "Any luck from you guys? Did Jackson's uncle meet you guys?"

Natalie tells them, "Yeah, but he wasn't much help. But he is aware of what Jackson is up too now, but I don't think he can stop him since Jackson has full control of this arms deal, and he can't fire him because he has full tenure."

Jason tells them, "Look, why don't we head back to the room and figure out what to do?"

Nathan tells them, "Yeah, before we go down there why don't we get something to eat? I don't think any of us had a chance to eat all day."

All of them say okay, and they all head to the elevator and press the button. All of them enter the elevator to take them to their secret room. Back at the secret room under the library that is their detective agency, a few minutes later, they're eating their pizzas and drinking their Diet Pepsi and Diet Dr. Pepper while working at the table.

Jason tells them, "Alright, Luke, I got ahold of your uncle. He said he's going to get us information about where the operation is, but I don't think he's going to find the deal anytime soon. But I do think he is going to find where Jackson's operation is at, and who he is working with, someone who is covering the tracks."

Nathan tells them, "What did you guys find out from Thomas?"

Natalie tells them, "Well, the same thing you did. He doesn't know where the operation's at, or the deal. It's some top secret military base. The only one who knows where it is would be Jackson. He also doesn't know what the weapons are, because Jackson is the one who authorized the whole thing. He's the one in charge of the operation."

Luke tells them, "I guess we're back to square one. We'll just have to wait until Uncle Steve calls me."

Nathan tells them, "I wish we could find some more information on where they are."

Jason tells them, "I guess we'll have to wait until tomorrow, until Steve calls us. He's the one who can give us all the info we need to put away Jackson. So, I guess that will be it for the day. We'll come back tomorrow and figure out what else to do."

Luke tells them, "Good idea. So I've been thinking, we can head home, or we got some new games on the computer upstairs, so why don't we just play some of those?"

Nathan tells them, "Well, I'd love to guys, but I've got a date with Helena."

Luke tells them, "Helena? My cousin? How'd you get a date with her? She's like impossible to date. Besides, I thought she only dated macho tough guys. That's what Uncle Steve told me."

Nathan tells Luke, "I'm sure that's a misunderstanding."

Luke tells Nathan, "Look, Nate, you've got to be careful. Don't make a move on her. Her father is really protective. This guy had Green Beret training. He could kick your ass in eight seconds if you even think about putting the moves on her."

Nathan looks a little bit frightened, "I don't think I should do that. I won't even kiss her, not on the first date. Maybe after a year or two, when her father actually likes or approves of me."

Luke tells Nathan, "That's a good idea."

Nathan goes over to the elevator, and Jason tells Luke, "Luke, you do realize your Uncle Steve never had Green Beret training? He could barely punch someone out without breaking his back. He spent the majority of his military career fixing computers. Plus, the guy actually likes Nathan."

"I know that, but I just want to watch him squirm for a minute," said Luke.

Jason tells Luke, "Heh, funny. Cute, but funny."

Luke and Tom gets up from their chairs and head to the elevator to reach Nathan.

Natalie is about to leave, but Jason says, "Wait, Natalie, there's something I wanted to talk to you about."

Natalie tells Jason, "What is it?"

Jason sees Nathan, Tom, and Luke leaving, so he has some alone time with her. Jason tells Natalie, "Uh, Natalie, I just wanted to ask. I know this is none of my business or anything, but do you–" Jason was about to ask her out, but couldn't find the right words, so Jason starts telling her, "I wanted to ask if you like the library. You know the head librarian is a friend of mine, his name is Joe, and he installed a new vending machine. I just kind of wanted to know if you liked the new vending machine he built."

Natalie tells him, "Uhm, I think so. Except I never went to the lounge, so maybe I'll take a look at it in a minute." Natalie gets up from her chair and exits.

Jason is upset, and tells himself, "God, what did I do. You idiot."

Natalie comes back for a minute, and starts kissing Jason on the lips, and they stop, and Natalie tells him, "You know, I was going to ask if you'd like to have a drink with me sometime, you know if it's alright with you. I know a college bar about a mile from this library, so I was wondering if you wanted to come."

Jason tells her, "I think it's kind of closed today, but you know, I have some drinks here, I have some beer or some champagne. You know, mostly I bring Joe down here so that he doesn't have to go to the bar. Anytime he gets off work and wants to unwind. Besides, he is the one who showed me this place in the first place."

Natalie grabs Jason by the hand, and picks him up, and they start making out for a few minutes.

Jason stops for a minute, and tells her, "You know, we've also got some scotch in the fridge too."

Natalie tells Jason, "Jason. Not helping."

Jason tells Natalie, "Oh, sorry. I've got to stop doing that."

They continue making out.

Back at Jackson's warehouse, Jackson, Gable, and Norville are waiting for the call. The phone rings, and Norville answers it, because he was sitting down in the office chair. He picks up the phone, "Hello? Hey Ryan. Oh, you got it? Alright thanks. Okay, I'll print it out in a minute." Norville hangs up the phone, and he starts printing the information about Jason and Nathan. Norville tells Jackson, "Mr. Lucas, good news, Ryan called, he's got the information about those two morons who spoke to you in the office. I'm printing out the information right now."

Jackson tells him, "Alright, go check out the information about these two, and find out who they are. And tell me how I can murder those little geeks for interfering in my operation and jeopardizing my deal." Norville gets up from his chair and head to the fax machine. Gable and Jackson get up from their chairs and join Norville. Norville grabs the information, and takes a look at it. Jackson tells them, "Alright, who are these guys anyway? And tell me, when can I put a bullet in their heads."

Gable tells Norville, "C'mon Norville, who are these guys anyway?"

Norville tells them, "Guys, you're not going to like this."

"So, who are they?" says Gable.

Norville tells them, "They're cops. Actually, one of them is a cop, and the guy that's working with him is a P.I."

Jackson is really upset, "Ahhh great, now I have a cop and his stupid P.I. buddy jeopardizing my mission?"

Norville tells Jackson, "They're names are Detective Sergeant Nathan Devers, he works in the robbery unit. He recruited his best friend Jason Boswell to track us down. Devers has been on this case for a year, but we always found a way to trick him. Not until he brought his friend Jason in to track us down."

Gable tells them, "So what? We can deal with Boswell and Devers. They're losers. They may track us down, but they're not smart enough to come after us. Besides, those guys are practically harmless."

Norville tells them, "You're not going to believe this, but Boswell? He's mildly autistic, he works in NOCOMO."

Gable tells them, "What is NOCOMO?"

Norville tells them, "It's a workshop where mentally handicapped people work. How do you think Boswell got to work there? Most of the time his job was to tear out paper and put in barrels, kind of like a recycling thing."

Gable tells them, "Well, what a way to save the environment. Come on this guy is a stupid retard, he can't come after us, he's too easy to kill."

Norville tells them, "Yeah, well Mr. Retard tracked us down in the first place. Devers has been on this case for a year and he couldn't track us down, but his pal did."

Gable tells Jackson, "So, Mr. Lucas, what should we do? We're not afraid of this geeky moron. He's just some mentally handicapped loser. He may have been lucky to find us, because he's mildly autistic, but he's not stupid enough to come after us. Even Devers couldn't protect him, and he's a cop, he's too easy to be killed."

Jackson tells them, "Gable, come here for a minute." Gable goes a little bit closer, and Jackson punches Gable in the stomach, and punches him in the face, and Gable falls down on the floor. Jackson tells Gable, "First of all, nobody talks about my plans, only I decide what the plan is. And you're right, Gable, he is an easy target, but right now I'm a little bit intimidated, because he knows everything, but he doesn't know where my operation is at, or where I'm going to make my deal with General Ashuk. So I'm safe. But I don't need him and Devers running around my operation, I want them both dead. Oh, and Norville, I need your help. I want you to call Ryan, and get some of my men to take these losers out. I don't need them running around my operation."

Norville tells Jackson, "Sure thing, Jackson, it's no problem."

Jackson tells Norville, "Oh Norville, there's one thing I forgot to mention."

Norville tells Jackson, "What is it sir?"

Jackson grabs Norville by the nose, knees him in the stomach, and gives him a roundhouse kick to the face. Norville falls to the floor and Jackson kicks him in the face three times. Jackson tells Norville, "First of all, that's Mr. Lucas to you. You call me Jackson, that's disrespect, like we're friends. We're not friends, you work for me, you're my slave. The only reason you're alive right now, is because I want you to kill those dorks for running around my operation. Both of you guys get up, and make the call to Ryan."

Norville and Gable are both hurt, but both of them get off the floor. Norville heads to the phone, and makes a call. Gable tells Jackson, "Uh, Mr. Lucas, how are we going to find these guys anyway, they could be anywhere."

"Norville before you make that call, any idea where to find those morons?"

Norville tells Jackson, "Well, sir, I read their file. I know he works at NOCOMO, but I called NOCOMO and he's taking a couple weeks off. Mostly he's spending some time at a college library, it's at Northwest Missouri State University."

Jackson tells him, "Norville, you know where they live right?"

Norville tells Jackson, "Yes sir."

Jackson tells him, "I want you to go tail them in the morning. I want you to go to Boswell's house, and follow him. He won't go anywhere without his pal Devers. Once they get to the college library, where nobody else is at, that's when I want you and your men to go out there and kill them."

Norville tells Jackson, "Yes sir." Norville picks up the phone and makes the call to Ryan, "Hey Ryan, listen I need another favor."

In the morning at the college library parking lot, Nathan parked his van in the parking lot. Jason and Nathan exit the car, and they're about to head to the library until they see a car parked right across the curb. Ryan is sitting in the black SUV, and Norville is in the passenger seat, and four of Jackson's men are in the back. Ryan sees Nathan and Jason getting out of the car, and Jackson tells Norville, "Alright, Norville, they're getting out."

Norville tells them, "Alright, let's get 'em." Norville, Ryan, and four of Jackson's men exit the car and head over to talk to Jason and Nathan.

After Jason and Nathan exit the car, Nathan tells Jason, "You know, there's something I wanted to ask you Jace."

Jason tells Nathan, "What is it Nate?"

Nathan tells Jason, "You know, yesterday when we spoke to Jackson, do you think he got suspicious and knew who we are? I don't think he bought our act when we questioned him."

Jason tells Nathan, "I don't know if he did buy it or not, but if he didn't I think he would've sent his men after us, because if I know one thing about bad guys it's 'no witnesses.'"

Norville's voiceover tells Jason and Nathan, "You're right about one thing Boswell. No witnesses. And too bad you guys stuck your noses where they didn't belong."

Nathan and Jason turn around when they hear the voice, and they see Norville, Ryan, and four of Jackson's men in the parking lot. Nathan tells Jason, "I was afraid this may happen."

Jason tells Nathan, "Don't worry, we can take 'em."

Nathan tells Jason, "Six against two? I don't think I like the odds. Besides, I didn't bring a gun with me."

Jason tells Nathan, "Well, neither did I. Besides, you know I never bring a gun with me."

Norville, Ryan, and four of Jackson's men take out their Smith & Wesson 4506s from the back of their jackets, and aim their guns on them. Norville tells them, "Hold it, it could be a trap. Search them. Besides, they said they didn't bring a gun, but I think they may be bluffing."

Ryan tells them, "What should we do?"

Norville tells Ryan, "Go search them."

Ryan goes to both of them and searches them. He tells Jason and Nathan, "Turn around, hands on your head." Jason and Nathan are being searched by Ryan, and Ryan tells Norville, "Well, they're clean."

Norville tells Ryan, "Well, shoot them. In the back."

What Ryan and Norville and their men don't know is that Tom was behind the passenger seat, and he opened his window gently, and turned the alarm on his cellphone up really loud. Ryan, Norville, and his men are deafened by the alarm.

Ryan tells them, "Ah, God, what is that?"

Jason sees Tom in the back of the car, and tells them, "You're right about one thing. I wasn't bluffing, I didn't bring a gun with me. No, but he did." Jason stomps on Ryan's foot, and Ryan's foot is aching.

Tom comes out of the car, and dives down. Tom has a Beretta 92F, he tells Jason and Nathan, "Get back!"

Jason and Nathan get back, and Tom fires his gun. Two bullets come out of his gun, killing Ryan. Tom takes out two other Beretta 92F guns and gives them to Jason and Nathan. The alarm is off. Jason and Nathan catch their guns. Jason turns around, and fires his gun, three bullets come out of his gun and hit Norville in the chest, and he dies. Six other bullets come out of nowhere, and hit the ground near Jason and Nathan, but miss them. The three of them dive down, and Jackson man 1 tells his men, "Shoot them!" Five other bullets come out of nowhere, and hit the trunk and bumpers, and three other bullets hit them as well.

Nathan tells them, "Cover me, I'm going in." Jason sees the target on Jackson man 4. One bullet comes out of his gun, and hits the road near Jackson man 4 but misses him. Nathan gets up, and dives down on the ground. Three bullets fire out of his gun and hit Jackson man 1 in the chest, and he dies. But three other bullets come from nowhere, and hit the road near Nathan, but miss him. Nathan rolls around for a minute, and sees another car, and hides behind it. Tom fires his gun, two bullets come out of his gun, and hit Jackson man 2 in the stomach, and he dies. Jackson men 4 and 3 keep firing. 4 sees Jason's foot, and one bullet comes out of his gun and hits the road near Jason's foot, but misses him.

Jackson man 3 tells 4, "We've got to get out of here, the cops may arrive."

Jackson man 4 tells him, "Not until we shoot these guys. Lucas' order."

Nathan sees Jackson man 3, one bullet comes out of his gun, and hits him in the leg, and Jackson man 3 is a little bit sore. Nathan comes from behind the car, and three bullets come out of his gun, and hit Jackson man 3 in the chest, long enough for Jackson man 3 to be distracted. Tom comes out of the car, and two bullets come out of his gun and hit the man in the forehead and he dies. Jackson man 4 was also distracted, and when Jackson man 3 was shot, Jason comes out from behind the car, and fires his gun, and three bullets hit Jackson man 4 in the chest, and he dies.

Tom tells them, "It's a good thing, I spotted those guys before we left. I knew you guys were being followed."

Jason tells them, "It's a good thing too. That's what I like about you Tom, you always have keen observation."

Nathan tells Tom, "That's the reason why he was my best partner back then."

Jason tells them, "One of you guys better call this in."

Tom tells them, "You think Jackson is going to send some more guys to come after us?"

Jason tells them, "I don't know, but if he does, we better keep a lookout. It may not be good."

Nathan tells them, "Well, we better be prepared. We better pray that Luke's uncle calls, because I think right now we're running out of time." Nathan takes out a cell phone from his right pants pocket to call this in.

Back in the secret room, Joe is hanging out with Luke and Natalie. Joe comes out of the elevator carrying a cell phone in his left hand, and tells Natalie, "Excuse me, Sergeant Xalatan, Luke? You guys have got a call. Luke, it's your uncle."

Luke tells Joe, "Hey, thanks Joe. I called my Uncle Steve yesterday, and told him to call the library. The guy we were trying to bust may have phones tapped, so we need to call outside the line, where the phones aren't tampered with."

Joe tells them, "Hey, I'm just happy to help. Here you go Luke."

Luke grabs Joe's cell phone, and Luke tells Joe, "Hey, thanks for letting us use the secret room, we owe you."

Joe tells Luke, "Hey, no problem. Anything to help my friends. Can you tell Jason I say hi? I just want to get in good with his mother, she's putting in a lot of money for the library."

Luke tells Joe, "Sure thing." Joe heads back to the elevator, and Luke answers the call, "Hello? Hey Uncle Steve. Yeah, I'll write this down." Luke has a pen and paper on the table, and he tells his uncle, "Okay, go ahead."

Inside the elevator that's heading to the secret room, Jason, Tom, and Nathan are waiting for the elevator to head to the secret room. Jason tells them, "Hey, I wanted to ask, what are the odds of Kristen Stewart winning an Oscar anytime soon?"

Tom tells Jason, "Well, that depends, if her next movie is Oscar-worthy. And even if she does get nominated, I highly doubt she'll win, she's a million-to-one shot."

Nathan tells them, "Yeah, tell that to Michael Keaton, Bill Murray, and Eddie Murphy. They were the front runners to win last time, and they all lost to a guy out of nowhere."

Jason tells them, "Man, wouldn't it be cool to see if Kristen Stewart could win an Oscar. She hit it big with the *Twilight* series, which was her big break."

Nathan tells them, "Well, like I said, it depends on what movie could get her an Oscar win. There's a million other actresses that could win. You forget Meryl Streep was nominated a million times, and she's lucky that she won a few."

Tom tells them, "Okay, one more question, last year we saw the Royals go to the World Series, but they chocked it in game 7, so do you think they have another shot to go to the series again?"

Nathan tells them, "Yeah, well it took them 29 years to get back in the World Series, and by getting another repeat, that's a million-to-one. The Yankees are lucky that they got a repeat, because they're the guys that everyone depends on."

Tom tells them, "Well, if they ever get another shot at the series, I'm sure they'll take it. Maybe this time they'll go all the way."

Jason tells them, "We'll see Tom. Because right now, we'll be lucky if these guys even win the pennant this year."

Inside the secret room, the elevator door opens, and Tom, Jason, and Nathan exit the elevator. Natalie tells them, "Hey guys, what happened to ya? What took you so long? We got a little bit worried."

Nathan tells them, "Let's just say we ran into some old friends in the parking lot."

Jason sarcastically tells them, "Yeah, we were just lucky that they wanted to stop by and say hi right before they pulled a gun on us, and wanted to kill us."

Luke tells them, "Oh my God. Man, I knew Jackson's men were going to come after us."

Natalie tells them, "Sometimes, I wish we could just arrest these guys."

Nathan tells them, "With what? We've got nothing. Besides, they may work for Jackson, but since they're dead I really doubt they'll confess that Jackson hired them to kill us."

Tom tells them, "Man, if only there was a way we could put away Jackson, and find Ashuk, and those military weapons, and that 20 million dollars of laundered money, we could put them away."

Luke tells them, "Well, I think our problem is going to be solved. I have some good news. My Uncle Steve called. He gave us all the information, he found on Jackson's operation, and the guys who has been working with him. He thinks he can lead us to it."

Jason tells him, "What's the bad news?"

Luke tells them, "He has no idea where the secret location that Jackson is going to make his weapons deal with General Ashuk is going to be. But, maybe his right hand guy can help us with that."

Jason, Luke, and Tom sit down in their chairs and start discussing. Jason tells Luke, "So Luke, what did you find out?"

Luke tells them, "His name is Gable Lucas. He's Jackson's half-brother. They share the same father, different moms. He works for the military government. The guy actually worked on computers, and he's an ex-Green Beret. He found that he was excluded from the army about three years ago when they found out that he was selling secrets to a Jordanian war lord."

Jason tells him, "That'll be Ashuk."

Tom tells Luke, "How come he was never charged? Didn't they have enough evidence to put him away?"

Luke tells them, "Nope, there wasn't enough evidence to Court Marshall him. Plus JAG never had a search warrant with him. And here's the biggest kicker: He works for JAG now. Because he was acquitted. He was thrown out of the army but JAG gave him a job to work with them. So now he's an associate to JAG. And that explains how he covered his tracks. That's one reason why Jackson was never investigated, because he had JAG on his payroll."

Jason tells him, "That explains a lot why JAG never investigated him, because his half-brother is on board with him and is a member of JAG."

Nathan tells Luke, "So, Luke, where is Jackson's operation?"

Luke tells them, "It's at 113 Hanover Street, it's one of the warehouses that Jackson owns."

Jason tells them, "I think that's where he's doing the work on the weapons, but he's storing them where his deal is at. All we have to do is find that location where he's storing all his weapons, and we've got him."

Luke tells them, "I have some good news. I think I know what these top secret weapons are. They're the new T-148 Flamethrower that they were creating for the army. They were going to use it for some top secret demonstration. That's what the defense company is willing to pay 20 million dollars for is those new flame throwers."

Natalie looks at Luke's notepad, and tells them, "These T-148 Flamethrower are pretty unstable. They were supposed to be in for repair to make them work better."

Luke tells them, "Yeah, last week they repaired the new flame throwers, and they were supposed to store them in this military warehouse. Only Jackson knows where the warehouse is, and where he stores it. But, it was never reported to the army, and the new T-148 Flamethrower were never stored in that warehouse."

Jason tells them, "If it was never reported, it means the army will be unaware that Jackson is actually selling the repaired T-148 Flamethrower to Ashuk. And if anyone finds out about this deal, they know they're going to blame Jackson's uncle for this because his signatures are all over those contracts."

Nathan tells them, "And Jackson will run off with all the money. So after he finishes the deal, and the army figures out that those flamethrowers are in the hands of Ashuk's men, it's going to be bad for America and this nation."

Tom tells them, "Not only that, but Jackson's uncle could go to jail for this."

Jason tells them, "Well, we're not going to let that happen, all we have to do is find that top secret warehouse where Jackson is storing those flamethrowers, and once we find those weapons and the stolen money, we'll put Jackson behind bars, and his uncle will get off scot-free."

Luke tells them, "Yeah, but like I said, we still don't know where that deal is going to be, it could be anywhere."

Jason tells them, "No we don't know, but Jackson's brother will. Luke, you know where we can find him?"

Luke tells them, "Yeah, tomorrow night he goes to the Nitro Club. It's a night club that Jackson owns. It's at 115 West Street, in Shawnee Mission. It opens at 8 PM, I think that's where we might run into him, since he manages the place."

Jason tells them, "Okay. So I guess tomorrow night, at 8 PM, we'll pay Gable a visit and ask him where that deal is."

Nathan tells them, "And if he doesn't tell us?"

Jason tells him, "We'll beat the snot out of him if we have to make him talk."

Tom tells them, "Well, if we're gonna play the good cop/bad cop roles, I hope this time I get to be the bad cop. Because I never got to play bad cop with Nathan."

Jason tells them, "We're not going to play good cop/bad cop. We're going to play the I beat the snot out of you if you don't talk role."

Nathan tells them, "Well, Tom, that's what we'll do. We're not playing good cop/bad cop. We're playing talk now or we kill you."

Tom tells them, "I like that game better."

Natalie tells them, "I hope you guys have another plan, because what happens if Plan A doesn't work?"

Luke tells Natalie, "Well, I have Plan B all in mind." Luke takes a piece of rock out of his left jacket pocket, and puts it on the table.

Natalie tells him, "Luke, that's a rock. How's that gonna help us with Plan B?"

Luke tells her, "This isn't an ordinary rock. This green button on top of the rock? If you press it, it's a GPS system. Anywhere the rock goes, you can track the movement. I have the password open and the tracking device on my laptop. We just put the tracking device anywhere, I turn on the computer, and we can track it anywhere."

Jason tells them, "If we can get the rock on Jackson's car, once he leaves with the car, we can track him on the computer and find out where he is. That way he can lead us to his arms deal with Ashuk."

Nathan tells Natalie, "Okay, once you find the deal, call us, and alert the rest of the cops, and tell them where it is."

Jason tells Natalie, "And we'll come running."

Natalie tells them, "Alright, I'm in."

Jason tells them, "Alright, we've got a lot of work to do before tomorrow night, so here's the plan. Nathan, Tom, all three of us are going to the Nitro Club to talk to Gable, and if he won't tell us where the deal is we'll be the snot out of him good. And if that doesn't work, we'll go with Plan B. Natalie, go to Jackson's warehouse, and plant the GPS device on Jackson's car. He's going to be travelling by limousine, so it'll probably be the only limo at the warehouse. Once you're done, call Luke. He'll stay here and he'll monitor the computer and see where Jackson is going. Luke once you find the location, give the directions to Natalie, and she'll give the directions to us. Then, Luke, you call the cops and tell them where to go."

Luke tells him, "Check Jace."

Jason tells them, "Alright guys, we have a lot of work to do. And I'm scared doing this too. But remember, our ass is on the line. Not just the military's but ours too. Besides, we know Jackson stole that laundered 20 million dollars, and made a fool out of the KCPD. He also made a fool out of the army. And right now an innocent person is going to go to jail if this arms deal goes through. Remember, we've got a lot of work to do. I just want to know if you guys want to do this. If you don't, I understand because this is a big sacrifice we're doing here." Jason looks at all of them, "And you're right, we're all going to die doing this. So am I. And Tom, I know you promised my mom you'd look after me, and you can tell her I'll be fine. But if anything happens to me, I have a letter for her that explains that whatever happens to me I was serving and protecting the people of Kansas City, and America."

Tom tells Jason, "Well, I promised your mother that I'd protect you, and I will. So you don't have to give her a letter, because I'm going to make sure nobody hurts you, that's my word."

Jason tells them, "Okay. Fair enough. Let's do it."

Nathan tells them, "Hey, you had us and when do we start. Let's do it."

Jason tells them, "Alright, let's do it." All of them do their fist bumps, and they're done.

Luke tells them, "Come on guys, we better start practicing. If we're going to go out, we're going to go out as champions, so we've got a lot of work to do."

Jason tells them, "Yeah, come on, let's get started."

Back inside Jackson's warehouse, in the manager's office. Jackson and Gable are in the office. One of Jackson's associates comes inside the manager's office, and tells them, "Excuse me, Mr. Lucas."

Jackson tells him, "What is it Roads?"

Roads tells Jackson, "I checked into the police scanner, and I also checked out the parking lot. Ryan and Norville and 4 of our men your dead."

Jackson is really upset, and punches a few papers off of the desk. Gable tells Jackson, "Hey, don't worry big bro. We can still take these bastards out. Hey, maybe they were goddamn lucky. If we got Boswell alone we could kill him easily. He's still some autistic loser, he can barely fight."

Jackson is really upset, and he goes over to Gable and slaps him in the face, and knees him in the stomach. Jackson tells Gable, while Gable is hurting, "You idiot. By the way, when did the stupid train come here? With or without Boswell, I still can't kill that son of a bitch, because if I know one thing about autistics, it's sometimes they surprise you. And you're right Gable, he is retarded, and he can't hurt me. That guy can barely understand anything or take care of himself, so he can't do anything to me. All I've got to do is put a bullet in the idiot's brain, and I'm home free. Besides, that guy was never a threat to me."

Gable tells them, "Yeah, but he's the one who figured everything out. The cops have been after us for a whole year, and we always covered our tracks, but he figures everything out in a few days, how do you explain that?"

Jackson tells Gabe, "I'll tell you what it is. Blind stinking luck. He may be damn lucky he survived, or even found us, but he doesn't know everything. That's one thing about autistics, they have trouble understanding emotions and feelings. That's why they have one of the worst communication disorders ever. And that's why they're easy to kill."

Gable tells Jackson, "So, what are we going to do Jackson? Should we send some more guys to take out Boswell and Devers?"

Jackson tells Gable, "Well, we don't have any time. Ashuk is going to be here tomorrow night. We have a lot of work to do. Is everything scheduled Roads?"

Roads tells Jackson, "Yes Mr. Lucas, everything's all scheduled. The T-148 Flamethrowers are ready to be transported to our secret location sir."

Jackson tells him, "Excellent. Right now, we're loading the final flamethrowers. As soon as we finish paying Ashuk, we'll open the safe so he can get the rest of the flamethrowers, and get them on the trucks so Ashuk can take them to his planes to start his revolution against the Jordanian royal family."

Roads tells Jackson, "I'll go supervise the loading of rest of the flamethrowers sir."

Jackson tells Roads, "Okay, you go ahead and do that. I'll come with you and take a look to make sure everything is right on schedule for tomorrow."

Roads tells Jackson, "Yes sir."

Roads leaves the manager's office, and Gable tells Jackson, "So, big bro, what are we going to do with Boswell and Devers? What happens if they try and find our arms deal?"

Jackson tells Gable, "If they do come near this arms deal, we'll kill them. But, we have to make sure that those idiots aren't running around

Kansas City coming after us. Once we finish this deal, you'll find them and take them out."

Gable tells Jackson, "Sure thing, big bro. But before I meet you at the deal, I have to be at the club, and supervise the area for a few minutes."

Jackson tells Gable, "Okay. With or without you, we'll still continue this deal. Just make sure you're on time, if you're not I'll kick the snot out of you all day. But even if you're not there, that's fine, because I'll handle this deal alone."

Gable tells Jackson, "Hey, don't worry big bro, I'll be there on time, I promise you."

Jackson tells Gable, "Alright, I'm going to hold you to that. And if you're not, you're going to get a serious can of ass kicking."

Gable tells Jackson, "Yes sir." Jackson and Gable exit the manager's office and go downstairs to supervise the deal preparations.

Back at the library, Jason, Nathan, Natalie, Luke, and Tom are preparing themselves for the huge bust of Jackson's arms deal with Ashuk. Natalie is practicing with the GPS signal with Luke. Luke is in the secret room at the laptop, and Natalie is outside the library. She presses the green button, and Luke is looking at the GPS system. Jason and Nathan are at the gun range in the secret room, and they're practicing their shooting. They're firing at targets, and they're hitting the bull's eyes. Natalie is in the parking lot of the garage, and she presses the green button again. Luke is at the secret room, still at the laptop, and he's putting his thumbs up. Tom, Jason, and Nathan, are drinking Diet Pepsi in the secret room for a minute, taking a break. Natalie is on the second floor, testing out the GPS system still, and she presses the green button again, and Luke checks the laptop and he holds a thumbs up. Jason, Nathan, and Tom are back at the gun range, and they're using cardboard cutouts in what they call the Judgment Range. Jason fires at a target, and puts through three bullets through a gunman. Nathan puts two bullets through a gunmen's head. Another popup comes out and Tom puts three bullets in the judgment arena. Natalie is in the training room, at a mat in the secret room, and she's practicing self-defense with Jason. She flips him on the mat two times. Nathan is practicing at a video game gun range at the harbor, and he shoots out six bad guys. Natalie is still practicing self-defense with Jason. This time Jason is pretending to hold a knife and comes at her, but Natalie knees him the stomach and tosses him on the mat again. Jason and Tom are practicing their live action video game with their video game gun, and they shoot six live action gunmen in a warehouse.

At the real warehouse, Jackson, Gable, and Roads are supervising the warehouse. A few of Jackson's men are storing the flamethrowers inside the boxes and putting them in the back a big rig truck.

Jason and Nathan are practicing at the shooting range again. This time they're shooting five more popups of gunmen. Nathan is practicing self-defense with Jason. This time Nathan tries to attack Jason, but Jason grabs him by the arm and flips him. Tom tries to attack Jason from behind, but Jason elbows him, and kicks him in the groin, then tosses him onto the mat. Natalie is back outside the library. She presses the green button on the rock again, and Luke is in the secret room, and sees that the laptop is working, and Luke gives another thumbs up.

Back in the warehouse, Jackson, Gable, and Roads are seeing the finishing touches of his men storing all of the flamethrowers in the big rig truck.

Natalie practices her GPS tracking again, and this time, she's on the roof of the college library. She presses the button, and Luke is giving a thumbs up. Back on the roof, Natalie is making out with Jason, because they needed some alone time, and her phone is ringing. Back at the secret room, Jason, Nathan, Tom, Natalie and Luke are sitting down in their chairs. Jason tells them, "Alright guys. You all know what to do?"

All of them say, "Yes."

Jason tells them, "Listen guys, I have to warn you. Something could go wrong, or something could go right, but we don't know. We could fail, but I don't know, and our asses are on the line. A lot of people are depending on us to solve this. It's not just Jackson's uncle whose life is depending on this, but ours too. We promised a lot of people that we were going to solve this. I need to prove to everyone one time that I can solve a case. Nobody ever asked me to do this, but Nathan, you came to me, and I appreciate that, and I owe it to you to finish this case. But guys, we started together, and we'll finish together. Say hello to Team NOCOMO."

Luke tells them, "Team NOCOMO for life." All of them put their fists together as a symbol for shaking hands and they're done.

Outside of the Nitro Club, Nathan parks his Grand Jeep Cherokee right outside of the club. Jason, Nathan, and Tom exit the car, and go inside the Nitro Club. Nathan tells them, "Hey guys, you ever been inside this club before?"

Jason tells him, "No, besides, I don't think I'd go in here if it was run by a guy named Jackson Lucas. That guy is the biggest kingpin in Kansas City. I would never go to a club he owned."

Tom tells them, "Hey guys, there was this question that I wanted to ask. Imagine if Jackson's guys tried to bribe us, would you guys ever take it?"

Nathan tells him, "Forget it, Tom, I would never take bribes. I'm not going to be like one of those crooked cops I usually work with. Besides, I would be lousy at covering people's tracks. Gable may be Lucas' brother, but he's really good at covering tracks, that guy is really smart."

Jason tells them, "Yeah, besides, one thing I learned about bad guys. You have to be one step ahead of them, otherwise they win. Besides, with or without the badges, we don't take bribes from criminals. We don't like being bought by assholes like Jackson."

Tom tells Jason, "Good, I was testing you. Listen, Jason, remember my promise. I promised I'm not going to let anyone hurt you, and I won't. I'll make sure bastards like Jackson never hurt you."

Jason tells Tom, "Hey I appreciate that Tom, and besides I'm a pacifist. But if we were in a life and death situation out there, I would definitely take a bullet for you, because that's what friends do. You're not just my bodyguard, you're my best friend, and I would definitely take a bullet for you."

Tom tells him, "Hey I appreciate that Jace. And don't worry Nate, I'll take a bullet for both of you too. Because I made a promise, and I'll make sure Jackson doesn't touch you either."

Nathan tells Tom, "I appreciate that Tom."

Inside the Nitro Club, Jason, Nathan, and Tom enter, and they see a waitress. Jason tells them, "Okay guys, we've got to find Gable. He could be anywhere."

Tom tells Jason, "We can't split up and find him because it's a big place. Besides, one thing I've learned, if you get lost ask for directions. That's one thing that every navigator does."

Nathan tells them, "That's before we had GPS."

Jason sees the waitress, "Hey, excuse me?"

The waitress asks him, "Hi, can I help you?"

Jason tells the waitress, "Yeah, excuse me. I'm looking for Mr. Gable Lucas. Yeah, I'm one of his new investors. He called me to take a look at this new nightclub and invest in this place. This is my business manager and my body guard. I'm paying big money to invest in this place, and he asked me to come by and take a look at it."

The waitress tells them, "Well, that's funny. Mr. Lucas didn't tell me you were arriving, or anything about investors."

Nathan tells the waitress, "Well, actually he called us last minute. He must be so busy running this club. Even the bouncer didn't know who we were. We had to slip him a 20 to let us in. He called us really last minute."

Jason tells her, "And we really need to see him. I have a contract to sign to put a lot of money in this club, but if he isn't here I guess I'll have to take my business elsewhere. And he'll be in a bad mood if I don't invest in this club, and once he's in a bad mood he'll take it out on you too."

The waitress tells them, "Mr. Lucas is in the V.I.P. room. Just go straight, and then make a right."

Jason tells the waitress, "Thank you, I appreciate that."

The waitress tells him, "Sure thing, besides, I don't want to lose my job for this." Jason, Nathan, and Tom head to the V.I.P. room.

Inside the V.I.P. room, Gable, Roads, and three of Jackson's men are sitting down and having a drink of champagne. Only Gable and three of Jackson's men are having the champagne, Roads is the designated driver. Jason, Nathan, and Tom enter the V.I.P. room, and see Gable. They go over to talk to him. Jason tells him, "Hey, Lucas. Hope it's not a bad time. Aw, man you guys ordered champagne without us? I hope you aren't hogging it, because I want to drink with you since we're all celebrating tonight."

Gable looks at Jason, and recognizes him. Gable tells them, "It's them! Shoot them!" Gable, Roads, and three of Jackson's men take out their Smith and Wesson 4506 from the back of their jackets, and aims their guns on them. Roads fires his gun first, and two bullets come out. Jason, Nathan, and Tom dive down on the floor as three more bullets come out of nowhere, and hit the floor, missing them. Jason, Nathan, and Tom roll over the floor right across the area, and they hide behind a booth. Jason, Nathan, and Tom take out their Beretta 92Fs from the back of their pants. Jason sees Roads, and fires his gun. Three bullets come out of his gun, hitting Roads in the head and he dies. Nathan fires his gun and two bullets come out hitting the wall, missing the target. Five more bullets come out of nowhere, hitting the wall, table, and chairs. Nathan fires his gun again, two more bullets come out, and hit Jackson man 2 in the chest, and he dies. Tom fires his gun, two bullets come out of his gun, and hit Jackson man 1 in the chest, and he dies.

Jason takes out an eraser from his left pants pocket, and throws it on the floor. Nathan tells him, "Are you out of your mind? An eraser? What're you thinking?"

Jason tells Nathan, "Watch!" The eraser shows a huge flash of light out of it, and it blinds Gable and the remaining Jackson man. Jason, Nathan, and Tom get off the booth, and Jason tells them, "Come on, let's get out of here, now!" Everybody in the club hears the gunshots, and they start panicking and rush to the exit.

Jason, Tom, and Nathan head to their car, and Tom tells Nathan, "Nathan I'm driving."

Nathan says, "What are you nuts?"

Tom tells him, "Just give me the keys."

Nathan takes his keys from his left pants pockets, and tosses them to Tom, and Tom grabs them, and Nathan asks Tom, "Why do you want to drive?"

Tom tells Nathan, "I know a short cut."

Nathan tells Tom, "Well, I'd love to argue right now, but we're in the middle of a shootout and we're going to be sitting ducks in a minute."

Jason tells them, "Just shut up and drive." Tom, Jason, and Nathan get in the car. Tom is in the front seat, Nathan is in the passenger seat, and Jason is in the backseat.

Outside the entrance of the Nitro Club, Gable and Jackson man 3 see Jason, Nathan, and Tom's car exiting the club. Gable is upset, and yells at Jackson man 3, "Ah shit! Why didn't you go after them? You stupid idiot! You should've gone after them!"

Jackson man 3 tells Gable, "There's too many people. I couldn't see a goddamn thing! What are we gonna do now?"

Gable tells Jackson man 3, "We can't let those guys go running around alive, it'll be our asses on the line. I know where they're going, follow me!"

Jackson man 3 tells Gable, "I was afraid of that."

Outside the Kansas City highway, Tom, Nathan, and Jason are inside Nathan's van. Nathan tells them, "Did we lose them?"

Jason tells them, "I don't know. I couldn't tell. All of us were getting out so fast we didn't even see anybody coming after us."

Tom hears a gunshot out of nowhere, and tells them, "I don't think we lost them."

Jason turns around, and sees that Gable and Jackson man 3 are driving a black SUV. Gable is shooting a Franchi SPAS 12 at them. Gable fires his gun, three bullets come out of his gun, but hit the road missing them. Jason tells them, "Aw, man. Now they're coming after us." Two more bullets come out of nowhere and hit their bumper. Gable's car tries to ram into their bumper, but Nathan's car speeds up. Gable fires his gun again, and this time four more bullets come out of his gun, and two of them hit their tail light, and the other two hit their back window.

Tom tells them, "We've got to lose them!"

Nathan sees a road closed sign on the right, and tells them, "I have an idea, just trust me!"

Jason tells Nathan, "Whatever it is, I don't think I'm going to like this!"

Nathan yells at Jason, "Trust me on this! We need to stall 'em!" Nathan sees his Beretta 92F gun in the seat, grabs it, opens the window, and fires at them. He hits their bumper. Gable fires his gun again, and three bullets hit the road, missing them. Nathan fires his gun again, hitting their headlight, but misses them. Gable aims his gun again, but he can't get a close enough shot, but he fires his gun two more times, missing both shots. Nathan takes a look at the road closed sign, but it is still two miles ahead, and he's trying to distract Gable.

Tom sees the road closed sign, and tells Nathan, "Hey, that road's closed! Are you out of your damn mind!?"

Nathan tells Tom, "Trust me, this is the only place to lose them!"

Tom tells Nathan, "If I die, I'm going to put a bullet in your damn head!"

Gable fires his gun, hitting the bumper of Nathan's car again. Nathan is still trying to distract Gable, while Tom gets close to the road closed sign. Nathan fires his gun, two bullets come out of his gun, but hit the road and miss them. Gable fires his gun back, three bullets come out of his gun, and hit the road, missing the car.

Jason sees the glove compartment for a minute, but he can't open it right now, but he has an idea, "I have an idea! You're right Nate. Tom just get to the road closed sign and crash it! When you get there, speed up to 60 miles an hour!"

Tom tells Jason, "What are you nuts?! 60 miles! What the hell are you going to do?!"

Jason tells them, "You know Jackson gave me something in return, so I'm going to give him something in return too!"

They see the road closed sign, and Nathan tells Tom, "Alright, floor it, now!"

Tom tells them, "I wonder if it's too late to update my résumé!" Tom turns right, and crashes the road closed sign, and speeds up to 60 miles an hour.

Jason opens the glove compartment, and sees a bag of marbles. Jason tells himself, "Thank you Uncle Steve. And by the way, you didn't lose your marbles after all."

Gable fires his gun, three more bullets come out of nowhere. Jason opens up his window and throws one of the marbles out on the road. It's a 2 pound grenade.

Nathan tells him, "What the hell is that?"

Jason tells him, "When we hit 60, let's just say somebody hasn't lost their marbles after all." Gable fires his gun again, three bullets come out of his gun, and hit the trunk of Nathan's van. Tom is burning rubber, and reaches 60, and sees an empty bridge.

Nathan yells, "Empty bridge ahead! Whatever it is, Jace, you better do it now, because we're going to run out of road!"

Jason sees the car is up to 60 now, and tells Tom "Alright, I'm ready!" Jason tells Gable, who is still firing at them, "Hey guys! Guess you guys lost your marbles! Good news, I found them!" Jason throws the bag full of marbles, but Gable doesn't really look frightened, until the marbles hit the van, and all the marbles explode, destroying the car, Gable, and Jackson man 3. Gable and Jackson man 3 are killed in the explosion. Tom stops the car, and parks it. Jason, Nathan, and Tom exit the car, and take a look at the explosion.

Nathan tells them, "What are those things anyway?"

Jason tells them, "Those are marble grenades. They're one or two pounds, they could destroy anything in one or two seconds. All you've got to do is aim and throw, and the marble explodes, and you've got that. It's one of the R&D devices that Steve created. Got to thank Luke for that, good think he gave it to me before we left."

Nathan tells them, "It's a good thing too."

Tom tells them, "I guess Plan A didn't exactly turn out the way we thought."

Jason tells them, "Well, we better pray Plan B starts, or we're in big trouble."

Nathan tells them, "I just hope Natalie is doing okay. If she gets caught, we're dead."

Back outside of Jackson's warehouse, Natalie is in her car. She's driving a Toyota Avalon, and is parked right across the street from Jackson's warehouse. Natalie has a CB radio in her passenger seat and grabs it, "Hey Luke. Alright, I'm at the warehouse."

Back at the secret room, Luke is on the laptop, waiting for Natalie to plant the GPS device on Jackson's car. He tells Natalie, "Okay Natalie, all you have to do is plant the GPS device on Jackson's limo and we're set."

Natalie's voiceover tells Luke, "I wonder if Cameron Diaz had days like this when she played Charlie's Angels, when she did stuff like this, planting tracking devices on people's cars. Besides, she was one of the best secret agents in that movie."

Luke tells Natalie, "The Charlie's Angels were P.I.s, not secret agents. They looked like secret agents, but they were private investigators."

Back at Natalie's car, Natalie uses her binoculars to find Jackson's limo, and she can't find it. She tells Luke on the radio, "I can't find the limo."

Luke's voiceover tells Natalie, "If there's no limo at the warehouse, then I don't think he's going to be driving by limo. He must have a town car."

Natalie looks at one of the cars at the warehouse, and tells Luke, "I think I found one of the town cars. Hey tell me, what do town cars look like?"

Luke's voiceover tells Natalie, "Well, it has to be a black car. Most people use Lincoln or Mercedes continentals."

Natalie looks at one of the black town cars and tells Luke, "I think I found one. I think it's a Lincoln Continental. That must be what he's using."

Luke tells Natalie, "I think that might be the one. Alright, just plant the GPS device, and we're home free."

Natalie sarcastically tells Luke, "If this is the wrong town car, I'm definitely going to put a bullet in your head. And trust me, I will."

Luke's voiceover tells Natalie, "I was afraid of that."

Natalie puts her binoculars down, sees the black scotch tape and the GPS device that looks like a rock, but Natalie is thinking for a minute, that if she uses the black scotch tape to press the button, it could pop right back up. She checks her glove compartment, and takes out regular scotch tape. She exits the car, and sees the black town car right across the warehouse parking lot. She sneaks in as fast as she can before Jackson sees her. Natalie tapes the rock behind the bumper of Jackson's town car. Also, she turns the GPS device on. She gets away quickly when she hears somebody coming out of the warehouse. She gets back in her car, and ducks down for a minute.

She grabs her radio, and tells Luke, "Don't do anything yet. I'll let you know when they leave."

Luke's voiceover tells Natalie, "Check."

Jackson and his men are outside the warehouse, and they all are getting in their cars and exiting the warehouse parking lot. Jackson's town car, three SUVs, and two big rig trucks are leaving the warehouse, and Natalie sees them. Natalie tells Luke on the radio, "Alright, Luke, they're gone, get started."

Back at the secret room, Luke turns on the laptop and sees the GPS device is working. Luke grabs his CB radio, and tells Natalie, "Alright Natalie, the GPS is working, they're heading to the Kansas City freeway."

Back on the Kansas City freeway, Nathan, Jason, and Tom are getting back in their car, until Nathan's cell phone rings. Nathan tells them, "It's mine." Nathan picks up his cell phone, "Hello? Hey Nat."

Natalie on the other end of the line tells Nathan, "Nate, Jackson and his men just exited the warehouse. The GPS device is on. They're heading to the Kansas City freeway."

Nathan tells her, "Hang on. Hey guys, good news, Natalie called. The GPS device is on, and Jackson is heading to the Kansas City freeway."

Jason tells Nathan, "That's great. Okay, Nate, keep us posted."

Nathan tells Jason, "Sure thing, man."

Back on the freeway, Jackson's men who are driving the town car, three vans, and two trucks, are driving to the arms deal, to meet General Ashuk.

Back at the secret room, Luke tells Natalie on the radio, "Okay, make a right, and get to West 123rd Street."

Nathan, Jason, and Tom are on the Kansas City freeway, where Tom is driving the van. Nathan tells them, "Okay, make a right and get to West 123rd street."

Back at the secret room, Luke tells Natalie over the radio, "Okay, go southeast."

Nathan tells Tom in the car, "Go southeast."

Back on the freeway, Jackson's cars are still driving on the highway.

Luke is telling Natalie on the radio, "Alright, make a left and head to Walnut Street."

Nathan tells Tom, "Left at Walnut Street."

Jackson's cars are still on the freeway, and back at the secret room, Luke is telling Natalie, "Okay, right on Maple."

Nathan tells Tom, "Right at Maple."

Jackson's vans are still on the freeway.

Back at the secret room, Luke looks at the laptop, and tells Natalie on the radio, "Okay in five miles make a right on Lincoln."

Nathan tells Tom, "Right on Lincoln in five miles."

Luke looks at his laptop, and is happy and thrilled, and tells Natalie, "Alright, I found the arms deal. It's in an abandoned hangar at Callaway Airport. Tell them to make a right, and go 10 miles, and you'll find the Callaway hangar."

Back in Nathan's van, Nathan tells Tom, "Alright, go 10 miles towards Callaway Airport. There's an old abandoned hangar that nobody ever uses. I think it's owned by Lucas Weapons."

Jason tells them, "Unbelievable, I can't believe he would use that place. That's where all the flamethrowers are stored at?"

Nathan tells Natalie on the phone, "Alright, Natalie, call Warner, and tell him where the deal is. Tell him to call in the cavalry."

Natalie tells him over the phone, "Okay, I'll meet you there."

Before Natalie leaves the warehouse, she makes a call to Warner, "Alright Captain, send a couple SWAT vans and helicopters, and inform the army that we found their missing flamethrowers and have them send in a couple squadrons. We'll try to distract them until you guys arrive. Bye." Natalie hangs up her phone and exits the warehouse to meet them.

Inside the abandoned airplane hangar, Jackson and 10 of his men are with General Ashuk and five of his guys, getting ready to start the arms deal. Three of General Ashuk's men are carrying briefcases. All of the boxes of flamethrowers are here, and one of Jackson's men is opening the safe that has all the boxes. He opens the safe, and takes one of the boxes out, and opens it with a crowbar, and puts one of the flamethrowers on the table. One of Jackson's men is carrying a briefcase and opens it, and it has the 20 million dollars of unmarked, laundered money that was stolen from the bank, and Ashuk is really impressed by this. Ashuk nods at one of his men and he puts his briefcase on the table and opens it, and it has 20 million dollars.

Outside the hangar, Nathan's van and Natalie's car have just arrived and parked. Nathan, Jason, and Tom are exiting Nathan's car, and Natalie parks next to them and exits her car, going to talk to them. Jason tells her, "Hey Natalie, how long is it going to take for the cavalry to arrive?"

Natalie tells Jason, "It's going to take 10 or 20 minutes for them to get here. That means this arms deal will probably be over and they'll be out of here before they arrive."

Jason tells them, "We'll have to stall them until they get here."

Nathan tells them, "So what do we do now?"

Jason tells Nate, "Well, Nate, we're going to do what we always do. We're going to distract them until the cavalry arrives."

Tom tells them, "Well, what happens when they see us and try to shoot us?"

Jason tells them, "Do what we usually do, we fire back. This is a life and death situation, so we do what we have to do."

Natalie tells them, "So, what's the plan?"

Jason tells them, "We just need one person to distract them, and we'll give them the element of surprise."

Nathan tells Jason, "What's the element of surprise?"

Jason tells Nathan, "You'll see in a minute."

Nathan opens up his trunk, and takes out a couple of Beretta 92F guns and hands one to Jason and one to Tom. He also hands another gun to Natalie. Nathan tells Jason, "I was afraid you'd say that."

Natalie tells them, "Well good luck, who are we going to get to distract them?" Jason, Nathan, and Tom look at Natalie and they all nod their heads. Natalie looks at them, "I hate it when you do that."

Back inside the hangar, Jackson and Ashuk's men are finishing the deal. They are about to close the deal, until Natalie comes inside the hangar out of nowhere. Natalie tells them, "Hey guys, I'm sorry to interrupt your business deal here. So, hey check that out. What am I seeing here? Aren't those the new T-148 Flamethrowers? How about that? Hey is that you Mr. Lucas? Didn't your company design those new flamethrowers? Wasn't that your ideas? Didn't you stiff the army out of those? Man, they're gonna be pretty angry when they find out you screwed them over and sold their weapons to a Jordanian warlord like General Kabob here. Hey General, I never liked those royal guys anyways. I think it's pretty cool that you're going to use those to burn up their fields and their castles too. I was trying to get to the art museum, there's a new tour, but I always get lost in Kansas City. I tried to go to the Arrowhead Stadium yesterday, but it was empty and I remembered that it's not football season! And I tried to get to Worlds of Fun today, but it was closed, isn't that crazy? Hey, have you guys ever been to the Truman Memorial Library? It's in Independence, it's only a couple blocks from here. Have you ever been there? If you ever went there I'm sure you want to burn it down with one of those flamethrowers. Sure, it's a historical landmark, and that's probably a felony, but hey you're going to use them to start arson in the Jordanian palace, right? But, hey, I'm just here along for the ride. Besides, I'm sure that was just a lucky guess, I bet. By the way, I forgot about the directions to the art museum, I was really planning on going there. How far is it from here anyway?"

Jackson, Ashuk, and their 15 men take out their Smith & Wesson 4506 guns and they all aim them at Natalie. Natalie tells them, "Hmm, this is a really bad time to bother you guys isn't it?"

Jackson tells her, "Well, actually it's a good time for me, because I get to shoot somebody, and I was really in the mood to shoot somebody. Kill that stinking bitch."

Natalie begs for her life, "Listen, I'm really sorry, I guess I was in the wrong place. And I'm unarmed. You don't really want to shoot an unarmed person do you?"

Jackson tells Natalie, "But of course, because it makes it easier."

They are about to fire at Natalie, until a marble rolls across the floor, and explodes. Natalie dives down before the explosion, and hides behind the boxes. Natalie takes out her Beretta 92F from the back of her pants. Everybody is so distracted. Natalie fires her gun, and three bullets come out of her gun, and hit Ashuk in the stomach, and he dies. When the smoke clears, five more bullets come out of nowhere at Natalie, but hit the boxes and the walls. Natalie fires her gun and three more bullets come out of her gun, but miss. Jason, Nathan, and Tom enter the hangar. Jason fires his gun, and kills Ashuk man 2. All three of them are on the right, and they hide behind the boxes and barrels. Nathan fires his gun, two bullets come out of his gun but miss. Jackson fires his gun, two bullets come out of his gun, just missing Jason. Tom fires his gun, three bullets come out of his gun, and hit Jackson man 10 in the chest, killing him. Natalie fires her gun, three bullets come out of her gun, and hit Ashuk man 1 in the chest, and he dies. Jackson fires his gun, and three more bullets come out of his gun, and hit the floor near Natalie but miss her. Jason is a little upset, but he fires his gun. Two bullets come out of his gun, but they hit the table, missing Jackson. Tom fires his gun, but hits the floor near Jackson man 3, missing him. Natalie fires her gun, two bullets come out of her gun, and hit the briefcase, missing Jackson and his men. Jackson man 8 fires his gun, two bullets come out of his gun and hit the box near Natalie, missing her. Natalie fires back, and three bullets come out of her gun, and hit Jackson man 8 in the chest, and he dies. Jason fires his gun, two bullets come out of his gun, but hit the floor, missing Jackson again. Jackson fires his gun again, two bullets come out of his gun, but hit the barrel, just missing Nathan and Tom. Ashuk man 4 fires his gun and two bullets come out of his gun, hitting the box, missing Natalie. Natalie aims her gun on Ashuk man 4, three bullets come out of her gun, but miss, hitting the floor. Nathan fires his gun, two bullets come out of his gun, and miss Jackson. Jackson fires his gun again, one bullet hits another barrel. Tom fires his gun, two bullets come out of his gun, but miss, hitting the floor. Jackson man 1 fires his gun, two bullets come out of his gun, and hit the wall near Natalie, missing her. Tom fires his gun, two bullets come out of his gun, hitting the table.

Nathan aims his gun on Jackson man 1, but he aims on the foot. He fires his gun, one bullet come out and hits the floor near Jackson man 1, and he is a little bit startled. Jackson man 1 tells Nathan, "Okay, you're really starting to piss me off." Jackson man 1 fires his gun, two bullets come out of his gun, and hit the box near Nathan, barely missing him. Jason fires his gun, two bullets come out of his gun but hit the wall near one of Ashuk's men, missing him. Tom's got a good target on Jackson man 1, he fires his gun, two bullets out of his gun, hitting him in the chest, and he dies. Jackson fires his gun, two bullets come out of his gun, and hit the wall near Jason, but miss him. Natalie fires her gun, one bullet comes out of her gun, and hits Jackson man 2 in the leg. Jackson man 2's leg is hurt, but it's enough of a target for Natalie to make her move. Natalie fires her gun, two more bullets come out of her gun hitting Jackson man 2 in the chest, and he dies. Jason fires his gun, one bullet comes out of his gun, and hits the floor near Jackson but misses him. Jackson fires his gun, but hits the wall near Jason, missing him. Natalie fires her gun, but her chamber is empty. She unloads the clip, and gets another from the back of her pants, and loads it. Natalie fires her gun, two bullets come out of her gun, but they hit the floor, missing Jackson man 4. Nathan fires his gun, two bullets come out of his gun, and hit Jackson man 5 in the chest, and he dies. Natalie fires her gun, three bullets come out of her gun, hitting Jackson man 6 in the chest, and he dies. Jason fires his gun, two bullets come out of his gun, and hit Ashuk man 3 in the chest, and he dies. Nathan has a marble in his left pocket and he throws it on the floor, and it explodes. Jackson dives down on the floor before the marble hits. The explosion distracts everyone enough for Natalie to fire her gun again, hitting Jackson man 9 in the chest, and killing him. Tom fires his gun, three bullets come out of his gun, but hit the wall missing one of Ashuk's men. Jason fires his gun, two bullets come out hitting the floor near one of Jackson's men, missing him. Natalie fires her gun, three bullets come out of her gun, but hit the wall near one of Jackson's men, missing him. Jason fires his gun, two bullets come out of his gun, and hit Jackson man 7 in the chest, and he dies. Jason sees Jackson, and fires his gun, but his bullet hits the floor missing Jackson. Jackson fires back, and three more bullets come out hitting a box, but missing Jason. Nathan fires his gun, two bullets come out of his gun, but hit the floor missing Jackson's men.

Jason looks at Jackson for a minute. Jason tells Nathan, "Cover me, I'm going in!"

Tom tells Jason, "What? What are you talking about?"

Jason tells them, "Just cover me, I'm going in!"

Tom tells himself, "I hate it when he does this."

Nathan sees Jackson man 4's foot, and Nathan fires his gun, his bullet hitting the floor near Jackson man 4. Jackson man 4 is a little frightened, but it's just enough to distract him. Jason gets up from behind the box. Two bullets come out of nowhere, but hit the wall. Jason is a little bit frightened because he's never done this before, and whispers to himself, "No guts, no glory." Jason starts charging in, five more bullets come out of nowhere, hitting the floor around Jason. Two more bullets miss him hitting the wall. Jackson turns around, and sees Jason tackling him. Jackson is Jason's target, so Jason tackles Jackson into the table, dumping the money and the flamethrower to the ground. Both of them drop their guns. Jackson gets up, grabbing Jason by the shirt, and knees him in the stomach, and punches him in the face twice. Jackson tells his men, "You guys keep stalling them, and finish them off. I've got a little unfinished business with this retard." Jackson grabs Jason by the shirt, and throws him into the hangar's office. Jason tries to get up, but Jackson kicks him in the stomach. Jason is hurting, and Jackson gives him a roundhouse kick to the face.

Nathan fires his gun, two more bullets come out, missing one of Ashuk's men, hitting the floor.

Jason gets up from the floor, and Jackson punches him in the stomach, and gives him another roundhouse kick to the face. Jackson kicks Jason in the stomach two more times. Jackson kicks him again, but Jason blocks his kick, and punches him in the groin. Jason gets up from the floor and knees Jackson in the face. Jason punches Jackson in the face three times, and tosses him to the floor. Jason grabs Jackson by the shirt, and knees him in the stomach, and punches him in the face three times, and he kicks him in the stomach, and gives him a roundhouse kick to the face. Jason is about to go over to him, but Jackson pulls a knife from his left pants pocket. As Jason is coming toward him, Jackson gets up from the floor and slices Jason's left arm. Jackson makes it a fair fight by dropping his knife, and punching Jason in the stomach. Jason's arm is hurting. Jackson drags Jason up against the wall of the office and punches Jason in the head twenty-two times, and knees him in the stomach and lets him drop to the floor.

Ashuk's man 5 fires his gun, two bullets missing Natalie and hitting the boxes. Jackson's man 4 fires his gun, two more bullets come out of his gun, hitting the floor near Tom, missing him. Nathan fires his gun, two more bullets come out of his gun, hitting the floor and missing Jackson man 1.

Jason tries to get up, his face is bruised, and his left arm is a little bloody, but Jackson sees him, and kicks him in the stomach again, and gives him another roundhouse kick to the face. Jackson tells Jason, "Nice try, retard. You know Boswell, I got to hand it to you, trying to come and get me. But you know what? I have to tell you why they made you nature's mistake. Because deep down only the strong survive, and nature's mistakes don't belong in a place like this." Jackson kicks Jason in the stomach again.

Jackson man 1 fires his gun, two more bullets come out of his gun, and miss Nathan. Natalie fires her gun, three more bullets come out of her gun, but miss one of Ashuk's men. Nathan grabs another marble, and throws it on the floor and there is another explosion to startle the men, but it doesn't faze them. Natalie fires her gun again, but it misses hitting the wall.

Jackson is still torturing Jason, and Jackson is about to kick Jason in the face, until Jason sees Jackson's knife. He rolls over and grabs it, and stabs Jackson's left leg. Jackson is sore and bleeding, but it doesn't really bother him because it's just a flesh wound. Jason gets up from the floor, but Jackson still kicks him, and he falls back down. Jackson takes the knife out of his leg, and grabs Jason by the shirt, and knees him in the stomach three times, and tosses him on the floor again.

Nathan fires his gun, two more bullets come out of his gun, but miss the men. Ashuk's men are pissed off and tell Jackson man 5, "These guys are starting to piss me off, and I want to shoot their stinking faces off."

Ashuk man 5 tells Ashuk man 4, "They're going to pay for killing our leader."

Ashuk man 4 fires his gun, five bullets come out of his gun, but miss Natalie again, hitting the wall. Tom has an easy target on Jackson man 4, and fires his gun, three bullets coming out, but hitting the floor missing them again.

Jackson gives Jason another round house kick to the face, and Jason is still hurt. Jackson is taking a little break for a minute, but he doesn't know that Jason is getting up. Jackson sees him, and punches Jason in the face, but Jason blocks his punch and kicks Jackson in the groin, and grabs him by the shirt, and takes him to the wall, and hits his head on the wall five times, and he elbows him in the stomach, and tosses Jackson on the floor.

Ashuk man 4 fires his gun, two bullets come out of his gun, but hit the wall missing Nathan again. Ashuk man 5 tells Ashuk man 4, "We've got to get out of here."

Ashuk man 4 tells 5, "No! Not until these wimps die for killing our boss!"

Ashuk man 5 tells Ashuk man 4, "They're going to pay for what they did to our boss. We were going to take over the Jordanian empire."

One bullet comes out of nowhere, and hits the floor between them. Ashuk man 4 tells Ashuk man 5, "You know what, we'll kill them another time. Let's get the hell out of here!"

Ashuk man 5 tells Jackson's men, "Hey, you can tell Jackson the deal is off!"

Ashuk men 4 and 5 are about to leave. Natalie sees Ashuk man 4's leg, and fires. She hits him in the leg, and he can barely move, until Natalie gets a target, and has him right on time. Natalie fires her gun, two bullets come out of her gun, hitting Ashuk man 4 in the chest and he dies. Nathan fires his gun, four bullets come out of his gun and hit Jackson man 4 in the chest, and he dies. Tom is about to fire his gun, but he's out, so he loads a new clip from the back of his pants. Ashuk man 5 was about to leave until a SWAT member comes from the back carrying a Winchester 1300 Defender. Three bullets come out of his gun, hitting Ashuk man 5 in the chest, and he dies. Tom fires his gun, three bullets come out of his gun, hitting Jackson man 1 in the chest and he dies while he was distracted by Ashuk's man's death. Tom and Nathan get up from the floor and so does Natalie.

Tom tells them, "Hey guys, I'm going to go help Jason, be back in a minute."

Nathan tells Tom, "Just hope he comes back in one piece."

Jackson is on the floor, and Jason tries to kick him in the stomach, but Jackson blocks his kick, and Jackson kicks him in the groin, he knees him in the stomach, and punches Jason in the face three times. He tosses Jason to the floor. Jason is bruised and hurt, and his left arm is bleeding. Tom sees Jason's gun, and grabs it, and he sees Jackson is about to shoot Jason. Jason is still wounded, but he gets up from the floor, and Jackson kicks him in the stomach again, and punches him in the face. Jason falls down on the floor. Jackson sees another gun on the hangar's desk, and he grabs the Beretta 92F, and aims it on Jason. Jackson tells Jason, "Well, here's what I've got to tell you Boswell: You came close to catching me, but like I said, retards like you should leave the detective work to real detective not nature's mistakes like you. Maybe you can remember that in the next lifetime." Jackson is about to fire his gun, until Tom comes out of nowhere, barging into the room, tossing Jason a gun. Jackson fires his gun, one bullet coming out of his gun, but Tom came out of nowhere while Jackson was about to kill Jason. Tom dives down, and takes the bullet for Jason, letting it hit his chest.

Jason sees his gun while Jackson is distracted, and he gets up from the floor, runs a little bit and grabs it. Jason aims his gun on Jackson, and he tells Jackson, "Guess what? I'm not nature's mistake. I'm nature's favorite person. And to tell you the truth, you've just become nature's mistake asshole."

Jason fires his gun, three bullets come out of his gun, and Jackson sees it, even though he was a little bit distracted, and Jackson tells himself, "What the hell?" The three bullets hit Jackson in the chest, and he dies.

Jason is hurt a little bit, and Tom gets up from the floor and he's fine. He opens his shirt a little bit and he has a bullet proof vest on. He tells Jason, "Well, Jace, just remember one important lesson. Always wear a vest."

Jason tells Tom, "I'll remember that."

Jason drops the gun, and tries to cover the wound on his left arm. Tom is a little sore from getting shot in the chest, but he grabs Jason's shoulders, "Like I said, Jace, I promised your mom that I'd protect you, and I'll keep that promise."

Jason tells Tom, "Well, I guess I do owe you one, because you said you'd take a bullet for me, and you did."

Back outside the hangar, where the police and an ambulance are outside. The paramedic inside the ambulance finishes patching up Jason's left arm. Nathan, Tom, and Natalie go to see that Jason's okay. Natalie tells Jason, "Hey, Jace, you okay?"

Jason tells Natalie, "Yeah, I'm fine. Besides, lucky for me it was just a flesh wound, nothing serious."

Nathan tells Jason, "Well, I guess we kind of do owe you this one."

Jason tells them, "Hey, Nate, I'm just here to help you out. I said I'd help you, and I did."

Nathan and Natalie's boss comes over to them, and talks to Nathan and Natalie. Captain Warner tells Nathan and Natalie, "So, I heard on the radio. Can you explain this case?"

Nathan tells Captain Warner, "Well, sir, it's a long story, and we've had a long night, but I can tell you one thing. We recovered the 20 million dollars from the hangar, and the mastermind behind this was Jackson Lucas. He's the one who stole all of that money, and it was embezzled from the a deal the military made with his company. He did it so that he could sell those flamethrowers to a Jordanian warlord who wanted to terrorize the Jordanian royal family. That's all I can tell you, and I can give you more detail later, but I couldn't have done it without Jason's help. He's the one who figured out everything, and we couldn't have done it without him."

Captain Warner tells Nathan, "I'm usually concerned about citizens working with us. Mostly because I don't want them to die or sue us, but I'm sure he signed a release form to work with you guys."

Natalie tells Captain Warner, "Yes, he signed a release form, and he technically worked for us. He's a private consultant for the Kansas City PD. We'd love to give you the form, but we sort of lost it after he signed it. I think we threw it away, but we'll get another one for your records."

Captain Warner tells Natalie, "Well, get him another one to sign. Man, I always hate when they lose those things. But, I would like to say congratulations to both of you. And congratulations Boswell, and thank you for helping us out."

Jason tells Captain Warner, "Thank you sir."

Warner tells him, "Besides the congratulations, I'm going to appoint you as my new official private consultant for the police force. We're going to give you three the Kansas City PD Medal of Honor for this, and I'm proud of you."

Nathan tells Captain Warner, "Uh, thank you sir."

Captain Warner exits the ambulance, and Jason tells them, "Thanks guys. I owe you."

Natalie tells him, "Hey no problem. Tomorrow we'll have to get you a release form to sign if you want to work with us fulltime, if it's okay with you."

Jason tells Natalie, "Hey no problem."

Back at NOCOMO, Jason and Luke are back at their ordinary jobs. Nicki comes over to see Jason and Luke, and tells Jason, "Um, Jason, Luke, you're friends from the Kansas City PD are here, they want to see you, they said it's really important."

Jason tells Nicki, "Must be another case."

Nicki tells Jason, "So, what is it? Armed robbery? Drug dealing? What is it?"

Jason tells her, "Sorry, Nicki, but I think that's police business."

Nicki tells them, "Okay, well good luck guys."

Jason and Luke get up from their chairs and Luke tells Nicki, "Hey Nicki, can you get Fred and Chester to cover for us?"

Nicki tells him, "Sure."

Back inside the cafeteria in NOCOMO, Luke and Jason see Natalie, Tom, and Nathan sitting down. Jason tells them, "Hey guys thanks for getting me out of this. Man, I've been working all day."

Natalie tells Jason, "You know we had a couple of weeks off and we wanted to celebrate with you guys."

Jason tells Natalie, "So, what did you tell Nicki to get us out early. Besides she already knows that we're working with you guys on a case-to-case basis."

Nathan tells them, "I told them there was a homicide. A drug dealer was killed in an alley, and they needed our expertise to help out."

Luke tells them, "You guys do realize that you work at MCU not homicide?"

Nathan tells them, "Okay, I was panicking. Besides, I told her that homicide called us in to investigate."

Natalie goes over to Jason and makes out with him for a minute, and she tells Jason, "Hey just remember, our date is at 8 PM tonight."

Jason tells Natalie, "Hey, I'll remember."

Nathan's phone rings, and he answers it, "Hello? Hey Captain. Really? Aww man, it's our week off. Well, okay. Bye." Nathan hangs up the phone and tells them, "Guys, I think our lie just became the truth, because we have a case. There was actually a drug dealer shot in an alley, and homicide called for our expertise."

Jason tells them, "Well, I guess we have no choice but to get to work. Come on, let's get started."

Nathan, Tom, and Luke exit the cafeteria and Nathan tells them, "I wonder if it's heroin this time, or actually cocaine. Mostly I can tell a drug dealer is on heroin, but cocaine? That'll be another story."

Luke tells them, "Maybe we should ask my uncle. Besides, we did help Lucas Weapons become richer when we saved Thomas from going to jail, and getting the flamethrowers to the army on time."

Tom tells them, "I hope he's there, because he is the only informant we know, and it's hard to get another one."

Nathan, Luke, and Tom exit NOCOMO. Natalie is about to leave, but Jason grabs her hand, "Hey, we still have a couple of minutes before we get to work."

Natalie tells Jason, "Well, we only need five."

Jason tells Natalie, "Fair enough." Jason and Natalie start making out.

THE END

Final Word

That's it and thank you for reading Bobby Cinema second Librarian detective series. I hope you enjoy reading this.

Printed in the United States
By Bookmasters